Jilly
Jackie

To Phil, thank you.

*Such as are your habitual thoughts, such also will be the character of your mind; for the soul is dyed by the thoughts*
Marcus Aurelius

Victoria Mansbridge

# A WALK ALONE

AUSTIN MACAULEY PUBLISHERS™
LONDON • CAMBRIDGE • NEW YORK • SHARJAH

Copyright © Victoria Mansbridge (2017)

The right of Victoria Mansbridge to be identified as author of this work has been asserted by her in accordance with section 77 and 78 of the Copyright, Designs and Patents Act 1988.

All rights reserved. No part of this publication may be reproduced, stored in a retrieval system, or transmitted in any form or by any means, electronic, mechanical, photocopying, recording, or otherwise, without the prior permission of the publishers.

Any person who commits any unauthorized act in relation to this publication may be liable to criminal prosecution and civil claims for damages.

A CIP catalogue record for this title is available from the British Library.

ISBN 9781849637831 (Paperback)
ISBN 9781849637848 (Ebook)

www.austinmacauley.com

First Published (2017)
Austin Macauley Publishers Ltd.
25 Canada Square
Canary Wharf
London
E14 5LQ

# Chapter 1

Emma's legs felt stiff as she tried to stand up. Unknowingly she had been sitting on the hard, cold kitchen floor for over an hour. It seemed that not a single thought had passed through her mind in that time and Emma wasn't even sure if she had been breathing. She had no recollection of the sound of her breath but she must have been breathing, she was still alive, after all.

She steadied herself against the worktop. Looking up, she caught sight of the grey flint wall just outside the kitchen window, blocking any chance of sunlight filtering into the room. She was caught between the curious feelings of a wave of nausea rising up in her as a wave of claustrophobia crashed down over her. She had to get out of the house. She needed to go for a walk. She always did her best thinking whilst walking and now she needed to think. Of course that meant getting down the stairs, which she did so very carefully, gingerly picking her way down, fighting the urge to gag, until she reached the lobby. She grabbed her coat and then she quietly left the house and headed for the beach.

Emma crossed the main road, then the car park and finally an expanse of golden sand until she stood at the water's edge. She looked slowly around her, trying desperately to slow down her breathing. She had to calm down. She had to work out what had happened this morning. The sea had calmed a little since yesterday. It was striped bright blue against a much darker blue, with bright white crystal caps on each rising swell of water. Emma tried hard to focus on these facts, to distance herself from the turmoil in her mind. Near where she stood the sea had a rhythm, hypnotic and beautiful as it coursed down on to the sand with a boom and swept back against the small stones in a long and insistent *schhhhh*.

Further out the sea was random, with no rhythm, rising and falling where it wished; playful and powerful together. It was a beautiful scene and Emma tried to recognise this as she fought with the tight knot in her throat. Above, the sky was a perfect springtime picture. A full range of weathers, all typical of one season, painted onto one huge canvas. It was so beautiful to see all the elements of spring in one sky.

It was a scene that would remain with Emma for the rest of her life. A perfect image, frozen in time. Even in her anxiety she could recognise that.

Over the sea, the sky was intensely blue. Tiny flecks of cloud served only to highlight the deep-bright blue. You could stare into it forever, up and up through its vastness. It didn't seem possible that the blackness of space was only a few miles above; surely a blue that pure would stretch to the end of the universe.

Emma let her head fall back as she looked up into the sky. She wanted to scream out to release some of the tension inside her. God, what had happened this morning? What had she done?

Turning away from the sea, towards the mountains, the sky revealed its trick of the day. As if to show the ground that anything it could do the sky could do better, clouds formed around the tops of the mountains, doubling the height of each peak. It became impossible to tell where the mountains ended and the clouds began. They towered up into the sky. Underneath the solid, real, hard mountain and above the ethereal, impermanent droplets of water, mimicking that below, caught in a massive game of Simon-Says. Small glimpses between the cloud-mountains revealed a darker, greyer, angrier sky.

She had to believe she hadn't done anything wrong. This was not her fault. She had to calm herself down and prepare herself for the rest of today.

Emma had lived in this bay, alone, for over a year. It was one of the most beautiful places she had ever seen. She had first visited here a few years previously and the approach by car down through the dramatic, wind sculpted mountains, along the heavily-wooded estuary and finally to see the sun glinting off the clear blue sea had touched her heart. She wasn't alone then; she had someone to share in her awe. She had wanted so much to never leave this place. She sacrificed so much to move here, to be able to stay here. Now it seemed this might be her last walk here ever.

Emma was no-where near ready to start facing that thought. Instead she turned back to stare at the sea, watching the seagulls, envious of their freedom. A gentle breeze washed over her and she allowed herself the luxury of wishing she could be part of that breeze, not physical, not solid, but a transient wisp escaping all the trouble that awaited her here.

So, this would potentially be her last walk here. Her heart thudded painfully at that thought. She had to make this walk count. Emma loved walking for two reasons, firstly to see the sea and the trees, to hear the birds and smell fresh air. The second was because walking often helped her to sort out her problems, think things through rationally and find solutions. Walking was good for the soul and good for the cellulite. Some of the major decisions and realisations in her life had been made whilst walking. So, she had to make this walk count on two fronts. She had to breathe in as much of the beauty she saw around her as she could. She also had a problem to work out, a large, life altering problem. She didn't know where to start and that feeling of helplessness made her want to cry. Somewhat unexpectedly her mind took her back to when she was a young child.

Young Emma sat on her bed engrossed in a book. As she finished the chapter she was reading she stretched out. She'd been sitting here for hours, propped against her pillows, reading. She wiggled her toes against her bright yellow duvet cover. The cover had been chosen to match the little yellow flowers on her wallpaper and the big, bright flowers on her curtains. Emma loved sitting reading in her room, though she was always half listening for when her parents would put down their work and be ready to talk or even, on rare occasions, play. The house was still quiet, her mum was working away studiously in the spare bedroom, and her dad sat staring intently at the papers he had spread out on the dining room table. The silence indicated it was still time to sit alone and read. Emma was conditioned to this way of life. Much of her time was spent sitting quietly, waiting patiently to be ignored. She only had one chapter left in her book and she wanted to take it as slowly as possible.

There was no point in running out of things to do until her parents were also finished. So instead she stared out of her window, towards the end of the cul-de-sac, where a green strip of field ran the length of the housing estate. The field was only about 300 meters across but about a mile long and from where Emma sat she could see a few trees and the river, which flooded regularly enough to ensure this parcel of land could never be built on. Emma loved the field; she liked to look at it with her eyes half closed so the other houses faded away and she could pretend she was a princess, living in a castle, overlooking her own land. This was a game she played often. She knew from stories that young princesses were often left in rooms or towers, alone, for many years until a handsome young prince would come and save them. Emma knew these stories were make-believe but was still young enough to hope they might hold some kernel of truth.

She never spent time imagining the castle she might live in, or the clothes she might wear. Instead she looked, with eyes half closed, lovingly at the field. She imagined it was part of her garden. She pretended there was a kindly old gardener who would teach her all about plants and trees and how to look after them. She would have a huge garden all to herself and she would get to decide how it would look and what would go where. She would have banks of big red flowers whose name she did not know, though of course, as the princess she would know the names of all the flowers. Best of all, there would be an overgrown path, twisting through bushes and trees, leading to her own secret garden, somewhere no one else knew of. Here the lawn would be made of flowers and attached to the big old oak tree would be a swing. Emma could spend hours imagining playing on the swing in her secret garden.

A noise startled her from her day dream. Her mother was

leaving the spare room; Emma rushed out to meet her at the top of the stairs.

"I'm going to cook dinner now. I'll call you when it's ready." Mum did not look happy. Clearly Emma's assistance in making dinner was not required, so she returned to her room and waited to be called down. As she sat down on her bed she noticed a small section of wallpaper had come unstuck over the radiator. Her heart started to beat faster and faster as she slid her finger nail between the wall and the wallpaper. It would be so easy to rip the entire strip of paper off. It would be so satisfying to do. Emma loved the feeling of ripping off wallpaper. She had to stop. She had to sit on her hands and make herself not do it. She knew she would be shocked, as always, at her own act of vandalism if she continued. She would stare at the bare wall knowing that it would mean a horrible telling off. She must not do it. She had done it so many times before and each time she promised faithfully never to do it again. It was too destructive. Emma sat battling with her conscience, her hands gripping her duvet cover, until she was called down to dinner. With immense relief, she left her room.

They always ate in the kitchen as her dad had taken over the dining room as an office. As Emma entered the room she learned that her mum's bad mood seemed to have something to do with work.

"... I bloody well told Bob that if I didn't have that file to work on over the weekend the 'you know what' would really hit the fan." Her mum paused for breath.

"The what?" Emma wanted to know what was going to hit the fan.

"Never you mind, just eat your dinner," came the snapped reply. So Emma sat and ate her dinner whilst her parents talked over her in what seemed to Emma to be a code that only grown-ups understood.

After dinner Emma was allowed to sit and watch TV for one hour, whilst her parents scuttled back to their respective makeshift offices to continue preparing for tomorrow. Emma sat close to the TV so she could switch between the three available channels. There was nothing much on so she didn't mind when, precisely 60 minutes later, a simultaneous cry came from the spare bedroom and the dining room.

"Bed time Emma!"

Once she'd brushed her teeth and changed into her nightie she stood at the top of the stairs and shouted, "Night!"

"Good night darling," her mum called from the spare room.

"Sleep tight love," her dad shouted up from the dining room. Emma had planned to read the final chapter of her book before falling asleep but as she entered her room she noticed the sky looked peculiarly dark. She knelt on her bed and looked out across the houses. Huge black clouds filled the sky. From far away a loud, foreboding growl of thunder built up until it felt like it was coming from inside the house itself. Then a massive bolt of lightning split the sky wide open and as it did the rain came.

And what rain! Emma wondered if this is what it would be like to be under a waterfall. More thunder roared out, more lightening crashed through the darkness as the storm built itself up into a massive frenzy. Emma rested her head on her arms which were propped on to the window sill and looked out at the storm. In the pit of her stomach, instinct told her she should be afraid. But she wasn't. She refused to give in to fear, princesses and heroes of all descriptions do not give in to fear. She watched the storm and felt its power, never flinching from it. Eventually, as the thunder and lightning moved away, Emma snuggled down into her duvet and felt very brave for having faced the storm. She was trembling but felt proud of herself for not crying. Emma smiled to herself as she finally fell asleep, tonight had proved to be a very exciting evening and she felt satisfied with her own bravery.

Twenty years on and Emma had no idea why she was thinking of the storm now. Maybe because it was the last time she felt proud of her own actions. Maybe because she needed to find some of the strength she had that night now. Her desire to cry had now passed but she wanted to scream at that little girl. She wanted to shake her and scream at her that she must never grow up. She must never let her life get to where it had today.

Reminiscing about storms was not going to help. If she really wanted to work out her problems there was no room for idle, day-dream distractions. She had to start at the beginning, get to the root of it and work it out from there. Slowly, rationally and methodically, she would work out what to do.

She needed to start at the beginning, but which beginning? Jess, or Ben? They were two entirely separate stories, linked only by her own part in them.

Of course, she would start with Jess. Everything started with Jess. If nothing else, this morning had shown her she still had quite a bit to work out there.

## Chapter 2

In 1986 when Emma was 13 years old a leaflet arrived at home one Saturday morning advertising an after-school hockey club open to all girls aged 11-16, every Wednesday evening 4pm-6pm. Looking over the garish yellow leaflet, Emma's mum remarked, "This would be perfect for you."

"Erm?" said Emma, looking up from her bowl of Coco Pops.

"After-school hockey, wouldn't you like to go along?"

"Not really," replied Emma. PE was her least favourite subject at school. She didn't really like things she wasn't any good at, and with a lack of any real hand-eye co-ordination, and an inability to run fast, she most certainly did not like sports.

"But love, if you don't try it, then you won't know whether you like it or not. Besides I worry about you being at home on your own so much. It would be nice for you to have a new hobby."

*No, it would not be nice for me to have a new hobby, especially not a sport, one that I don't like anyway,* thought Emma, but she kept her counsel to herself. Mum had clearly made up her mind that Emma was going to go, probably as some sort of personal growth thing – the hardest thing of all to fight against. Why she even cared was beyond Emma's comprehension, what made hockey so important all of a sudden? Emma thought hard.

"What about my homework?"

"Your homework has never been late has it?" There was a sharpness to her tone. Emma had to tread carefully. Her parents held schoolwork in ridiculously high regard.

"No, never, but Wednesday is science homework night. Hockey would interfere with my schedule." Surely this was the winning shot, Emma relaxed a little, safe in the knowledge there would be no hockey. She had invoked the word 'schedule' – something both her mother and father were almost religiously devoted to. They both lived and would probably die by their work schedules. Everything bowed to the schedule. Nothing could interfere with it.

Would today be the day that Emma finally got her way? Would she finally win one of their arguments? (Her family did not argue; they discussed things rationally, with no raised voices. Raised voices were not permitted and were met with stony silence, until Emma was finally convinced to do whatever her parents had known all along they would get her to do.)

"Never mind dear, just try it this once. You can do your science homework today instead."

"But we're going shopping together today; you said I could have some new jeans." Emma was pouting slightly, the sting of her mother's hypocrisy hit hard. Apparently Emma's schedule was a lesser god, one not to be worshipped as her mother's was. Besides, she'd had her eyes on a pair of stone-washed, tight-fit jeans and she wanted them so badly. She never had nice new clothes to wear. Her parents just didn't seem to understand the importance of jeans.

"Oh Emma, I told you I have to go into the office today, you know I did," said with such a sharp smile that sliced Emma's heart. "In fact I'm running a little late" (unlikely) "… I must dash, I'll see you later? Okay?"

And that was it. The sting of her mum's lack of understanding and hypocrisy, coupled with her bloody self-righteous devotion to her career, brought tears to Emma's eyes. Nothing could come between her mum and her career. She had once patiently explained to Emma how hard it is for a woman to work in a man's world. How women had to be twice as strong and make more sacrifices to succeed. You'd have thought that by working for a poxy advertising firm her mother was single-handedly spearheading the feminist movement. Even at the tender age of thirteen Emma knew this was nonsense. Her mum was just selfish. She loved her job, loved the power she had in the office and would gladly sacrifice time at home with her daughter, under the banner of progress, just so she could spend more time at her desk.

Emma would have complained to her dad, but he was just as bad and Emma had been screamed at enough times to know better than to disturb him when he was working. His time was always spent working and his excuse could hardly be feminism as well. They didn't care about Emma, or Emma's lack of stone-washed jeans. Even as she thought this, Emma knew it sounded silly. That didn't stop salty tears mixing with her sweet Coco Pops. Breakfast was ruined, as was Emma's day, and by the looks of it, Emma's Wednesday evening too.

She worried for the next few days. School was bad enough without having to go and meet new people after it as well. At least at school she occasionally learnt interesting things. Hockey was not one of these interesting things and Emma despaired of having to go and play. More than this she loathed the idea of being amongst a group of strangers. She never knew how to start conversations and hated the way it seemed to come so easily to other girls. At school she had Jenny and Helen for break and lunch times. The three of them weren't exactly close friends but they bandied together to avoid the awful stigma of being alone. None of them had ever been formally ostracised by their peers, instead they were just ignored. Emma was considered to be boring and Jenny and Helen were intelligent and therefore branded nerds. Emma's attempts to cajole them into joining her at hockey were met with derisive stares.

The following Wednesday Emma made her way, after school, to the local recreation centre. As she approached she saw a group of girls all wearing nice bright tracksuits, some even had matching leg-warmers. Emma's heart sank. She was still in her school uniform. She had her PE kit in her bag, ready to change into, but these girls had arrived ready prepared, already changed for hockey. And not into their PE kits either, but into nice tracksuits that they must have especially for non-school sports. Why had nobody told Emma? Why wasn't there anyone who could give her a heads-up on what was the proper thing to wear and where the hell you should change into it?

The changing rooms were locked; the after-schools club had only hired the hockey pitch, not the facilities. There was a disabled toilet next to the reception desk that Emma managed to sneak into, here she quietly swapped her uniform for her PE kit. Once changed, she sighed and prepared to meet her peers whilst dressed inappropriately for the surroundings. Her black Woolworth's plimsolls were no match for the other girls' trainers. If you have been lucky enough to live a life free from loss, pain and betrayal, this is about as bad as it gets for a thirteen year old girl.

Emma made her way over to the group of girls and stood near them, but not amongst them. The chatted away happily, not including Emma in their conversation. Somewhere nearby a whistle blew and as one unit, plus Emma, the group moved towards a sickeningly healthy, energetic and enthusiastic looking woman in her thirties.

"Hello girls, welcome to the first session of our hockey club," beamed the animated stranger with a whistle. "We're all here so we can excel at sport, so we can really get into hockey, understand the importance of rules, get fit and have some fun along the way."

Oh dear lord, this was worse than Emma had imagined. First of all, whenever an adult tells you you're going to have fun, you can almost guarantee the reverse is true, otherwise why would they have to tell you? Secondly, Emma was not there so she could excel at sport, that unrealistic aim had been abandoned years before. Finally 'understand the importance of rules' really made Emma's heart sink. This whistle blowing stranger (Mrs Wilson) was obviously determined these sessions would be as much about personal growth as about sport.

Mrs Wilson had indeed read a book about encouraging teenagers to grow into healthy, productive adults. As a result she was going to make a group of girls run around in the freezing cold for their own good. Could it get any worse?

"Come on, come on, you're late!" shouted Mrs Wilson, "you must try to get here on time. You're making the other girls wait and that isn't fair on them now is it?"

The group turned as one to look at the poor unfortunate soul who had dared to show up late. Some of the girls giggled, turning the new arrival bright red. The girl stood next to Emma, who gave her a shy smile. Emma's smile was returned with a grateful beam.

Over the next hour they were made to warm up (star jumps and lots of jerky twists) and then split into teams to have "A quick knock-around, see what standard your hockey skills currently are," Mrs Wilson had explained. Emma and the late comer were put on the same team for a quick 10 minute skills testing game. At the end of ten exhausting minutes they were allowed back to the sidelines whilst the next teams had a go. Emma stood breathless, next to the equally panting late comer.

"Hi, I'm Jess," she gasped.

"Emma." She tried for a smile but it came out as more of a grimace.

"Not fit." This was part statement about Jess herself and part question for Emma.

"Not fit," agreed Emma, nodding and rubbing her ankle where a girl twice her size had smacked her with a hockey stick in order to get the ball. It wouldn't have been so bad, but the girl was on Emma's team.

"You like hockey?" Jess asked, her breath returning, meaning complete sentences would soon be possible.

"No!" came Emma's emphatic reply. "You?"

"Nope. I'm only here because Mum used to play for the county and she wanted to see if I could follow in her footsteps."

"Do you think you will?" Emma was starting to like Jess, she smiled easily and seemed as unwilling to be there as Emma herself. She waited a little apprehensively for Jess's reply; it could make or break the newly found kinship.

"Not bloody likely! I love my mum to bits, but being smacked around the ankle by a piece of wood on a freezing cold afternoon is not my idea of fun." Jess grinned broadly. "I said I'd give it a go, and I have. So far it's a big loser in my book. Mum will understand. You?"

Emma sighed, "Mum really wanted me to come and I'm

not sure how I'm going to get out of this."

"But you want out?"

"Oh yes!"

"Just tell her you didn't make the team, tell her they aren't interested in girls who aren't already good."

*That's bloody brilliant,* thought Emma.

"That might actually work." There was every chance her mum might have already forgotten her previous conviction to get Emma out of the house more. And, well, if hockey wasn't for her at least she'd tried. She could even pretend to be disappointed not to have made the team. She could actually turn this to her advantage. She wondered if a sympathy pair of stone-washed jeans would be pushing it too far.

"Come on, let's get out of here," said Jess.

"Can we do that?" Emma asked a little incredulously. Surely you couldn't just leave somewhere when you were supposed to be there.

"Of course we can, come on."

Mrs Wilson seemed engrossed in the match in progress. They looked around and slowly backed away towards the rec building.

Jess kindly waited whilst Emma changed back into her school uniform, they pooled what little money they had and went across the street to a café and ordered one Knickerbocker glory and two spoons. Over ice-cream they bonded over their mutual dislike for hockey and geography and their love of cats (which neither had), ice-cream and Blondie. Jess was so easy to talk to, she invited conversation. She had beautiful blond curls and the happiest pair of smiling blue eyes you could imagine. They laughed a lot over their ice-cream. It was the easiest conversation Emma had ever had in her short life; she had never before met anybody who could incite such articulation from her. Though they attended different schools they lived only a mile apart, easy walking or biking distance, and so arranged to meet the following Saturday.

On Emma's mum's part, whilst she didn't completely believe the story regarding hockey practice and not making the team, she did decide that if her daughter was prepared to make up such an elaborate lie then she must have really disliked hockey. Who was she to push her into something she didn't want to do? However, there was certainly no question of Emma getting a pair of stone-washed jeans out of it. No way.

# Chapter 3

That Saturday afternoon Emma and Jess went to see Top Gun together at the local cinema. They laughed together and cried together over a large buttered popcorn and a pack of Maltesers. At the end of the film Emma declared her undying love for Maverick and Jess for Ice Man. (Different tastes in boys would surely stand their friendship in good stead for later years). And that was it. From that day on they met at Jess's house every Saturday. Some Saturdays Emma would sit with Jess in her room and listen to Blondie, swapping gossip, reading Just 17 and discussing *Neighbours* story lines. Other times they would walk by the lake in the local park, or along the stream in the field that separated their houses. Emma finally had her first ever best friend.

Eventually the Saturday visits to Jess's turned into regular sleepovers, where they would stay up late in their pyjamas, listening to The Cure and developing theories about life. They'd had such little life experience but that didn't stop them forming such big theories about it. Theories flow so easily when you're talking to someone who really understands you, someone who can finish your sentences and know exactly what you mean by 'thingamabob'.

Emma loved Jess's easy manner and confidence; she seemed at peace with the world even whilst trying to change it (there was very little that the teenage Jess did not campaign for; though only young she had marched on Downing Street as often as the police who patrol it). Jess for her part found Emma to have a fantastic sense of humour (you haven't lived until you've seen Emma's impression of a giraffe). She also warmed to Emma's kindness and modesty, in a way she felt that Emma had great potential that no one else seemed to see and she was determined to bring that out. All Emma really needed was to gain some self-esteem, to stop believing that she didn't understand the world and to realise that she was capable of making the world whatever she wanted of it. Emma herself didn't know this, probably would not really understand it if she did. Probably never would, at least not until it was far, far too late. But Jess still had faith in her.

About 6 months after they met Jess discovered (at the grand old age of 13) a key she believed would help to Emma understand the world and her place in it. It was a way for both of them to reach a greater understanding, but Emma mostly. She found some books on dream analysis.

That Saturday Emma arrived as usual at about 10 o'clock, wearing a rah-rah skirt that had been fashionable approximately 4 years ago. Jess usually had a tape playing in her room but today the only sound was her excitedly flicking through new-found books.

"Emma, you're not going to believe this."

"What is it?"

"The answer to everything," Jess announced, making a sort of 'ta-dah' magician's assistance's flourish with her arms, which made them both giggle.

"Okay, really what is it?"

"Dream analysis," Jess paused for effect, and seeing no effect was apparent she continued "It's amazing. It's your unconscious mind interpreting your thoughts and the world and everything."

"What?"

"No, honestly, it's all here in these books. Did you know your dreams can be messages from yourself?"

"What?" Emma hadn't the faintest idea what Jess was talking about.

"Look, come here, help me go through this book and it explains everything."

It was raining outside and with nothing else to occupy them they spent the rest of that day and most of the evening pouring over Jess's new books. They decided pretty quickly that they didn't like Freud. They both felt a bit uncomfortable with the idea that *everything* is about sex, sometimes death, but mostly sex. After lots of giggling they decided to reject Freud.

Jung, however, now he was a different kettle of fish. Jess

liked Jung. She liked the idea that dreams were a way of making you look at alternatives, that the unconscious mind gave you scenarios to help you understand yourself better. She believed Jung was saying that by getting to know and interpret your dreams you would understand both yourself and the world better. Yes, Jess decided they were Jungian.

Emma didn't really know what ego meant, or what interpreting the unconscious meant. She had no idea what it meant to be a Jungian, but it seemed they were ones and she had no real problem with that. If Jess said it was right, then it probably was. Besides, she'd always felt that life should come with some sort of guide or map. Whilst this wasn't exactly Ordinance Survey, it was better than nothing.

The fun part came later. Luckily the book describing the Freudian and Jungian ideas was discarded once Jess decided they were Jungians. The next book was far more accessible to Emma as it was dedicated to actual dream analysis itself. It told how dreaming of dandelions meant a wonderful future for you but dreams about lions meant you were in danger. The book gave such simple, easy ways to interpret the present and foretell the future. It was a key for understanding the world. It seemed insane to them both that not everyone was in to dream analysis; it felt like they had stumbled across the secret to understanding everything. – Why hadn't their parents told them about this years ago? How come not everyone in the world was into this? Grown-ups, so caught up in the mundane had forgotten to be amazed at the world and all its answers. They pitied their parents and anyone who didn't understand this great advancement in human understanding. The rest of the night was spent looking up just about every dream they could ever remember having and then trying to remember what had happened the day after the dream in order to prove the book right. Of course, having already decided the book was right made it much easier to find evidence to support their belief.

From then on in whenever they spoke on the telephone or met up on a Saturday the book, their guiding light, would be pulled out and their dreams examined. Emma couldn't always remember her dreams so sometimes she made them up to keep Jess happy. Jess loved dream analysis and Emma just wanted Jess to be happy. Their friendship, of course, covered more than just the esoteric and they would speak on the telephone each evening after school. Once the dream analysis had been covered they would move on to the more mundane.

As the 6 o'clock news started on the BBC, Emma dialled Jess's number as usual. She had to wait until 6 o'clock for the cheap rate calls; in fact she came to always associate the start of the news with Jess.

"Jess?"

"Hi Emma. So?"

"So?" Emma wasn't sure what she was being asked.

"So, what did you dream last night?" Jess asked excitedly. "I've got the book here ready."

"Oh, okay. I dreamt that Mum, Dad and I were standing in the field at the bottom of our road and you know when the sun shines down through the clouds and it looks like shafts of light coming down? Well the light beams were all around us and I was with them, in the light, but I was also looking at the three of us from the pathway, if that makes sense? "

"Uh huh."

"Then this boy, I don't know who he was, came out and started throwing strawberries at us and I was on the side trying to stop him. But I was still with Mum and Dad as well." This was not a made up dream. This is what Emma had spent the night before processing in her sleeping mind.

"Bloody hell," said Jess, "hang on a minute." She flicked through her book. The dream was a bit too specific to have a definition of its own but she came across strawberries first so decided to start with them.

"Okay, strawberries indicate temptation or sexuality..." To which they both gave a simultaneous "Ooohhh" and then giggled.

"Bloody Freud, he gets everywhere doesn't he?" Emma joked. "But are you sure it's not strawberry jam?"

"Eh?" Jess queried.

"Well, it's just when I woke up I was thinking about when me and Mum, ages ago, went strawberry picking and she was going to make jam, but never got around to it and the strawberries all went mouldy."

"Could be, could be," Jess reasoned. "Okay, let's try sunlight. Oh, listen to this, sunlight represents radiant energy and goodwill."

"Oh brilliant." Emma liked the sound of this.

"So your dream means you are a sexy, enlightened person with lots of good will."

"Excellent!" Emma liked this even more.

"Yep, you are the ultimate femme fatal and very nice with it." They both laughed at this. Satisfied with Emma's dream they moved on to Jess's.

"Right, I dreamt last night that I was in a car and it could fly but whenever I wanted it to fly it would land and whenever I wanted to land it would fly."

"Bugger."

"Bugger indeed. I've already looked it up and it means that I have ambition and a sense of freedom but the not flying bit probably means I'm frustrated."

"Oh, what do you think the frustration bit means?" Emma worried; she assumed that it might have something to do with her. Emma found it hard not to assume things were about her.

"I think it's because I can't wait to be older. 16 seems like such a good age to me. I can't wait to be 16. It will be brilliant, we'll be able to get out of school, go to college, make our own decisions. It will be fantastic."

"Yeah!" Emma agreed emphatically. "Oh, that reminds me, you'll never guess what happened at school today!"

"What happened?"

"Well, you remember me telling you about Ms Daniels?"

Jess remembered; Ms Daniels was Emma's favourite teacher at school. And so the conversation went on. With the analysis over, the mundane took its place. As usual, Emma went on to recount tales of her school day and Jess laughed at the funny bits, shared her anger at the unjustified bits and bitched beautifully where applicable. Jess would then tell

Emma about her day, to which Emma would dutifully listen and respond as necessary.

Whilst Jess loved these chats, to Emma they were more than just idle gossip. Jess helped Emma to put her day into perspective. She slowly helped negate the vague feeling Emma had that she was always out of step with her surroundings; it also no longer bothered her to be the only girl in her class without a boyfriend. Somehow Jess always managed to make the things Emma worried about most seem trivial. Once they were made trivial, Emma could stop worrying about them. Jess's pragmatic approach to life balanced out Emma's teenage neuroses. Emma needed Jess in her life. Their daily conversations were ones Emma could never have with anyone else in her life; in fact, there *was* no one else in her life.

Back at the beach, Emma stood still again to look out to sea. Her walks were often punctuated with long periods of standing and staring. It seemed somehow rude to walk along the beach's edge without contemplating the sea. Like going to a christening just for the free buffet without once mentioning how cute the baby looks. She smiled as she thought again about Jess. Christenings were the basis one of their many theories. For the devout a christening is a time of great celebration. The non-devout only hold them for the presents. They stand up in church promising to guide their child in the light of God, but are really wondering if anyone bought the lovely, little Nike trainers they've been hinting about.

A beating she had once narrowly avoided at school made her think of just how often her thoughts and actions were guided by 'what would Jess do?' It did not, even now, occur to her that Jess had not actually saved her that day; rather, her own misplaced honesty had saved her. To Emma that was irrelevant, it was Jess that had saved the day. It was always Jess that saved her.

Thinking of their big life theories reminded Emma of another dream analysis session that had happened at Jess's house one Saturday. Again, this was not a made up dream, but rather one Emma had really dreamt. Jess was sitting, as usual, crossed legged on her bed when Emma arrived that Saturday morning.

"Jess, I had such a mad dream last night!"

"Tell me!"

"Well, I was walking around a really beautiful old ruin. The building was too crumbled to tell what it had been but there was still a large stone wall and some smaller walls but the whole thing was covered in green plants and ivy and trees growing out of everywhere. As far as I could see the trees and greenery went on and on. It was really, really beautiful." Emma paused at this point, wanting to ensure Jess had the full impact of how the scene looked. Her pause was also partly for dramatic effect.

"Go on," Jess encouraged.

"Then I realised where I was. I was in heaven."

"Seriously!" Jess exclaimed.

"Yep. It was heaven. It was my heaven. There wasn't anyone else around, no angels or anything like that. But it felt so peaceful I knew without any doubt that it was heaven. You know how in a dream you just know."

"True," Jess agreed.

"I had this feeling of being really calm, of just knowing that everything and everyone was okay."

"Wow, that's quite a dream," Jess agreed as she reached for her book.

"That's not all. Then I went to hell."

"No way! What was hell like?"

"It was exactly the same place."

"The same place?"

"Yep. It was exactly the same place. Only the feeling was different. I felt really anxious and worried. Like there was so much I needed to do but didn't know where to start or what it was I had to do. It felt horrible. I was searching around trying to find the feeling of heaven again but I couldn't because I was in hell and because it was the same place I didn't know how to get from one to the other." Emma stopped. The anxious feeling of the dream had not yet left her and talking about it made her feel it all the more. She tried to get back the feeling of dreaming of heaven but it escaped her.

"Bloody hell," Jess whispered, sensing the weight of her friend's emotions. They both sat in silence for a moment before Jess asked the question burning her mind.

"Was God there?"

"I didn't see him."

"Oh." Jess had been hoping for something a little more concrete. "Do you believe in God?" She asked.

"Yes. No. Wait, I don't know." Emma really did not know. She just always assumed she did believe in God but no one had ever asked her directly before. It made her think. It made her think she wanted to know what Jess believed.

"Do you believe in God?"

"I don't know." Jess's reply seemed a little sad, she wanted to believe in God and had spent quite a while thinking about it, but when it came down to it she just wasn't sure.

"It just seems, I don't know, so unlikely I guess."

"Well neither of us are religious," Emma reasoned.

"Maybe that's it," Jess brightened a little, "maybe I just don't believe in religion."

"How do you mean?"

"Well, okay," Jess took it slowly whilst she tried to organise her thoughts, "I want to believe there is more than just, you know, this." She gestured around her room. "But why does the church get to say what God is and what makes Him angry or happy?"

"Or Her." Emma was proud of her idea that God may not actually be a man.

"Good point. You see, exactly! Who decided God is a man? Who decided it's wrong to be gay or… or get divorced? Why is it wrong?"

Emma didn't know how to begin answering any of these questions, but luckily Jess wasn't looking to Emma for answers, just discussion. Besides which she was on a roll.

"I mean divorce doesn't seem to be the terrible sin it was a few years ago – did God decide She didn't mind anymore?" Jess liked referring to God as 'she'; it seemed to back up her argument. "Why should something be wrong for so many years and all of a sudden it not be wrong anymore?"

"Don't you agree with divorce?" asked Emma, missing the point.

"No, it's not that, it's just that religion can't say 'this is the truth, it's definitely the truth and that's all there is to it', then a bit later say 'oh well never mind, we're not that bothered anymore'."

"Maybe religions change; you know, evolve with the world and society and everything."

"Yes, but God either is or She isn't. how can you have something that is absolute but that changes at the same time? It doesn't make any sense." Jess was making herself quite annoyed; to her, inconsistency smacked of untruth.

"Just because religion got it wrong doesn't mean God doesn't exist." This was probably the most profound thing Emma had ever said. Jess looked at her.

"You know you might be right." She gave Emma a big hug and her mood lightened considerably. Jess wanted to believe there was a good and kind god who would right all wrongs but religion always seemed to her to get in the way of that belief. Emma had hit the nail on the head for her, given her a way to have her belief but without having to question it through a filter she felt to be too inconsistent. Emma just beamed, delighted that she had cheered her friend up and said something intelligent at the same time. It was a red letter day for her.

They spent the rest of the day theorising on the actual meaning of heaven and hell, and more importantly how to get to each of them.

"Maybe…what if, you have to judge yourself?"

"Well that sounds okay" reasoned Emma.

"No, it would be worse. I mean, you could convince a kindly, loving grandma type god that you were sorry, and you had good intentions, but can you really convince yourself of that, if you know it's not true?"

It was a big concept for them to understand. They hated the fact that there could be no proof either way, just a feeling, a belief. Finally Jess turned to the book to see what answers it could provide. It told them that dreaming of heaven denotes the desire to find perfect happiness, whilst hell highlighted repression, a feeling of being emotionally crushed. It seemed such a mundane explanation after their entire day of theorising. It felt unsatisfactory and they eventually put the book to one side and continued discussing the afterlife until it was time to join Jess's parents for tea.

Emma's need for Jess was made particularly apparent by an unfortunate incident at Emma's school. Emma survived it okay, but felt she never would have without Jess's support. One Saturday morning Emma arrived at Jess's looking sullen and red-eyed. She marched into her friend's room and threw herself on the bed. Through stilted sobs and enthusiastic nose-blowing she recounted to Jess the horrible scene from the day before.

Somehow one of the older girls at school had got it into her head that Emma fancied her boyfriend. The fact is, she had got it into her head because a girl in Emma's class, wishing to ingratiate herself with the older girls, had made the rumour up. Emma, of course, didn't know this. All she heard was a rumour that she was going to beaten up by a girl 2 years older than her.

Generally at school Jess and Emma managed to avoid being regular targets for the bullies. Instead they walked a fine line of keeping their heads down and above all obeying the cardinal rule of trying to never do anything that might result in them being noticed and therefore beaten up. Being accused of fancying an older, cooler girl's boyfriend was a nightmare situation. The only possible outcome would be years of being kicked, pushed, tripped and having the contents of her bag thrown over the playing field.

Indeed, the evening before as she'd walked home from school she'd been chased by three girls who'd knocked her to the ground before they ran off laughing. Emma had hurt her nose, scuffed her cheek and cried all the way home. She had mud on her white school shirt. Letting herself into her house, she'd called for her mum and dad, knowing only too well it would be at least two hours before either of her parents came home. So Emma had sat on the kitchen floor, alone, eating a chocolate mini-roll. Then she'd taken her shirt into the bathroom, washed out the dirt and dried it with a hair dryer before putting it with the rest of her uniform into the laundry basket. Then she'd run a bath and sat in the hot water feeling utterly miserable.

She gently washed her face and put her head under the water, holding herself under, trying to feel safe and secure. She was locked in her own home; they couldn't get her whilst she was in the bath. That thought comforted her a little. She broke free of the water, got out and rubbed herself dry with a big, course towel, carefully patting the soft, delicate area around her nose and cheek. Then she'd gone back into the kitchen for another chocolate mini-roll and waited until Saturday when she could see Jess.

On hearing this sorry tale of woe, Jess's first instinct was to give Emma a big hug. That helped a bit. Then Jess set herself about the task (as any good friend would) of finding every single expletive her young mind could think of to describe the perpetrators of this situation. 'What an ugly, cow-faced, dog, bitch!' Working herself into a real rage, Jess used every possible combination of insults she could possibly think of, until, verbally exhausted she exclaimed with disgust and defiance "I bet she's got shit stains in her knickers!"

Emma laughed so hard she nearly choked; a laugh full of happiness and joy at having a real confidante, a real true friend in a time of hopelessness. Jess laughed too and the pair of them howled until tears came down their cheeks.

The rest of the day was spent with dreaming up hundreds of scenarios in each of which this older girl was horribly humiliated and Emma made good, rising above all at her school to be crowned queen of the world. That would show them. Jess always made things right, always managed to put Emma back together again when she was feeling broken. They laughed a lot that afternoon and when it came to the evening, Silvia (Jess's mum) even let them order pizza to be delivered for tea. In the midst of anguish and despair it was a fantastic

Saturday as always.

Monday morning. Emma felt sick as she put on her freshly washed school uniform. The inane chattering of Radio 1 was not helping. She turned off the radio and the house fell deathly silent, save for the gurgling of the central heating. Her parents had left for work, as usual, in separate cars almost an hour ago. Monday morning was for breakfast meetings in the office. She thought of them, her mother happily sipping on what would probably be her fourth coffee, nodding to those around her in the boardroom. Her father sneaking yet another croissant from the plate in the sales office wondering if he'd beaten the other execs in last week's figures. Both blissfully unaware of the danger their daughter was about to face.

Morbid images flashed through Emma's mind; a beating that went too far, her blinded yet resilient, maybe winning a childhood bravery award? *Stop it*! She commanded herself and left for school with a stomach full of angry butterflies.

The day was uneventful all the way up to morning break, at which time a small crowd gathered around her. A kangaroo court. *Oh God, this is it,* thought Emma. Even in her fear she managed a wry smile. How did the crowd know? Were invitations passed out? 'Dear so and so, you are cordially invited to the trial and subsequent beating up of Emma'. How did everyone except her seem to know now would be the time, this the place? The few friends Emma had at school were nowhere to be seen, she was all alone. It was not so much that her friends had abandoned her in a time of crisis, but they had recently begun to distance themselves from Emma as they became increasingly tired with every sentence from her mouth starting with "My best friend Jess…"

The older girl walked towards her. Something Jess had said about shit stains in knickers flashed through Emma's mind. It didn't seem so funny now. What would Jess do? If she were here, what would her approach be? She clutched her bag with ever whitening knuckles, as if the bag might give her comfort, as if it might know what to do. *Just breathe,* she told herself. Now she really felt sick.

"Oi! I told you to leave Pete alone!" This was an odd

opening, as they'd never actually spoken before. Emma cast her eyes over the crowd; Pete, the Casanova in question, was indeed among the crowd. Bloody hell, was she about to be beaten up on the grounds that she was where he was, and he was only there because she was about to be beaten up? Hang on, that doesn't make any sense. *None of this makes any sense. This is stupid.*

Emma's mind whirled, she thought about Jess and about the best thing to do. Then she opened her mouth and words, which seemed to come from nowhere, but were actually coming from her mouth said, "I wouldn't touch your Pete with a bloody barge-pole, he's pig ugly and you're welcome to him!"

*Oh God, had she really said that?* Oh shit, she had just made things so much worse. What the hell had made her chose honesty now?! Not the best policy! Surely not the best policy!

Emma waited to feel the sickening thud of the other girl's fist against her cheek. Instead she heard a voice.

"You're not wrong, love, he is bloody ugly and all!' It was Pete's best friend. Pete had him instantly in a headlock and they were laughing. Laughing! They fell to the ground! Play fighting! At a time like this!

And that was it. The crowd started to laugh and engrossed in the play flight, moved gradually away from her. Emma had stated her case; the kangaroo court had considered its verdict and decided there would be no beating today.

The older girl narrowed her eyes as she looked at Emma, all the fight gone out of her. What use was a fight with no audience? What victory would that be? None at all. Realising perhaps now that she had put herself in a foolish position by accusing a younger girl of being associated with her boyfriend, she stared at Emma, her eyes narrowed to tiny slits and she hissed, "Piss off!"

*Gladly*, thought Emma.

# Chapter 4

Emma felt again now the force of emotions her dream so many years before had engineered. The afterlife was all a bit too much to try and contemplate now, Emma couldn't afford to lose herself again in idle theories. She needed to return to the present. She carried on along the beach, skipping back to miss the occasional rouge wave that came in too far, one that had apparently not heard the tide's call to retreat.

She now reached the harbour wall. A beautiful old stone wall, yellowed and greyed with age but bright in the sun's light. Stone steps, covered with water at high tide were now accessible, if a little slippery. Emma carefully walked down them and stood on the wet and silty sand below, under what, twice a day, would be the harbour's high tide mark. A few small dinghies floated on what was left of the water. In a few hours this would be flooded with water; it would be impossible to stand here. Emma liked that, liked the feeling she was doing something that not everyone could do, at least not all the time anyway. She crossed the soggy sand to the steps at the other side and carefully climbed them. The harbour looked so peaceful. No boats returning laden with fish and no accompanying screaming sea gulls. A few dinghies bobbing silently and a discarded piece of fisherman's netting were her only company. It bought to mind a few lines from a poem she had once read,

*Three men in a boat, they went out to tote*
*For fishes the whole evening through*
*But was it sea-bass or mackerel en mass that took them out into the blue?*

A lump caught in her throat as she was once again thrown back to her younger years.

Jess had something to show Emma. She was quite nervous about it, as it was a thing never seen by anyone else. She'd already pulled the blue folder out of its hiding place twice that morning, looked at it and then returned it to the safety of its secret spot. For a third time she went back to her book shelf and again pulled the folder out from where it sat, completely obscured from view, next to her secret diary. She sat on her bed and started to flick through its pages. The early entries made her smile. They were so childlike, clumsy and innocent.

As she'd grown up though her poems became less concerned with simple rhymes and seemed to her own critical eyes to have developed some merit. Oh, if only she could be sure they were any good. Her blue folder had been with her since she was 7 years old. So many nights had been spent snuggled into bed, scribbling away on scraps of paper, the best of which would be securely fastened into her blue folder. She had no idea if her poems were any good or just childish drivel. She needed to show her work to someone, get a second opinion and discover whether or not this was something she could do. Was poetry a talent of hers or merely an indulgence? She worried her blue folder may just be another version of her diary but in rhyming couplets. She worried it was immature. She had never felt so insecure about anything in her entire life. She could have shown her parents, but as teachers she dreaded that they may just mark it out of ten, correct her grammar and then hand it back with a silly smile.

At 10 o'clock precisely Emma came bounding into Jess's room.

"Good morn…" Was as far as Emma got before Jess blurted out:

"I have something to show you!" Damn it, that was not how she wanted to introduce her poetry, she wanted to do it casually, as though it were nothing in the world. Now here was Emma, mouth opened wide, staring at her, waiting for the big announcement. Jess tried again.

"Good morning Emma love, sorry, sit down, I didn't mean to make you go all wide-eyed and startled looking!"

Emma felt a little aggrieved at being criticised for her

natural reaction but sat next to Jess nonetheless.

"Okay, no one has ever seen this before," (this pacified Emma little); "it's nothing really. Well it is and it isn't." It was all Emma could do not to grab the folder out of Jess's clutched fingers. "It's all the poems I've written, well not all, but anyway. Some of them I was really young when I wrote them. But anyway, I want you to have a look at them. No, not now. I mean later, tomorrow, when you're on your own. Have a look and tell me if you think they're any good."

"Really?" Emma was both touched by the confidence her friend was giving to her and also desperate to have a nose through her work. She never knew Jess wrote poetry.

"Yes, I need a second opinion. Look it's nothing really, I just thought you might like to have a look and let me know what you think."

"Let me see them now!"

"No, only after you've gone home, you can't read them whilst I'm here!"

Emma's curiosity was a powerful beast though. She wanted to see them now and so for the next half hour or so she in turns pleaded with and scolded Jess who in return gave way to her insecurity and at first refused coyly, politely and finally quite harshly until it was agreed that Emma would take the folder home, read through the poems and then give her feedback the following Saturday.

It was not the best sleep over they'd ever had. In fact it was one of the worst. Jess worried that she should never have offered to show her work to anyone else whilst Emma sulked a little at not seeing it right this instance. By the time it came around for Emma to go home Jess nearly managed to orchestrate it so that the folder stayed with her but just at the last moment Emma ran back and insisted on taking it. So Emma left with Jess's most intimate thoughts clasped together in a blue folder. Jess waited for the feedback.

Once safely ensconced in her own room Emma opened the folder and did what she had been dying to do since she first heard of its existence. She scanned the pages for her name. When she realised she was not going to be mentioned by name she read a little more closely to see if she was mentioned by description instead. She read and re-read the poems until eventually she had to accept that she was not in any way a part of any of Jess's poems. She did wonder if perhaps the little blue bird might be her, but no, reading on it was clearly just a bird Jess had once seen.

So that was it. In Jess's most private and most expressive writings Emma did not even warrant a mention. Nothing at all. No ode to friendship could be found, nor either a throwaway line in any poem. Nothing. Emma huffed, sulked and discarded the folder. She never did read it to check the technical merit of Jess's work nor to see if the poems were any good at all. She never read it again and it was never spoken of again by either of them.

# Chapter 5

Emma did something then she would never normally do. She sat on one of the benches overlooking the harbour. Emma shied away from doing anything that might bring her into contact with other people unnecessarily. A sit on a harbour bench might encourage inane conversation with a tourist. But as there was no one else around, Emma sat. Besides, today was not really an ordinary day.

Emma had made a conscious decision to tell Ben about Jess, to open up her darkest feelings, lay them bare for him so he could see her as she really was. So he could see what it was that made her who she is. She felt this was the only way to the deep understanding that true love is dependent on. So, with a feeling of utter kinship, she led Ben to the pool and they both sat under the shade of a large umbrella, their feet dangling in the cool water and Emma began her story.

Hang on; thinking about Ben now is jumping ahead. It's not right; this story needs to be thought through in order, so all the pieces can fall together properly. However Emma couldn't help but think that it was Ben's reaction to what had happened with Jess that had somehow led her to today. The story with Jess had happened over 10 years before, but it was Ben's reaction many years later that led to today, though somewhat indirectly. In all honesty, it was very indirectly. Emma slowly began to face the possibility that maybe it was her reaction to it all that had led to today, just as her actions 10 years ago led where they did. She had blamed herself for so many years and rightly so. It was stupid to try and blame other people now.

She cast Ben from her mind, plenty of time for that later; for now she concentrated on Jess. Jess was always on her mind, she was always there in the background, forcing thoughts on Emma that she didn't always understand. Now it was time to face the memories she had worked so hard and so futilely to repress.

A Thursday in August 1989, three years after Emma and Jess first met, GCSE exam results day. Emma and Jess went separately to their respective schools to pick up their results. Jess, for her part, felt excited; she had done the best she could and now was the moment of truth. Emma felt sick.

Emma had studied hard for her GCSEs and much had been sacrificed. Her parents decided a month before the exams that Saturdays should no longer be a fun day spent with Jess, but rather a day for extra revision. Neither Steve nor Denise, her dad and mum, were on hand to help their daughter revise. It was expected that Emma would sit alone in her room and absorb the contents of large textbooks. Emma felt this was extremely unfair, she needed a break from study and her Saturdays with Jess provided the perfect escape, but this was denied her. So for all of April and much of May, with fun off-limits, Emma had done as she was told and sat studying whilst nursing a feeling of resentment at what she believed was an unfair regime imposed by her parents.

For hours she quietly read her way through textbooks, set herself questions, wrote short essays and went again and again over the same material. To alleviate the boredom she imagined herself passing, in her day dreams she could feel the thrill of collecting grades far above those predicted. Gradually she'd turned the frustration and boredom of study into something positive. She worked harder than she ever had before. She had done her bit and now it was time to reap some reward by achieving the good grades she felt she deserved. She still felt sick though.

At Emma's school the results were displayed on a giant board, no anonymity here, everyone could see everyone else's results. Emma scanned the board, looking further and further down, desperately trying to find her name. She had worked so hard, studied for so many hours. Where was her name? Where was it? She had sat for nine subjects but already had gone past all the people that had passed nine, eight, seven, then six then five, and then finally, she saw herself. Her name, and her four passes. Her head felt thick, like she was under water, short of breath and fighting for clarity. There were two teachers on duty, one with congratulatory smiles and one with tissues.

Emma didn't know which way to turn. Four passes was fine, it meant she could still sit her A-levels. It also meant that for all her study she had failed five subjects. Her eyes filled with tears; she tried to concentrate, look harder at the board.

Had she passed maths and English? Yes, just. She'd passed religious studies (like that would ever come in useful) and she had passed geography. She didn't even like geography. She had failed French, economics and all the sciences.

Emma felt so angry with herself. *A doctor?! Ha!* She had once thought she could be a doctor and she couldn't even pass GCSE biology. Her tears burnt full of hot anger and frustration. For all her hours of study and hard work, for all the time she had spent really applying herself (*God, how teachers love that phrase, 'apply yourself'*) for all that she had missed out on, she had proved herself to be just average. She wanted success and it had eluded her. She heard an incongruous laugh and looked round. Jenny Adams. Jenny Adams who hadn't done a scrap of work, who wore too much makeup and short skirts and had a boyfriend well into his twenties, had passed six. *Bitch!* thought Emma. *Bloody bitch!* Emma felt betrayed, betrayed by a stupid exam system, betrayed by teachers who had raised her expectations, betrayed by parents who expected far too much from her. Most of all, she felt betrayed by herself. She just wasn't who she thought she was; not the bright, intelligent, beautiful woman she wanted to be. If she really, really worked hard she could just about pull herself up to average. It wasn't fair. It wasn't right.

Emma walked quietly out of the school, passed the screeching groups of her classmates all full of congratulations, passed the small sobbing groups and kept her head down. She walked to a small, secluded spot amongst the trees at the far end of the playing field. She put her head against the cool bark of one of the trees and stood shaking and sobbing her heart out. She sobbed for the missed opportunity, for the failure. The four passes meant nothing to her. All she could see were the failures, the black and white proof that she was not good enough, or at least not as good as she thought. She stood for about an hour, by herself, feeling wretched, by turns crying with sadness and crying with frustration.

No matter how bad you feel, eventually you stop crying; there just aren't that many tears. So, eventually Emma stopped crying. She started walking, just headed off in no real direction. Walking made her feel a bit better. Like she was moving away from her failure. Only she wasn't, she carried it with her. But now her feelings were changing, she no longer felt so wretched; she no longer just wanted to hide away. Instead she was feeling reckless. She wanted to do something, something hard and stupid and dangerous, but she didn't know what. She did know, however, that she wanted to get drunk.

She changed direction and started to head to Jess's house. She didn't know what they would do, but Jess always made her feel better. Jess would put it all in perspective for her. After about half an hour she reached the house, stood outside and tidied herself up a bit. She tried to adopt a casual air; she didn't want Jess's parents Bob and Silvia to know of her failure, not yet anyway, not until Jess had made her laugh about it, made her realise she was still fantastic and that it didn't matter. The door was unlocked as always and Emma let herself in. No sign of Bob or Silvia, but upstairs she could hear voices. Two female voices. She shouted hello but no one heard her over the din of excited chatter coming from upstairs, so she wandered up to Jess's room.

Through the open door she could see Jess laughing and dancing around, she looked joyful. As she whirled round she caught sight of Emma and stopped, suddenly.

"Ems!" she called out, a little too loudly, "come in!"

Emma entered the room and there she saw Sarah.

Sarah was a girl in Jess's class, Jess had mentioned her before but Emma had never really been interested. She was Jess's best friend, anyone else just wasn't important. But now, for the first time, she came face to face with Sarah.

"Can you believe it?" screeched Jess, "Nine As and a B!" She grabbed Emma's hand and danced her around, trying to do a little jig, which Emma resisted. Not that Jess noticed. She was just too happy. She was swept up in the joy of success. Sarah laughed at their display, much to Emma's disgust. Jess was red faced from exertion and laughter as she breathlessly explained,

"Sarah and I got exactly the same results, can you believe it? The same grade for the same subjects! I had to bring her back here to celebrate! I'm so glad you're here, now we can plan our triumphant celebrations!"

She hadn't even asked how Emma had done. She had her ten passes and that was all that mattered at the moment. It wasn't that Jess was being selfish (though this was Emma's interpretation); she was just too happy. Sarah was also completely swept up in the moment and did not recognise Emma's discomfort. Sarah and Jess had a strong bond of happiness that afternoon that excluded Emma and they didn't even notice. *Ten bloody passes,* thought Emma bitterly, *includes home economics – who could care less about that?*

"Come on, what shall we do? How shall we celebrate our victory over exams? Come on! Think, my lovely ladies!" Jess's happiness was beginning to border on nauseating.

"Let's get drunk," said Emma. She feigned a smile, trying to mimic the happiness she saw around her whilst consumed with bitterness.

"Let's!" exclaimed Jess.

*My God,* thought Emma, *is she not even going to try and dissuade me? Is she really so wrapped up in herself she doesn't care that I want to get stupidly, dangerously drunk? Fine, I will then.*

"Yeah!" agreed Sarah (*oh, like you have any say in this,* thought Emma). "Let's get dressed up and go down the pub," Sarah continued gleefully, happy to have someone to share her joy and success with (her own best friend was on holiday in France for two weeks, so for now Jess and Emma would do).

Within minutes Transvision Vamp was screaming from the stereo, the contents of Jess's wardrobe were thrown on to her bed, make up boxes were flung open and the preparations for underage drinking began. Jess rummaged through her clothes, pulling out a beautiful silver top. Emma loved that top, now finally she might get a chance to wear it.

"Here, try this!" Jess threw the top at Sarah.

"Is that going to fit?" asked Emma, now on bitch overdrive.

"Yeah, 'course it will." Sarah said as she threw it over her head. My God, ten passes and she's still too stupid to work out when someone is taking the piss.

"What's your dad got?" Emma shouted over the music.

"You want to wear his trousers?" Jess shrieked. Sarah howled with laughter at this.

"No, I want to drink his beer." Emma had always had a problem with grinding her teeth and now they seemed in danger of shattering altogether.

"Oh, good idea!" Sarah approved heartily.

*Like we need your bloody approval,* thought Emma.

"Yeah, he won't mind, besides, I PASSED MY GCSEs!" Jess screamed the last part.

*Oh, for God's sake get over it,* thought Emma, *it's not like you solved world hunger.* Jess scampered off to see what she could find. Only Wendy James screaming 'Oh baby, I don't care' from the stereo broke what otherwise would have been silence in Jess's absence. In Sarah's case a silence borne out of careful and critical study of herself in Jess's mirror, in Emma's case a silence was borne out of contempt.

Jess returned with two bottles of red wine and three glasses.

"Erm, corkscrew?" Emma asked the question in such a way as to heavily imply that Jess was an idiot.

"I'm such an idiot!" Jess laughed and ran off again. Nothing, it seemed, was going to burst her bubble today.

"Oh honey, I don't care!" Emma sang along, trying to convince herself.

Soon the wine flowed freely, more so in Emma's direction, who drank far more than her fair share. Jess and Sarah seemed drunk enough on success to need much wine.

Two bottles of wine, a box of small French beers and two hours later, the girls were ready to hit the pub. Silvia and Bob had returned home full of congratulations for their clever daughter. What a bright girl, they were so proud. Caught up in Jess and Sarah's excitement Bob even handed over £20 for their night out. Only later, as the proud parents sat eating their chicken pie, did it occur to them that they hadn't asked Emma what her results were. Never mind, they could ask her tomorrow, she was bound to be staying over. Perhaps tomorrow Silvia should take the girls clothes shopping for a treat? Get Emma something nice as well; she never seemed to have any nice clothes of her own.

Sitting back at the harbour Emma thought back to her conversation with Ben, around the pool in Spain, years before. Had she skipped over the details of the way she felt that day? Had she made it clear enough? Had she only started the story when the girls were already in the pub? Was that telling it right? Maybe she hadn't told it right.

Emma thought with a sinking feeling back to that pub. The last time she had ever gone in there.

The pub door opened on to a raised platform on which was a pool table with red baize and a few chairs pushed against the walls. The bar was further down, reached by a few steps, with tables and chairs crammed in a line next to the wall. The floor was a bit sticky and the toilets had obviously not seen a bottle of bleach in many years, but that didn't matter. This pub would serve anyone; underage, drunk, high, it really didn't matter. Despite the less-than-luxurious surroundings. to an underage drinker, ensured of a pint, this pub was a beautiful sight. Making their way to the bar meant pushing through a group of lads, for tonight was the night for the pool team to practice. Which basically meant tonight was the night for a group of local lads to drink their own body weight whilst holding a pool cue.

"Oi! Oi! Make way for the ladies!" they'd called as the three walked in. Having been there since finishing work at 5 o'clock, the lads were already pretty drunk and bowed with tipsy flourishes as the girls walked passed.

"Morons," Sarah muttered under her breath to Jess and Emma. But Emma was pretty drunk herself and didn't mind the attention.

They made their way to the bar and ordered three pints of cider and black, which Jess paid for. Emma chose a table by the bar but near enough to the pool table, nearer than Sarah or Jess would have chosen. Jess raised her glass.

"To our current success and future prosperity!" she toasted, being deliberately formal and solemn, to which Sarah giggled and clanked her glass against Jess's. Emma simply nodded and drank, and drank, and drank until her pint was two-thirds empty.

"Ah," she said with satisfaction, smacking her lips together. Rather than raising an eyebrow at this (was Jess really so blind she could not see that Emma was unhappy? *My God, does she not know me at all?* thought Emma), Jess instead smiled at the challenge and knocked back half of her pint in one slug. Sarah tried to join in and managed a measly quarter of her pint. *Wuss,* thought Emma.

"So, what are you doing this summer?" Jess asked Sarah.

"Don't know, Sunita will be back from France in two weeks, then I guess we'll just hang out and celebrate not being at school."

*Dear lord, this is boring*, thought Emma. She felt dangerous and wanted excitement, something fun and distracting. She finished her pint.

"Your round," she said to Sarah as she slammed her pint glass down. This was part order and part challenge, almost daring Sarah to contradict her so she could start a pointless argument. Partly also daring Sarah to finish her bloody drink so that at least she and Jess might feel part way as drunk as Emma, so at least she might feel some sort of connection to them.

"Right-oh," said Sarah, without the slightest hesitation, and downed her pint. Sarah was a nice person, no real malice to her, but at this point Emma just wanted to hurt her, maybe even humiliate her, just to make herself feel better.

"I'll have a vodka and coke. Double." *Go on; refuse to buy it,* Emma thought belligerently.

"Yeah, double vodkas all round!" Sarah beamed as she swung round towards the bar. Then grabbed the back of her chair, swayed slightly and carried on towards the bar.

*God damn it, is this girl just going to agree to anything? Bloody wuss.*

"So, Emsy," began Jess. She was drunk, drunker than she had been before. A lack of food and drinking too quickly was beginning to catch up with her. She needed to partly close one eye to see Emma clearly and her words were becoming more slurred and more cutesy.

"So, Emsy," she continued, "my Emsy, what shall we do this summer? What shall our plans for world domination be?"

Emma was tempted to just ignore the question, pretend Jess hadn't spoken, but looking round the bar she spied the guys at the pool table.

"Let's get laid." She looked Jess square in the eyes, not an easy thing to do as Emma was herself now squinting a little.

"Uh?" Jess hiccupped.

"Yeah, we've left school, we're 'adults'," said with extra emphasis on the word adults, somehow managing to make it sound like a rude word, "I think I'm gonna get laid; see him? He'll do, he's been looking at me since we came in here." The lad in question had once, by coincidence, caught Emma's eye when looking round the bar. Emma was drunk enough and bitter enough to consider this a come-on.

"Oh, sex!" Jess made the word sex drag on for far longer than a sober person would. "Mmmm, maybe." She nodded solemnly, as if she would definitely give this suggestion careful consideration. *For God's sake!* Emma's mind screamed, how far was Jess prepared to let Emma's self-destruction go?!

For Jess's part, she was as drunk as she'd ever been and happy with the world. Happy enough and drunk enough not to be able to see the suffering her friend endured. Besides which Emma could be a bit over-dramatic at times and probably wasn't really going to have sex right now. The idea of having sex right there in the pub, the inappropriateness of it, made

Jess involuntarily burst into shrieks of laughter. Unaware that Jess was laughing at her own private thoughts and not at Emma herself, Emma felt angrier than she had ever been in her short life, filled with rage and bitterness and hatred of anything or anyone that might dare to be happy at a time like this.

Frankly, on some level Emma knew this was all getting a bit out of control, that she needed to get a grip and stop behaving like such a bitch. But on another, more conscious level, she just couldn't help herself. She wanted to give into her anger.

Sarah returned with their drinks.

"What's this?" Emma demanded of Sarah, as she handed her a vodka and coke.

"The finest vodka and coke the cellar of this fine establishment produces." Sarah wasn't being sarcastic, she was in a silly mood, a funny mood, she was happy and wanted others to laugh with her. She was also drunk and took far longer than needed to say the word 'establishment'. Emma, no surprises here, misinterpreted Sarah's comments for sarcasm.

"Get me one with a diet coke in, like I asked for." Emma was really pushing it now. Jess intervened.

"Oh Emsy, get it down you, besides we've had no tea, the calories in the coke can be like dinner for us."

Emma knocked her drink back in one swig.

"Fine."

She stood up, not quite sure where she was going, the lad who had caught her eye was deep in conversation and she was just (only just) sober enough not to go and interrupt, she did have some (very little at this point) pride after all. Instead she swung round towards the toilets. The swing nearly caught her off balance and Jess and Sarah failed to suppress a giggle at this. *Bloody children,* Emma thought disgustedly.

Whilst in the ladies, Emma's drunken mind justified her behaviour. She was far more mature than either Jess or Sarah; they were just idiots, still concerned with exam results. Whilst Emma herself was a true lady, mature, grown up, beyond caring about such trivial matters as results. Yeah, she would show them, she'd have sex and prove herself to be a true adult.

Poor Emma and her delusional, drunken thoughts, could not possibly know that back at the table Jess had suddenly, through her own drunken fog, realised she had not yet asked Emma about her exam results. Hadn't Emma received the same grades as her? No wait, that was Sarah. As a true friend, Jess had to immediately make amends and find out how Emma had done. As Emma walked out of the ladies, from far across the other end of the pub came, what would be in any other circumstance, a friendly yell.

"Em! What were your test results?"

Oh dear. An unfortunate choice of words, shouted too loudly in an unfortunate setting. The entire pub stopped and looked at Emma and laughed. Half wondering if she were pregnant, half wondering what potential illness she had (HIV being the big issue in all the press at the time), but laughing nonetheless at her obvious embarrassment. Emma managed, somehow, to give a fitting answer.

"Negative!" she screamed back. The pub cheered, happy that the young girl standing in the corner by the toilets wasn't going to make them uncomfortable with some news of reality.

The answer, of course, threw Jess somewhat off-balance. She smiled a sloppy grin at Emma as she crossed the room towards her.

"No, see, what I meant was..." she began to explain as Emma approached. But Emma was not listening. She was now beyond furious. She could kick Jess for making such a fool of her. She stormed passed the table and directly towards John, the lad who had once, by accident, caught her eye.

"All right," he said in greeting as she got near him.

"Yeah, want to help me celebrate my negative test results?" Emma asked with what can only be described as a leer in her eyes.

For his part, John was neither an idiot nor a particularly bad person. He was, however, an 18 year old lad. And this particular 18 year old lad was as driven by his libido as much as any other. All he saw in front of him was an okay looking girl (nothing to be embarrassed about when telling his mates later) who was coming on to him in a way suggesting she would be happy to go further than might normally be expected. *Game on*, he thought.

"Yeah, whatever," in his mind he was the Steve McQueen of cool. "You want a drink?"

"Mmm, double vodka and coke, please."

And so the tone of the evening was set. For the next two hours Emma hung round the pool table, laughing and flirting, becoming louder with each drink. She could barely stand. Jess sat watching this display with Sarah. She was getting worried. At first she just thought Emma was up to some sort of game, just being silly and having a little flirt. That she would return to the table at any moment with a round of drinks for all of them, possibly with John's phone number tucked in her purse and they would gossip and laugh about her new 'boyfriend'. It would be fun.

But it became increasingly obvious that Emma was not going to return to the table. In fact she didn't seem able to move more than one breast-width away from John. This was getting silly. *What the hell was Emma doing? She couldn't really like this boy so much after such a short space of time? She was acting, well, like a tart.* And why the hell did she keep throwing such odd looks at Jess? Jess did not like this one bit. As she became more engrossed by what was happening at the pool table, Sarah was just becoming more bored. This night had been fun to begin with, but frankly Jess's friend Emma seemed like a bit of a bitch and Jess herself had gone a bit quiet and moody. *Sod this,* she thought, *I'm off home.*

"I'm calling it a night," she said.

"Uh?"

"I'm going to call a taxi and go home, you want to share one?"

"No, Emma's staying at mine tonight, I better wait for her."

"Suit yourself; I'll see you, yeah?"

"Mmmm," was the distracted reply.

"Bye then."

"Oh, sorry, yeah, bye Sarah, you all right getting home?"

"Yes, I'm going to order a taxi."

"Oh yeah. Take care, see you soon."
"Take care getting home yourself, yeah."

Sarah waited outside for her taxi, the evening had taken a slightly odd turn and she was glad to be out of the pub. Half an hour later she was lying in bed thinking, *Wow, that Emma really is a bit of a bitch.* She then threw up into a bucket she had the foresight to bring upstairs with her and fell asleep.

Back at the pub Jess, rather than sit alone at the table, made her way over to Emma. For the last round Jess had ordered a pint of water, too much drink and not enough food had caught up with her. She felt a bit sick and over above all she felt very tired.

"Em, you coming home?"

Emma ignored the question.

"Em! Are you coming home now?"

"What? No! I'm waiting until last orders."

"I want to go now though."

"Well bloody go then!"

"Aren't you staying at mine?"

"Don't know where I'm staying actually." Emma leered suggestively at John and moved closer to him. This was getting a bit much, Jess tried one last tactic.

"Em, come to the ladies with me?"

"Oh for God's sake Jess, you're potty trained aren't you? You don't need me!" This was nasty, horribly nasty and Emma knew it. John didn't, he howled with laughter.

"Fine!" shouted Jess as she stormed out of the pub.

The concern she had felt for her closest friend now turned to real anger. She was furious with Emma for behaving so badly. What the hell did she think she was doing? If alcohol made her into such a bitch this was definitely the last night she would ever drink with her. Bloody stupid cow. Call herself a friend did she? She could piss off.

Jess was too wound up to wait for a taxi and so stormed down the road towards home, her thoughts consumed with finding inventive new ways to describe Emma as the ultimate bitch. She could not believe she had been worried about Emma when all evening she had been behaving like such a bitch.

At the pool table, clinging to John, Emma did feel a momentary pang of guilt. She had treated Jess very badly. *Oh, screw her!* For a reason Emma could no longer remember tonight was all Jess's fault somehow anyway. John managed to untangle Emma long enough to go and buy another round of drinks. Emma knocked her drink back in one swig. She had to hold it in her mouth for a second, uncertain whether she could actually swallow it or would have to spit it on the pool table. Luckily she just managed the former.

In the next half-hour up to closing time she just about managed to finish one more drink. Then the lights came up and it was time to go. The pub's bright lights made everyone move out pretty quickly, partly as their eyes hurt in adjusting to the new light and partly because this was not an establishment you wanted to be able to see too clearly. It looked rank.

Outside the group of lads decided, with much jostling, shouting and urinating up the side of the pub, that they would go for a kebab. Emma didn't want a kebab; the thought made her stomach turn. She did, however, want to remain clinging to John. She grabbed him and kissed him. It could possibly have been a seductive kiss but they were both so drunk it was more of a mutual slobbering over each other. Emma moved back against the wall, she was having real trouble standing up now. The lads all whistled and jeered as they left the 'love birds' alone and made their way to the take-away.

Moving further back into the shadows of the alleyway next to the pub, Emma and John fumbled through each other's clothes. Emma's head was swimming. Thankfully through the slobbering Emma managed to break away long enough to mumble the word 'condom'. John had earlier in the evening moved the condom he had been carrying around hopefully for the last two years into a more accessible position. He now retrieved it from his front pocket and rolled it into place. After a few sweaty, slightly painful minutes, Emma lost her virginity. That was it, done. One further slobbering kiss from John and the whole experience was over.

Being a true gentleman, John flagged down a taxi, bundled Emma into it and stuck £5 in through the driver's window.

"Take her home mate," he said as he slapped the taxi roof with his hand and swaggered off to the kebab house. His friends were about to be regaled with a (mostly fictitious) tale of the great seduction and his role as stud. He hadn't even had to pretend he would call her. Sadly for John, had he known more about sex, he could have hung round for at least another 10 minutes or so before going off to brag to his mates. The fact he followed after them so quickly forever earned him the nickname Quick-Draw John.

Emma made the taxi drop her at the end of her road. She was feeling quite a bit more sober now and realised the importance of not waking her parents as she sneaked unexpectedly into the house.

She crept into the bathroom to wash herself down. As she quietly washed she reflected on the evening. This was not how she had wanted to have sex for the first time. She had imagined romance and a beautiful candlelit room; a large bed made up with soft sheets into which she would tumble, laughing, with her great love. A piss-soaked alleyway next to a pub was a poor substitute.

Oh well, done now. She felt very tired and tender. She did not want to think about Jess. That would have to wait until morning. She knew she had a hell of a lot of hard work to do there, a lot of ground to make up. But that could wait; all she wanted to do now was fall into bed. So she did and fell into an almost unconscious sleep which lasted well into mid-morning the next day.

# Chapter 6

The next morning Emma woke up with a feeling of urgency. She had to get up and do something and in the brief instance before the full power of her hangover hit her like a steamroller, she could not quite remember what is was she had to do. Then it came to her, both the memory of the night before and the gut wrenching, head pounding, brain splitting, eye piercing hangover.

She was not sure which was worse; the unfathomable pain (this was her first real, proper hangover) or the memory of how she had behaved. Sex with a stranger, her first encounter of that kind, well, she would just have to work out and deal with her feelings about that later. For now, she had a much more urgent task. Just as soon as she could lift her head from the pillow she had to go and make amends with Jess. Oh God, she had treated her awfully. She had ignored her, been rude to her and finally humiliated her in front of a pub full of strangers.

Jess would understand though, wouldn't she? Once Emma explained to her how she had been feeling yesterday, she would understand where all the venom came from, wouldn't she? Jess wouldn't care about a pub full of strangers, would she? No, if Emma could just explain it all properly, the full extent of her failure, then Jess was sure to understand. Yes, she would be angry, but eventually she would come round. They were best friends and one drunken night of stupidity shouldn't come between that.

Emma almost had herself convinced that maybe her crimes weren't so bad when compared to avalanche of failure she had experienced yesterday. She would talk to Jess and eventually they would be okay again and then maybe Jess could start the process of making Emma feel better about the whole sorry affair.

In the other room, the telephone started to ring (or shrieked like a banshee as it sounded to Emma). Could it be Jess?

Maybe Jess was worried about her and wanted to see if she was okay. Or maybe she was calling to tell her she never wanted to see her again. Oh God, Emma felt nuclear missiles launching from inside her head, making their way to her stomach and she wanted to die. She could hear her mother's muffled voice talking in to the phone. Okay, maybe the call wasn't for her. She still had time to call Jess and be the one to make the first move. That seemed important somehow. Right, she had to lift her head up and get out of bed. Slowly.

Jess had stormed out the pub the night previously, full of anger directed at Emma. She stomped down the road, her eyes blazing and her mind reeling with expletives aimed at her would-be best friend. *Stupid, bloody ignorant, selfish cow,* she thought. *Bloody well talk to me like that, will she?* As she passed the fish and chip shop two lads were about to call out to her, make a few lewd suggestions, but as they caught sight of the look on her face, they thought better of it and moved back out of her way. Jess didn't even see them. She was consumed by her own thoughts.

As she marched along, tiredness started to take hold. She had been drinking for many hours and was beginning to feel the ill effects. She wobbled a little as she walked. She slowed down to a gentler pace of stomp. *Bloody Emma, honestly. What was she going to do with her?* The violent action of her forced march made her feel a bit sick and she stood for a moment, her back against a wall.

As her fierce pace stopped, so too her anger started to dissipate. She sighed to herself. *Bloody Emma. What had been her problem?* As Jess slowly (somewhat tentatively) resumed her journey home she started to wonder what had caused Emma to behave as she had. She thought the world of Emma and knew there must be something more, something that had turned her into such a cow for the night.

As she stumbled along she thought back to the 'negative' test results. *Had Emma failed her exams? Is that what this was about? Oh lord.* Jess, in her kindness, started to feel a bit guilty. Perhaps her own celebrations and good fortune had soured Emma's mood. Perhaps the fact that Jess, as her best friend, had not seen there was something wrong earlier had pushed Emma to behave the way she did. Still, that was no excuse.

Jess was nearing her house now. She would call Emma tomorrow, get her round, sit her down and they would have a good, long talk about tonight. Everything would be alright; they would sort it out and go back to being best friends who have fun together, maybe with a bit less alcohol in future. That's what they would do. It would be okay.

Jess felt much happier now, calmer. She hated fighting with Emma; it was not something they had ever really done before. This was new. It would be sorted out and hopefully not happen again.

Jess was really finding it hard to walk now. She just wanted to be in her own bed and sleep away tonight. As she staggered along, she pushed herself off each lamppost to help propel her home. All she could think of was bed, even sorting out Emma was now stored at the back of her mind. She was concentrating so hard on just getting home that she was quite oblivious to her surroundings. *Nearly there. Bed soon. Nearly there.* She wobbled a bit. Was she still on the path or in the road? *Hang on, need to keep going forward. Oh, this is hard. Just keep going forward. Mmmm, bed soon.*

She didn't hear the car behind her. The car behind her didn't see her. Was she in the road, or did it clip the curb? No one knows. All Jess knew was that suddenly she wasn't going forward anymore. She was going up. She didn't have time to register what was happening before her upward motion stopped and she fell. She fell down hard and smashed her head against the pavement. The car was gone before she even hit the ground. The driver knew he had hit something. He wasn't sure what, but he had hit something and he needed to get out of there. This wasn't his car. So he just kept driving and didn't look back. He sped away as Jess's skull crashed against the ground. Her head smashed down and crushed against the hard pavement. Her eyes were open in a fixed stare.

She didn't see the car drive away. She was already dead.

# Chapter 7

Sitting on the harbour bench, Emma tried to focus on the digestive biscuit-coloured sand before her. Her vision would not stay solid and instead dissolved the scene into tears. A few large drops made their way down her cheeks. She had to stop this. She could not afford the luxury of breaking down now. She still had so much more to work through. Part of her wanted to jump up and keep walking, to physically shake the sadness off. But sitting here, part of such a calm and beautiful scene, was allowing her think clearly, to think about Jess and all that had happened. So she resolved to sit a while longer.

The day she had learnt of Jess's death was still a confusing mess in her mind. She still could not put it into any chronological order. She had spoken to the police to confirm she had not witnessed anything. She had spoken to Bob and Silvia. She had spoken to her own mum and dad. She knew those conversations had taken place, but those conversations meant nothing. All the while her mind had screamed at her that she could not talk to the one person she needed to; the one person she had to talk to. More than this, so much more than this, her mind had screamed at her the one truth she had carried ever since – that it was all her fault.

Just the week before Jess had dreamed of having a lion as a pet. Emma had convinced her that having the lion as a pet meant she would conquer fear, not that she was in danger as the book initially suggested. They both liked this theory so they accepted it. But the book had been right. Jess was in danger and that danger was Emma herself.

If only she had been walking with Jess as she should have been, if only she hadn't shouted at her and embarrassed her, Jess would not have been at that place at that fateful time. It was Emma who had put her there. It was Emma who insisted they get drunk. It was Emma who had wanted to go to the pub.

It was Emma who had behaved so badly.

It was Emma who had killed Jess.

Emma knew this; her guilt drilled itself into her mind, set up camp and would never leave. To begin with it was the guilt that was hardest to bear, that and the loss. But worse was to come.

No one understood. That was what made it so hard. No one understood that she was the one who had killed Jess. No one punished her, no one shouted at her, no one made her pay for her terrible crime. At the funeral Silvia had tried to put her arms around Emma, to comfort her. Silvia recognised what a painful loss this was to Emma. But Emma had frozen at this display of support. Her arms had hung down her side as Silvia pulled her closer. She couldn't reach out to Silvia. She couldn't find any solace in Silvia's attempt to reach out to her.

Because Emma was the one who had killed her daughter. She was the reason Jess would not grow up into a beautiful woman. She was the reason Jess would never get to change the world. It was all her fault and nobody else could see it. Nobody was prepared to punish Emma so she did it herself.

Over the next few months Emma turned in on herself. She became obsessed with the conversation that was always running in her mind. The conversation where she told Jess that she was sorry. It haunted her because she knew it was a conversation she would never, ever be able to have.

Her parents were so understanding. All through the summer they understood. At school in September, her teachers understood. Everybody understood that Emma had suffered a terrible loss and needed to be treated carefully. Everybody understood.

Except they bloody well didn't.

No one understood; no one comprehended that Emma was not feeling just loss. She was consumed with guilt and every gentle overture, every kind word, every understanding smile just made her want to scream at the world, 'I killed Jess and it should have been me!' Emma should have been the one to die. Jess had a future, she had kindness, and she had all the qualities that made her a fantastic person, someone to love and cherish. Emma had nothing, *nothing* to offer the world. If life were at all fair, she would have been the one to die. The fact that she had to live on and face what she had done every waking moment was the cruellest irony of all.

The guilt Emma felt was further enhanced by her isolation. She was suffering because of what she saw as her crime. But it was more than that. Emma had lost her confidant, she had lost her ally. She had lost the one person who could have reached out to her and helped her understand what she was going through. Jess knew Emma well enough to have seen her predicament for what it was – a sense of misplaced guilt. But without Jess's counsel Emma continued steadfastly down her destructive path.

Emma's world was now one where she was the evil villain; not a femme fatal, not an intelligent, beautiful woman, but rather a cruel bitch who had bought about the death of an innocent young girl. During this time Emma also stopped analysing her dreams. It seemed wrong to seek guidance and advice from the source Jess had introduced her to. How could she benefit from such a powerful tool when she had no right to? There was no point without Jess.

After the funeral, Emma stopped speaking. She had nothing to say to anybody. So why bother? If she didn't speak then no one would talk to her. She could be left alone to nurse her guilt. She went into her bedroom and sat alone all summer. Her parents accepted that she needed time to come to terms with her grief. So they left her alone.

As the weeks turned into a month and it was time to return to school to start her A-levels, they began to lose patience a little with her. Her mother would come into her room and sit beside her on the bed and talk into the silence. She talked about never forgetting Jess, how she would always be a part of Emma, but now it was time to get on with life.

Emma had wanted to slap her mother. How dare she? How bloody dare she? How could she honestly think that Emma was anywhere near ready to return to normal yet? Did her mother just think: *Oh well you murdered your best friend, hey-ho, time to move on?* Emma forgot, of course, that her mother didn't know she had been the one to kill Jess. In her fury she just stared at her mother in silence, her eyes dead, her face expressionless until eventually her mother left her room and did not return for another of these chats.

Emma went to school to do her A-levels, because what else was she going to do? She went to school because that was where she was meant to be. But still she didn't speak. She had appointed herself judge, jury and executioner at her own trial so she had no need to talk. She was too busy condemning herself in her own mind. Her teachers were unaware that she was not learning. At home as she sat alone in her room at night, her parents were unaware that she was not studying. She would sit for hours with an open book in her lap but her mind was far from Shakespeare. She was pleading with Jess to forgive her.

Eventually she would start to speak again. The catalyst was her parents – well, her mum really. It was now February 1990, six months after Jess's death. Emma was alone, as always, in her room with an open, unread book. Why would she always open a book? Why pretend to study? She had no idea; it was just a habit she had formed. There was a knock at her door and both her parents entered. This was new, mum and dad coming in together. *Blimey, it's a posse.* Emma would have once laughed at that. So would Jess.

They had news. They needed to talk to Emma because it concerned her. Emma looked at them both in silence. It had not occurred to her that once she stopped speaking the house had fallen quiet. All her thoughts concerned only her and she had not noticed anything beyond. If she had noticed she would probably have put it down to a silence out of respect for her feelings. But that would have been wrong. The fact of the matter was, her parents had stopped speaking many years before.

To be honest, it suited them both pretty well. Denise and Steve's home worked like a business, each knew their role and fulfilled it well enough. Neither particularly missed the love or the passion in their marriage. Each had had little indiscretions on the side, but nothing serious, nothing they need admit to the other. However, an offer had been made, something to upset the balance. Denise had been offered the chance to relocate to her business's high-profile New York office, to head up a new division. It was a dream come true. Steve knew it and would certainly not stand in his wife's way, even if he could. They still had a mutual respect and he knew what this meant to her. However, there was no question that he would go with her. And, it seemed, no question that Emma would be going either.

Denise had been offered the job three months ago but had asked for a deferment because she had 'family issues'. Her office had understood. But now they felt that the extra three months had been quite long enough to deal with an upset teenager and so it was time for Denise to make her decision.

And so she did. She would be leaving in three weeks.

So, Emma's family was about to be ripped apart. Her mother was about to leave for the other side of the planet. She had no idea when she would see her again. She honestly had no idea if she would see her again. This surely meant it was time for Emma to say her first words in over six months. She rose to the occasion.

"Okay."

# Chapter 8

Was this really helping? Sitting here by the harbour? Was the peace and calm and beauty really helping Emma to piece together where it had all gone so horribly wrong? She decided no. She got up and quickly began to pace along to the next part of her journey.

For the next part of her walk she needed to join the road a while before she could turn down the steps to the estuary. This was the most beautiful part of the village. The houses here perched against the edge of a mountain, a mountain supposed to contain gold, which was itself gold with flowering gorse bushes. Emma barely glanced at it. She thought instead of the time following her mother's departure. The months of living with a dad she barely saw. Though she was talking again they hardly spoke because they had so little to say to each other. On the second Saturday of each month at 3pm GMT her mother would phone from America.

"Hello, Emma darling."

"Hello Mum."

"How is everything?" Denise would ask hopefully, wondering if she might get an answer beyond a grunt that seemed to indicate 'fine'. As long as Emma kept using non-committal grunts her mother couldn't push her any further into conversation. At first Denise filled the silences with details of her new life, conscious that Emma was barely listening, until she, too, stopped talking. What could she do when she was so far away? In their first long distance call Denise managed to fill almost 45 minutes, but as time wore on their calls trimmed down to less than 5-6 minutes. There was only so much Denise could ask and only so much Emma could grunt.

The following February, less than a year after Denise had left she had to attend a conference on the second Saturday of the month. She'd meant to call Emma the week before but had been too caught up in preparing her presentation. She was going to do it the week after but the day just slipped away from her. By the end of the month Denise still hadn't called. It was hard being reminded month after month that she had no relationship with her daughter. It was hard trying to drag conversation out of someone who didn't care if you were speaking to them or not.

So Denise managed to put Emma in a little box in her mind. Emma became a little dark shadow that would creep out only occasionally to remind her of her failure. The shadow's cold, icy fingers would grab the back of her throat, at times when she least expected it, making her catch her breath and for a moment feel horribly disconcerted. The rest of the time she contented herself with the idea that her daughter no longer needed her, that she had done a good job of making her independent, so it didn't matter whether she called or not.

Since it was easier not to call, that was the path she took.

Back at home Steve was working very long hours; at least, that was what Emma would have assumed, had she bothered to think about it. In fact he had resumed an affair which had tailed off some 18 months previously, and it was going pretty well. There was, more often than not, food in the house. If Emma felt hungry she would cook something. If her dad felt hungry he would cook something. Each was polite enough to always cook extra, so invariably there were plastic containers in the fridge full of leftovers. If Emma noticed something was dirty, which was very rare, she would usually clean it and if Steve noticed, he would clean it himself.

As such the household ticked along well enough. Sadly, however, it was a house occupied by two people who were becoming increasingly estranged. It bothered Steve. He wanted to be a good dad, partly because he hated to fail at anything, but he hadn't the faintest idea how to reach his daughter now. Emma mused that the bond of friendship was so much closer than that of child and parent, but only because she had never had a friendship run its natural course and drift apart.

She needed to shake off this feeling of regret. It was not

helping and was not the purpose of this walk. She needed to get back on track. She needed to start to bring Ben into it.

She had moved to London after her A-levels. She had failed them badly enough to ensure university was out of the question. She had studied hard for her A-levels, in fact, study was pretty much all she had done for those two years. Two long years of sitting alone in her room staring at books, staring at the wall and then back at the books. But the books contained words that were not important, that had no meaning to Emma. She had tried to absorb the information they contained, even convincing herself she was succeeding, and so when the day came and the envelope with her results finally arrived it seemed the cruellest blow.

She'd failed everything. She was a failure. It was written in black and white.

Final proof of what Emma herself suspected and what was now writ large on a sheet of A4. She was a failure. She had allowed herself to begin to believe that maybe two years of staring at books might pay off, that maybe she could make something more of her life, maybe she could pass and perhaps even go to university. Her results slapped any such optimistic thoughts right out of her. The tiny window that had opened inside her that may have let some light back into her life was slammed shut.

Emma couldn't believe she had been so stupid. Not stupid in that she had failed her exams, but stupid in that she had actually believed she might pass. A year after Jess's death, out of boredom more than anything else, she had started to take a mild interest in her study. It distracted her from the only emotion she ever felt – guilt. As the second year wore on she began to convince herself that perhaps she could pass her exams. Perhaps she could still prove herself as an intelligent woman. Perhaps she might in some way be able to honour Jess by taking her place in the world. If she could prove herself as having a strong mind then maybe she could go on and achieve all that Jess would surely have achieved. Maybe in this way she could make amends with Jess. Maybe it need not be that

Emma had denied the world of all the good work that Jess would have done as Emma could do it in her place. If she could pass her A-levels it would put her on the right path. She could atone for her crime.

Her failure was a massive slap in the face. Who was she to think she could replace someone as amazing as Jess? She had no right to even think it. She had killed Jess and would be forever punished for it by her own failure. Thinking any differently was just pure arrogance. She had allowed herself a brief period of hope and when this was taken away she was left feeling even more desperate than she had at the time of Jess's death. She had dishonoured Jess by pretending to be as good as her. Emma's guilt increased ten-fold. Her feelings of self-loathing increased. She had done a bad, evil, terrible thing. She had been responsible for a death. She hated herself and everyone else should hate her too. She retreated even further into her silent world full of punishment and guilt.

If Jess had been alive she would have made Emma laugh at herself. She would have helped her to realise that A-level results do not define a person. She would have helped her to understand that whole world was still open to Emma and that her achievements could still be great. Emma could still be and do whatever she wanted. But Jess was not alive and Emma was left without her guidance, so instead of choosing a new path on which to find her place in the world she retreated from life and instead concentrated on her guilt. She also vowed never to read another book again; they contained nothing for her.

She left home and headed for London. Why not? There was no reason for her to stay at home and London was large enough and faceless enough for no one to ever really have to know her. She could lose herself there. No one had to know who she was or what baggage she carried.

Steve felt it was for the best. It was doing his daughter no good at all to just sit in her room and wallow. He felt her desire to leave home was a positive step; his daughter was trying to start her life again after her period of mourning. So he encouraged her, gave her a little money and off she went.

She had rented a smelly, damp, over-priced bedsit. She

couldn't afford a bed so she bought a second-hand mattress and put it on the floor. Home. At least now she had an address and so could start to look for work. She took temp work, drifting from one office to another. A fair amount of her time was spent in telephone boxes waiting for her temp agency to call her back. The city was a like a maze, she never knew where she would be from one day to the next and she spent most of her free time glued to an A-Z. She was jostled on buses, crammed into tube trains and ignored at work. She would have been desperately unhappy except that she was beyond feeling. All cried out. Instead she did what she was told, showed up where she was meant to be and learnt to become more and more insular. She found it was possible to go for days without really speaking to anyone. It became almost a competition to her, to see how long she could go without interacting with anyone. She didn't phone home, there was no point; she had nothing to say.

Eventually an office she spent three weeks at decided they needed her full time. Well, not her particularly, but they needed someone and she already knew the computer passwords and so from all round apathy they took her on full time.

She could now afford a new place to live. Not that she really needed one; all she needed was her mattress, a place to wash and an old portable TV she had picked for £10. She did not, unlike most people her age, have a stereo. She had stopped listening to music after Jess's death. All their old favourite records made Emma's heart feel like it might bleed with pain and unhappiness. She never listened to the radio just in case they played something that Jess liked, or even worse something that Emma knew she would have liked, were she still alive.

Looking through the paper she'd spotted an ad for a one-bedroom flat not far from the office and at only slightly more than she was paying now. She didn't even bother to see it first, just sorted out all the details over the phone, took in her first month's rent and deposit to the letting office and picked up the key.

She carried all her possessions to the new flat on the bus (she ditched the old mattress and would buy a new one, well – new second-hand one anyway). Letting herself in, she looked around her new home. Far more palatial than her last place, this one actually had separate rooms. It comprised a tiny bathroom, even smaller kitchen, a single bedroom, and a lounge. This meant she now had four internal doors, instead of a dirty curtain to separate the sleeping area and toilet area of her previous place. It still smelled of damp though. She put the TV on the floor in the lounge, hung her clothes in the wardrobe and put her two pots in the kitchen. Home.

Over the next few days she picked up a kettle, a battered old settee, a bed and even a small table for her TV to sit on. She now had the perfect setting to while away her life in. At 19 this was Emma's ambition, to while her life away. Of course, she no longer ever thought of being a doctor. She tried to never think of anything that had happened before today. She tried to train herself well in the art of forgetting. And if thoughts did start to crowd in, she always had her TV.

# Chapter 9

In London, Emma's life settled into a routine of going to work, eating, distracting her mind with TV and then sleeping. Her sleep was often punctuated with bizarre, surreal, yet frighteningly real dreams. There was no need for her to analyse these dreams, their meaning was obvious – guilt. In her recurring nightmare she held Jess's shattered and broken body, desperately trying to put her back together but Jess's bones crumbled and turned to dust in her hands. Sometimes it wasn't even Jess she was trying to put back together. Sometimes it was her mum, or her dad, or even once, a girl she had seen in an office she was temping at. The dream of Jess sickened her, but she felt so much worse when the body was not Jess's. When it was someone else she felt like she was being disloyal to Jess.

She would wake up more tired than when she had gone to bed, momentarily wondering which was the dream and which the reality. She would throw back the covers and lie there, cold, looking around the room, reminding herself that indeed this was her life. She muddled through each day, sometimes feeling little more than a zombie, the walking dead. The bitter irony of being alive without having a life.

Emma lived like this in London for 3 long years. Christmases and birthdays came and went uncelebrated, serving to tighten the knit on her shroud of misery. She tried very hard not to think about her future, though her own death did preoccupy her thoughts often. It was as if her life had become one very long, slow suicide attempt. She would not take her own life in a rash and desperate way; rather she would let it slowly seep away. She felt she had set up an impenetrable way of life that protected her from other people and protected them from her. She didn't consider herself to be lonely, she felt her life was justified – as it should be. Besides, she was in a continual one-way conversation.

For so long now Emma had ring-fenced part of her mind – part of her was always, eternally pleading with Jess to forgive her. Forever involved in a one-way conversation, no matter what else Emma was doing there was part of her whispering to Jess, "I'm so sorry," or, "I didn't mean it to happen".

Then one day, Jess answered back. She was there in Emma's mind talking to her. They were together again.

"It's okay," were the first words Emma heard.

"What?" Her first reaction to Jess after all these years was not entirely articulate.

"It's okay," the voice whispered again.

"Jess?" Emma choked the word, she was speaking aloud though her friend was not, the voice came from within Emma herself.

"Yes." The voice replied.

"Jess, is that really you?"

"Yes, I'm here. I've always been here."

"Why didn't you speak before? Where are you? Why are you with me now? Why did you leave me for so long?" Tears were pouring down Emma's face. She was elated, desperately sad and confused. She didn't understand what was happening.

"It's okay, I'm here. I've always been here with you. You just couldn't hear me before."

"Why now?" Emma had been alone for so long she felt suspicious of this voice. Could it really be Jess? Could she really ask her the one question that had burned away at her for so long? Would Jess finally answer her?

"Why now? Because now you can hear me. I've been talking to you for so many years, why did it take you so long to hear me?"

"I don't know. Oh Jess, is it really you? Are you really here with me?"

"Yes."

"Jess, please, please tell me, do you forgive me?"

"You didn't kill me."

Emma sobbed. She sobbed hysterically and laughed and hugged herself as hard as she could.

# Chapter 10

Denise had taken up gardening. It wasn't something she discussed with her colleagues, it being so incongruous with her super sharp career image, but it was something she enjoyed. Her own secret little pastime.

When she first moved to America she'd lived in a company owned apartment. Its stainless-steel surfaces and black trim were all high spec chic and modern. After a while she had to find her own place to live and so had rented a beautiful 3 bedroomed house just outside of the city. It reminded her somewhat of the house she'd shared with Steve back in England. It was far more homely than the apartment, with stripped wooden floors and comfy rugs scattered about. She liked to have a little green space to escape to after long hours spent at the office. She always thought herself happiest when immersed in work but it was good to balance that with something more, something less cerebral.

The house had a garden befitting its size and rather than let it overgrow with weeds Denise decided she wanted it to look nice. She wanted some flowers and a tidy lawn. She could have easily hired someone to take care of this for her. Whilst her life in America was full with lots of work related social gatherings, her lack of true friends meant she did have a few hours to kill each week and so decided the garden would be her project. She planted azaleas and roses, amongst other things, and had a new lawn laid of native sun turf grass. After a couple of years of careful attention the garden was looking lovely. Only her hostas were spoiling the show. Something was eating them almost as soon as they grew, so they looked like they were born dying. Unhappy with this, Denise bought a large plastic container full of slug pellets and surrounded the hosta bed with them. That would show whatever it was that was eating her plants.

It was the following Saturday, the second of the month, when she went out to do some weeding that she saw the snail. It was in amongst the slug pellets and seemed to be trying to writhe itself out of its shell. Denise's first instinct was to kill it, put it out of its misery. She hesitated though, wondering if this were normal behaviour for a snail. Frankly she had no idea what normal behaviour for a snail was. She didn't want to kill something that wasn't suffering.

Then a box in her mind opened and a dark shadow crept out and grabbed the back of her throat with its icy fingers. Her breath caught in her throat. She didn't know what to do; she was happy to kill insects by proxy with a few pellets, but she didn't want to crush this snail unless it needed it and she couldn't be sure either way. This was stupid – she should just stamp on the snail and get on with her day. She couldn't though because irrationally, ridiculously she sat on the grass and looked at the snail and it reminded her of Emma. As the snail writhed around Denise didn't know if it was in pain or not and she honestly didn't know what to do about it. She had so much power over it and had no idea how that power should be used.

She hadn't thought about Emma for months and months and now suddenly here she was in snail form asking her to do something and she didn't know what it was. A feeling of despair and an expected wave of insecurity washed over her.

She jumped up, went inside and poured herself a large glass of wine. As she poured she chastised herself for being stupid enough to get freaked out by a snail. She was obviously a bit run down. Then she sat on the sofa and made herself enjoy the fine red she was drinking. What else could she do?

# Chapter 11

Emma was elated. She was walking on clouds and the whole world seemed to be such a beautiful place. Jess was with her. Jess was always with her. At work Jess kept her company, made her laugh at the foibles of her colleagues, whom she had never really noticed before. The work day flew past now she had Jess for company.

Home time was the best time though. In the past Emma had never been the first to leave the office, she had nothing to go home for. Instead she would work until her work was done, whether this took an extra half hour or not. Now, however as soon as the clock hit 5, Emma would race from the office to get home. It was only once they were alone together that they could start to fill in the last few years of conversation.

Emma had so much to tell Jess, of all her guilt, of all her loneliness. Jess's reply was always the same.

"I know, I was there."

Emma talked and talked. There was so much she had to say. So much she had to tell. To begin with, Jess's voice was reticent. She did not know where she had been for the many years since last they'd spoken. She did not know how she was here now. She didn't know why Emma could not hear her before. Since the mystery could not be solved Emma ignored it. She was so excited to have Jess back that nothing else mattered. Jess forgave her; that was all she needed to know. Gradually Jess's voice became louder. Initially reticent to speak, wanting instead only to hear Emma, she slowly began to engage more. She began to laugh again and sound, well, just like Jess. There was absolutely no doubt in Emma's mind that this was indeed Jess. It was her best friend and they were together again.

The first Saturday after Jess's return Emma raided her bank account and they went shopping. Emma bought a full stereo system, a turntable, a double cassette deck, an amplifier, and a radio all in one big, black unit. They were about to leave the shop when the sales assistant suggested some speakers might be useful so Emma bought a small pair of speakers as well. Then they went to Woolworths and Emma just about cleared the music shelves. Luckily they had a good selection of 'old' music so she bought everything they had by The Cure, Blondie, Siouxsie and The Banshees, The Cult and The Clash. Then on to new music. Emma didn't know any new bands – she had so carefully avoided music – but she had once heard a snippet of a song called Waterfall by The Stone Roses. It was such a beautiful song that Emma hated it because she knew Jess would love it. It had made her heart hurt the first time she heard it knowing that Jess would never get to hear it. Now she was able to buy their whole album to play to her.

She was so excited that even though she was smiling, tears were running down her cheeks as she picked the tape off the shelf. If she had been on her own she would have looked quite disturbed, but she had Jess with her. If you're with someone else, no matter how disturbed you look, people tend to leave you alone assuming your companion will look after you. As Emma in her excitement was now talking aloud to Jess, people were happy to leave her alone.

They had bought far more than Emma could comfortably carry on her own. The stereo felt so heavy that she had to stop every few paces so she could re-position the weight and just rest for a minute. Even though she was struggling she didn't care. It was going to take them ages to get home and she didn't care. She couldn't stop laughing she was so happy. For well over two hours she dragged, pushed, lugged and man-handled her new play things towards her flat, all the while laughing and singing. She was exhausted when they finally made it through her front door, boxes and bags crashing everywhere. Still she had enough energy to set up the stereo (miraculously unbroken from the journey home) and stay up all night with Jess playing music, laughing and talking, just like they had on so many Saturday nights so many years before.

# Chapter 12

As Emma had no social life, there was nothing but work to interrupt her conversations with Jess, and even at work they would be continually chatting away together. Emma had very quickly learnt she could talk to Jess without having to speak aloud, so they were free to talk as much as they wished without anyone ever noticing Jess was there.

It came as a huge shock when she discovered something was going to break her routine. It scared her. It seemed the company for whom she now worked would be holding an event. The company had three offices based in and around London and it was decided that the staff from all the offices would come together, there would be brief presentations detailing the successes and failures of each office, after which the staff were to be treated to dinner and drinks. It was something of a team building exercise, something to bring staff and management closer together, so the staff might feel more involved with the company they worked for. Attendance was mandatory.

Emma felt sick. She did not want to go out and socialise with her colleagues. That would mean talking to them. She had developed a way of working competently enough but without having to engage with her colleagues. She worked in data entry so really all she had to interface with each day was a computer. Now she would have to go out to a place she did not want to go to and sit with colleagues she did not want to speak to. She wanted to be alone with Jess. Working was bad enough and she didn't want to have a precious evening taken away from her too. To Emma this just seemed cruel. Jess didn't seem to mind, as ever Jess quite liked the idea of an evening out. But then, she had always been more sociable than Emma.

Her initial reaction was that she would just call in sick on the day of the event. This seemed like a brilliant plan. However, it soon became apparent that this was not an option.

Attendance was mandatory and no excuses, save perhaps childbirth or a death in the family, were acceptable. Emma couldn't quite bring herself to fake the death of one of her parents and so the only option seemed to be to attend. There was a time she would have just resigned, but now she had Jess to think about as well, it wasn't just her own wellbeing at stake.

She felt agitated in the days leading up to the event. All she could think was that she didn't want to go. She wanted to know more about the event, to see what she was letting herself in for, but that would mean talking to someone, maybe even taking them into her confidence and she wished to avoid this at all costs. It seemed she had no option other than to accept that she was going to have to attend and there was nothing she could do about it. So, on the day, as fatalistic as ever, Emma made her way, alone, to the venue. Obviously Jess was with her, but as ever, she had no human companion.

She hadn't once considered what she might wear; she would, of course, wear one of her two work outfits. She had picked out the black outfit without even thinking about it. If she had spared a thought, the black one, as opposed to the grey, would certainly have seemed more fitting. More funereal.

The company had taken over a conference room at a hotel in central London. On arrival Emma saw the room had been set out with a top table for the directors and senior managers and three large tables. On each of the large tables was a central card indicating that the staff from each office was to sit together. Oh how she had prayed for individual tables, so she could sit alone at the back somewhere and spend the evening unnoticed. As ever, her prayers had gone unanswered.

Emma found her way to the table for her office and chose a chair as far away from the top table as possible, as far out of any potential limelight as possible. The two chairs on either side of her were, as of yet, unoccupied. Her colleagues at the other end of the table were in deep conversation and paid her no attention. As she settled herself down her thoughts were bitter, she did not want to be here. And anyway if this stupid event was supposed to bring staff and management closer together, why the hell were they all sitting on a top table and not amongst the staff? Not that Emma wanted to sit anywhere near her manager, but the layout of the venue belied the supposed intention of this event. Emma felt like she had been lied to, brought here under false pretences.

*Look at them all, sitting there on their top table, as if at any moment a bride and groom might join them. Pompous twats,* she thought. She was feeling angry and bitter. No surprise then that as more of her colleagues arrived the chairs nearest to Emma remained unoccupied. Good. Maybe she could just coast through this evening without having to engage with anyone.

Sadly, fate conspired against Emma. It seemed there had been a slight mistake on the part of the venue. The larger office based in Acton had not been allocated enough places at their table. Emma's office had been allocated too many. Rather than have everyone swap tables now, it was decided instead that the late comer from Acton would just have to sit at Emma's table. This was fine with Ben, the late comer, as his flatmate Rob worked in Emma's office. So Ben sat down next to Rob. In one of the chairs next to Emma.

*Stupid bloody venue*, thought Emma. *Stupid bloody man from Acton.*

Emma sat through the presentations, fiddling with her napkin and staring at the table. When finally the meal was brought out Emma stared intently at her soup whilst eating it. She did not raise her head, she did not get eye contact with anyone, nor was she engaged in conversation. So far everything seemed to be going well enough and actually the soup was delicious. The beef wellington main course was also pretty good as well.

Now, to be fair, what happened with the desserts was not actually the venue's fault. They had made enough to go round. It's just that the top table was, of course, served first. The chocolate mousse was one of the most delicious ever made and the marketing director quite happily insisted on a second portion. *Marvellous idea,* thought the sales director, and she too tucked in to a second portion. Emma's table was served last and by the time they got to poor Emma in the corner there were none left.

A waitress very discreetly apologised to Emma. Would she like lemon cheesecake instead? *No*, came the curt reply. No one else at the table noticed Emma's lack of pudding. Why would they? They barely noticed her at all. Emma was furious. She loved puddings. She hadn't wanted to come to this pointless waste of an evening. She didn't want to be here at all and now the only thing that could possibly have been one little ray of sunshine in this whole debacle had been denied her. *Bastards, everyone is a bastard.* Emma clutched her dessert spoon until her knuckles went white. Why couldn't this evening just be over? Why did she have to sit here? Why was Ben taking so bloody long to eat his dessert? Emma stared at his plate. It wasn't just chocolate mousse, in the centre it had a rich chocolate sauce that oozed out and on top it had shavings of both white and milk chocolate. Ben was eating it but without paying it any real attention, he was too engrossed in his conversation with Rob. How could a plate of chocolate perfection be wasted on a man who wasn't even paying it any attention? Emma would have worshipped that plate; she would have eaten the mousse with all the care and attention it deserved. The injustice of the whole evening just seemed too much.

Jess had, of course, been with Emma all evening, whispering to her, distracting her from all that was really around her. She was quieter in a crowded place like this, without the freedom to talk as much as they would at home. However Jess was there, with her mischievous sense of humour.

"Take some."

"What?" Emma whispered back in her mind.

"Go on, take some of his pudding. He doesn't seem bothered about it. You should have it. You want it. Go on. Quick!"

The dessert spoon she clutched in her hand was thrust into Ben's mousse. She pulled off a large chunk and stuck it in her mouth. It was something of an aggressive act and incredibly rude, but no one seemed to notice it had happened. Emma stared down into her lap as she sucked on the incredibly large mouth full of mousse she had purloined. She felt much better for it. She had in her own quiet little way stuck two fingers up to the whole event.

Emma believed her deed had gone unnoticed. Ben, however deep in conversation he appeared to be, had indeed noticed half of his pudding had just disappeared. A sidelong glance at Emma confirmed her as the culprit. He was bemused. It seemed that sitting next to him was an incredibly shy, quiet girl who was actually quite pretty, but who stole puddings when no one was looking. How odd. He decided not to say anything in front of the rest of the table.

Coffee was served and having gulped hers down Emma saw her opportunity to leave. People were mingling, chairs were being moved so as to facilitate gossip between the offices, no one would now notice an empty chair. So Emma, as unobtrusively as possible, gathered together her things and made her way to the exit. She felt a slight wave of relief come over her as she neared the door. She had survived the evening and managed not to speak to anyone. Most people would not consider this a successful evening, but to Emma it was a triumph.

She was so close to the door when behind her a voice just behind her said, "Excuse me."

Emma, assuming the voice was a member of the hotel staff probably about to tell her she had dropped something, turned.

She didn't know that Ben was aware she had taken some of his pudding. She didn't know that she had somewhat intrigued him and that he had been watching her since the dessert incident. She didn't know he was fascinated by her lack of interaction with those around her. She didn't know that she'd caught his attention and so, on the spur of the moment, he had decided to go after her when she left. As she didn't know any of this, Emma was pretty surprised to turn round and see Ben.

Emma very rarely looked directly at people, it might invite conversation. But Ben had caught her a little by surprise, so when she turned she did look directly at him.

"Hi, I'm Ben."

"Yes," she replied.

"Erm, from in there," he gestured towards the general area of the conference room.

"Yes," she again replied. Well, this didn't seem to be going anywhere so he tried a different tactic.

"You stole my pudding." Ah, that was maybe a bit too direct. Emma adopted a defensive stance.

"No, I don't mean stole, it's just that..." he trailed off. Emma was staring at him. She had no idea as to why they might be engaged in this ridiculous conversation, it's not like he'd paid for the pudding, the company had. She was about to turn away when he continued.

"What I mean is, you like pudding, I like pudding, maybe we could, you know, go out and get some pudding?" That was pretty pathetic. Ben knew it, even Emma, inexperienced as she was, knew it. Generally girls were easier to talk to than this, Emma was making it really hard and he felt a bit off-guard, a bit flustered. He did, however, have a supporter; one that he could never possibly have guessed at.

"He's flirting with you," a tiny voice said to Emma.

"Shhh," she whispered back, trying not to giggle. It was so wonderful to have her best friend back.

"Talk to him."

She could see Ben looked uncomfortable and embarrassed and whilst she may have been out of practice when it came to conversation, she heeded the voice in her mind. She asked, not unkindly, "You want more pudding?"

"Well," he said with a half-laugh, "I guess that would be a bit much right now; that chocolate was pretty rich."

"Uh huh," it was non-committal, but veering towards agreement.

"But I wondered if in the future, you might want to go out and get pudding. Together." This was possibly even more pathetic than his first attempt.

"What, not a whole meal? Just pudding?" This felt strange to Emma. Not only was she talking, she was even encouraging conversation by asking questions. In fact, she was bordering on flirting. She was starting to feel a bit flustered herself. Emma concentrated on avoiding people. It had never occurred to her that other people also tried to avoid her. The reason she was able to do her job without interacting with her colleagues was because they didn't want to talk to her. She came across as sullen, moody and arrogant and they were quite happy to avoid her. As she never came into contact with anyone else it had been many years since someone had tried to talk to her. Ben wanted to talk to her and Emma found herself responding to his direct approach. It had been so long since anyone had paid her any attention and whilst she believed she would avoid an encounter like this at any costs, actually it felt nice.

Besides, Jess was encouraging her. "He seems nice; why not keep talking to him?" Emma was having an actual conversation with a third person and the world hadn't ended. So, okay, let the conversation continue.

"Right," said Ben, "please let me have one more go at this and I'll try to stop sounding like such a pathetic idiot. Would you like to go out for dinner with me on Friday night? A full three courses?" He looked at her and tried not to look too desperate. He'd been turned down for dates in the past but this one he really wanted to go on. He wanted to know more about this woman; on first impressions he quite fancied her.

Emma's mind whirled. She'd been asked out on a date. No one had ever asked her out on a date before in her entire life. What should she say? She was blushing and fiddling with the buttons on her coat. Of course she should say no. Of course she should. But she didn't want to. Someone had noticed she existed and it felt good.

"Go on Emma, say yes. Let's go out on a date. Go on." She knew Jess was teasing her.

"You don't really want to go, do you?" She couldn't believe Jess wanted to go out again, tonight was surely enough?

"Yes." Jess encouraged her to do what a few weeks ago would have been unthinkable.

So, she said, "Yes."

"Great, great," said Ben, he felt relieved. He gave Emma a big smile. She smiled back at him, a small smile and then turned her head to look at the door. She was about to leave. Oh! Wait! He couldn't let her go yet, he had to make arrangements.

"Do you know Luigi's?" He asked.

"Yes." Emma passed the restaurant on her way to work every day. Ben knew the restaurant as he'd met Rob there after work a few weeks ago.

"Meet you there on Friday, say, half past 7?"

"Okay." As Emma turned to walk away a little smile played about her lips. Ben watched her walk away, just as she got to the door he called out to her again.

"Erm, sorry, but, erm, actually, it's just," he signed, "what's your name?" He looked suitable sheepish.

"Emma" she called back, gave him a withering look and stormed out of the hotel.

"I can't believe you talked me into that." Emma did not want to have to spend yet more time out of the house, away from their uninterrupted conversation. She almost felt a little bit cross. A bit manipulated. But, of course, she could not be cross with Jess.

"Oh, it will be fun. It's about time we started to go out more."

"You're not bored with me, are you?" Emma felt horrified at the thought.

"Of course not," such a gentle whisper, "it will be fun."

# Chapter 13

Denise and Steve's divorce was neither messy nor protracted. The arrangements made when Denise left for America suited them both well so the paperwork was little more than a formality. They probably wouldn't have bothered with it except they both liked to tie up loose ends. That and the fact they were both getting re-married. The affair Steve had resumed after Denise left had reached a new level and a date had been planned to make it official. Denise had meanwhile met a charming man at one of her client organisations and things there had also developed on to a new level. Each knew of the other's nuptials though no personal cards were exchanged on the matter.

Steve's fiancée knew of Emma, the two had overlapped in Steve's life though they had never met. Sitting one morning at the breakfast counter in their kitchen she broached the matter of Emma's invite to their ceremony. Steve stared at his wife to be. He hadn't thought about Emma for months and months. She should have been on his mind, only natural during the planning of a wedding, but she hadn't been at all. The realisation was something of a slap in the face. It was the realisation that he was no longer really her dad. He hadn't the faintest idea how to get in touch with his daughter – he had no idea where she was. He went to the garage, got out his mountain bike and went off by himself for the day. He rode as hard and as far as he could and when that didn't work he went home and poured himself a large vodka. He turned up the stereo, put on his headphones and drank until Emma was safely placed back in the little box in his mind where she should always reside.

# Chapter 14

For the next few days Emma put the thought of the date out of her mind, concentrating instead on being with Jess. This worked fine, but it was never going to delay the approach of Friday. 5.30pm had to come around eventually, and so here it was. Emma was home from work and had only one task – nothing to distract her from it – she had to get ready to meet Ben.

"I don't think this is a good idea."

"Why not?"

"I don't want to go out on a date. I want to stay in with you."

"Oh come on! For goodness sake, you have to go out at some point."

"No! No I don't. I've managed absolutely fine without going out for years." There was a certain petulance to Emma's voice.

"Yes, but I'm back now, so we should go out to celebrate."

"Why can't we go out just the two of us?"

Jess laughed at this; not a cruel laugh, rather a gentle one. Emma couldn't help but smile too. Obviously, the idea of the two of them going out together was not an option.

"Okay, well why can't we stay in just the two of us?"

"Emma, we have been through this." The patience in Jess's voice was wearing thin. "Come on, it's time for you to get ready." She sounded like she meant business.

Emma hadn't spent an evening with a friend getting ready to go out since August 1989. Under any other circumstances the guilt she would feel at this would have driven her, sobbing, into the foetal position. But as it was Jess she was actually getting ready with there was no need for guilt. Instead she enjoyed the process. Jess helped her pick out what to wear. A very easy task since she only had one suitable outfit. They joked about Emma's inability to apply make-up properly and for a while Emma even forgot that she felt like she was being sent to a firing squad. Then, without warning, insecurity hit.

"What if he's not there?"

"Of course he'll be there."

"But how do you know, what if he doesn't show up?"

"Why would he ask you out if he wasn't going to show up?"

"Maybe he's realised he made a mistake." Emma's face was flushed bright red.

"Don't be so stupid!" Emma knew Jess probably meant this to sound more encouraging and less like an insult.

"But why would anyone want to go out with me?" Emma had spent a long time doubting herself; it was a hard habit to break.

"Oh stop being so pitiful! He wants to take you out for dinner. You need to eat dinner. Therefore, get ready and meet him for dinner. Stop behaving like this is such a big deal." Jess sounded really cross and for a moment her words and tone stung Emma. Then she realised her best friend was simply trying to jolly her along. Okay, she would go and stop worrying about it.

"Look, how's this for a plan? You show up 10 minutes late, you walk past the window, if Ben's there you go in. If not, we come straight home. Okay?" It was a good plan. Emma felt happy again, at least for now she and her best friend where getting ready to go out and that was enough for her for the moment.

At 7.45pm Emma walked past the restaurant. There, sitting alone by the window at a table for two was Ben, playing with a bread stick. Emma went in and joined him.

"Hi." Ben stood up as she walked in and held out his hand to shake hers. Jess laughed at this overly formal start to the date. Emma just stood there, looking at the table. For a moment she wasn't in the restaurant, she was with Jess, wanting to know why Jess was laughing. What was the joke? Why didn't Emma get it?

"Shake his hand you idiot!" Jess's voice seethed through

her mind.

"Oh, hi." Emma finally managed to get the words out, shake Ben's hand and sit down.

*Wow, this Emma's shy,* thought Ben to himself.

"Would you like to look at the menu?" Ben handed Emma a red leather bound menu.

"Thank you." As Emma looked over the list of meals there was silence at their table. She tried to concentrate on the words in front of her but it was so hard to do. Her own mind was filled with what a mistake this evening was, how embarrassing it was to be sitting here in silence with a man she did not know. Jess's voice in the meantime was calling on her to make conversation, say something, anything. It was too hard to concentrate with all this going on.

"Is there anything on there you like the look of?" Ben also felt the silence was a little too much to take.

"What?" Emma was distracted, it took a minute before she realised he was talking about food.

"Do you know what you would like to order?"

"Oh, hang on a second, let me just think." This was both a request of Ben and a plea to Jess. Emma needed to focus on the menu. Choosing what to eat was far more difficult than she imagined it would be. Emma wanted to order the salmon. She loved salmon. But Jess would have ordered the mussels. Jess would always have the mussels if she had a chance. Emma didn't know what to do; she wasn't sure who she was ordering for. It had been a very long time since either she or Jess had been out for a meal. It seemed only fair really that she order what Jess would want. After all it was her fault that Jess hadn't been out in so long.

"I'll have the mussels." Okay, that was one hurdle over. The great exertion of deciding what to have was followed by more silence.

"What are you having?" She'd done it! She had made conversation. This didn't feel too bad at all.

"The salmon."

"Oh." Emma didn't know what to say now. Thankfully they were both saved by the arrival of the waiter. They ordered the salmon, the mussels and a bottle of white wine. Ben looked around the restaurant, trying to spot something that might act as a conversation starter. Emma, meanwhile, was distracted. She could hear Love Cats by The Cure in her mind. It had been one of Jess's favourite songs. She liked listening to Jess singing, it was far better than sitting here with a strange man.

"So, do you like Italian food?" Ben was clutching at straws; he was usually a little bit better at dating than this. Jess laughed at his attempt.

"Yes, which is lucky." Emma had made a joke, a very small one, but her first joke in years. Ben laughed encouragingly. This gave Emma an excuse to laugh. Not with Ben, but at him, with Jess. Ben took this as a good sign.

"I love Italian food. I like cooking and my pasta usually turns out okay." Ben gave a rueful smile as he said this.

"It's your turn, say something," Jess ordered.

"Oh, yes, erm, yes. I don't cook much but I do like food." Oh dear, Emma seemed only able to communicate at the level of an 8 year old.

Again, they were saved by the waiter. He bought over their bottle of wine. Ben poured Emma a glass. Thankfully they both had something to do now, other than play with bread sticks. They both gulped down their first glass and agreed it was 'very nice'. And bless that waiter for he then came over again, this time with their food order. If Emma were paying for this evening she would have tipped him well. Ben was also thrilled at the arrival of the food. Now they had something to talk about. His salmon looked delicious and he commented on it.

"It does look nice," agreed Emma, jealously. She looked down at her own plate. It had been prepared to the highest standard and was undoubtedly wonderful. But to Emma the little greeny-brown mussels floating in white wine and garlic looked vile. She hated mussels. She'd ordered them for Jess and Jess didn't even seem to care. In fact Jess didn't seem to be speaking to Emma at all. Instead she was quietly humming her way through The Cure's greatest hits. Emma felt very alone with her weird, alien-looking dinner.

"How's yours?" Ben asked.

"Great. Yeah, really great." She had to try some. It was the only rational course of action. She couldn't sit here with a full plate of food whilst Ben scoffed his. Hesitantly she picked out one of the smaller ones. It quivered on her folk. Oh, why did it have to quiver? It made it look all the less appetising. She closed her eyes and popped it in her mouth.

"Mmmm, yum!" The humming stopped and in its place came full appreciation of the food. Emma wanted to turn cartwheels she was so happy. She had done a good thing for Jess. Even more than this, Jess had appreciated what she had done. She felt so happy. She was making Jess happy, she was making things right.

Her happiness even extended as far as deciding to include Ben in the evening's entertainment. It occurred to her the one thing she could talk about was books. Her obvious drawback was that she had hardly read anything since she was a child. After the failure of her A-levels she'd felt wronged by books. What once had been a great love had turned to bitterness. She hadn't wanted to read anything in years. By delightful coincidence, however, Ben had also read all of the Famous Five books and so the rest of meal was spent reminiscing over story lines whilst Emma force-fed herself mussels and Jess made little 'yummy' sounds.

After the main course it seemed only right and proper that they should have a chocolate pudding each. The conversation had turned from childhood books to childhood in general and they chatted away easily enough. Emma was careful to keep her childhood stories to a minimum, preferring to hear Ben's stories instead. When Emma did speak it was only about her early childhood, nothing including Jess. Jess was her own private friend and there was no way she going to share her with a man she hardly knew. She wasn't going to share Jess with anyone. Jess didn't seem to mind. She was engrossed in the chocolate pudding.

It had been a struggle initially to get the conversation started. Ben knew this, but he felt he had achieved it in the end. He gave himself full marks for this. He had managed to turn around what could have been a disastrous evening. He was feeling quite proud of himself. He also knew he wanted to see Emma again. Yes, she was a bit difficult to get through to, but that might change in time.

The bill was presented to Ben along with their coffee. The evening was ending so he knew now was the time to ensure he got a second date. He was realistic enough to know there wasn't much hope of this evening going any further, so he had to give himself a second chance.

"So, you like Italian food. How about Chinese?"

"Is he trying to be coy?"

"What?" Emma was a little surprised, it was the first direct comment she had heard from Jess in a while.

"Chinese food, do you like it?" Ben tried again.

"Not so coy now, that was a bit more direct."

"What?" There was laughter in her head at her confusion as she tried to concentrate on both Ben and Jess at once.

"Don't listen to me, answer him."

"What?"

This threw Ben off-guard. *Wow, she really is a challenge,* he thought. "Well, I wondered if perhaps next time we go out we could go for Chinese food."

"What?" Emma had not considered a second date. It hadn't even entered her mind. She was only here because Jess told her to be. She didn't think she was going to have to do it again. Emma had said 'what' four times now. Ben felt he should tread more carefully, he liked a challenge but he wasn't going to scale Everest.

"Why don't I take your phone number, then maybe next week give you a call and we could maybe go out again? If you like." He tried to sound keen yet nonchalant, an impossible oxy-moron.

"I don't have a phone." It was true. Emma had never had a telephone. Why would she need one?

"What?" It was Ben's turn now. He'd never met anyone who didn't have a telephone.

"I don't have a phone. But you have my work number." Oh dear. She hadn't meant to say that. She was now encouraging a second date and she hadn't even had a chance to discuss it with Jess.

"Okay, I'll call you at work next week." Ben smiled as he said this.

They put on their coats and headed outside. As they were about to go their separate ways Ben leant over and kissed Emma on the cheek. *Blimey!* Apart from a game of kiss-chase when she was 7, this was her first proper, sober kiss. Her cheeks burnt as she walked home.

# Chapter 15

Emma had left the harbour far behind her. She walked slowly now and as she turned to walk along the estuary she started to think back. Back to other walks. To a day when, as a child, she had climbed a red hill. The scene in her mind looked dreamlike, the golden sun giving a sepia effect. The trees were all muted greens and browns and greys, as if painted with watercolours. The occasional bright yellow flower screamed its presence with its colour and a white flannel flower demurely added a touch of softness to the harshly textured landscape. To her right the trees fell away down a sharp, sudden incline. After a steep 50-meter drop the incline lessened to a slope which continued all the way down to the ocean.

Emma had felt so happy, alone, but so happy on that hill. Walking forward she had chosen a spot and lain down, raising her head and shoulders so that at eye level were a multitude of beautiful yellow and green and red and blue blooms. Their small petals ruffled occasionally by the breeze, the flowers bounced slightly as butterflies launched themselves from one sweet source of nectar to another. Lifting her head slightly further she could see the blue ocean below mirroring the clear, cloudless blue above. Flies buzzed by and sometimes a petal carried by the warm sweet air. The birds produced a plethora of sounds, some haunting, some fierce, some melodic, all with their own beauty.

Even whilst lying on that sweet smelling grass she missed this place and hadn't even left it yet. She wanted to be here forever in this natural, sensually narcotic world.

It was odd that she would be thinking of this now on her long walk by the beach, as it was the same thought that had occupied her on her walk back to her flat after her date with Ben. The date itself had been too confusing, too out of the ordinary. Emma didn't quite know what to think of it and so instead she had lost herself in a long-forgotten day dream. It was a coping mechanism she used often.

"What are you going on about?" It was Jess's voice.

"Sorry?"

"You. What are you going on about? You've just had your first date and you're thinking about flies! You were always easily distracted but for goodness sake try and concentrate on the matter in hand."

"What matter?"

"Well, are you going to see him again?"

"I don't know. I don't want to. I don't want anyone else in my life, just you." Emma paused. "What do you think I should do?"

"Well, as your life seems to consist of nothing other than work and oddly irrelevant day dreams, I think you should see him again. You need to get out more."

"Why?"

"What do you mean 'why'?"

"Why should I get out more? I have a best friend, I have you. I just want us to be together, like we used to be. I don't see why anything need come in the way."

"It's not getting in the way. This is about you having a life, talking to people, being with real people."

"You're real."

"Obviously I'm real! But I can't be the only thing in your life!"

"Why not?"

"Because *I* need more!" Jess's voice sounded exasperated.

"You're bored with me aren't you?" Emma accused, her eyes filling with tears. She had reached her flat now and as she entered she threw herself on to her old battered settee.

"Why does this have to be about you?" Jess's voice now had an accusing tone. "Why is it always about how upset you are, have sad you've been, how confused you are now? Why can't you just live a normal life?"

"Because," a large sob broke Emma's sentence, "because you... you know why!"

"So, everything is my fault?!"

"No, that's not what I mean. I just mean that when... when it happened and you left, I felt so... so..."

"Oh here we go, here it comes. Yes, you were so upset. I've heard this before you know."

"I know, I'm sorry. I'm so sorry. Yes, look, don't worry; I'll go out with Ben again. I'll go to lots of places. We'll have fun together I promise."

"Whatever."

This was the first argument Jess and Emma had ever had. They had always supported each other, always been on each other's side. But tonight Jess sounded derisory, she was badgering Emma and her tone was not soft and gentle as it used to be, but rather harsh and unforgiving. More than anything Emma wanted this to stop. Of course she didn't want to see Ben again but she would do anything for Jess, anything to make her happy.

Even now, back in the present, as she neared the estuary on her walk, Emma was still not exactly sure why Jess had been so mean that night and why it was so important that Emma have someone else in her life.

Ben called her at work on the Wednesday. Friday night, Chinese restaurant, 7.30pm. All arranged. Jess would be pleased.

# Chapter 16

Jess was indeed pleased that a second date was to go ahead. All day Wednesday she treated Emma to the pleasant humming of a catalogue of songs from the '80s. It was nice for Emma. Besides it gave her a chance to get on with some work. It's very difficult to concentrate when you have someone constantly whispering in your mind. When there was silence from Jess it was even worse. Akin to trying to sleep next to someone snoring. Like a tense, sleep-deprived partner Emma would wait quietly for the noises to start again, terrified in case they did not.

They always would start again though. Jess's recent sour mood, it seemed, extended beyond Emma to almost everyone they saw. Jess had always been a happy, positive person, always able to see the good, not only in situations, but also in people. Now she seemed only to notice faults. Death had really changed her.

It was nice for Emma to have a confidant, someone to share life's little foibles with. It had been a long time since she had had anyone to talk to and as such it had been a long time since she had really listened to anyone. Jess encouraged her to listen and frankly she was amazed at how stupid everyone sounded. She probably wouldn't have noticed were it not for Jess pointing out such things.

In the ladies' room one day, as she sat in a cubicle, two of her co-workers came in. One of them, Linda possibly, was crying.

"I can't–" (sob), "believe–" (sob), "I lost the invoices." Hard nose blowing from the crier. Was it Linda? It sounded like it could be.

"It's okay, these things happen. We know they're in the office somewhere, we just have to go through the files and find them." Was that Angela using such a soft tone?

"I'm so–" (sob), "sorry."

"It's okay…" The rest of Angela's comforting speech was drowned out by the sound of mirthless laughter in Emma's mind.

"What?" Emma whispered silently back to Jess. She was surprised to hear laughter. Linda was obviously upset, she was having a bad day and was just having a quick cry. It happened, nothing funny about that.

"What?" came the sarcastic reply. "What? How pathetic is she?! I mean seriously, a few lost bits of paper, oh big deal. Christ, has she never suffered anything real in her life?" There was real contempt in Jess's voice. "Can't she find anything real to cry about? Wow, if that's the sum total of her despair then hurray for her!"

"She sounds so upset though," Emma reasoned.

"Oh come on! Honestly, you've suffered far more than her and I don't see you crying. You're strong, she's just pathetic, don't try to justify what she's doing."

Jess was probably right, when they were children she had always been so much better at recognising situations for what they were. She always understood the world so much better than Emma, so she was probably right. Emma gave a sneering laugh. Yes, Jess was right and Emma was so much stronger and better than her co-workers. It was great to have Jess back again.

Linda was having an awful day. She felt tired, over worked and demoralised. She wasn't made to feel any better when that strange woman from data-processing, the one who never talked (Emma, was it?) walked past her in the corridor an inexplicably gave her one of the dirtiest looks she had ever seen. What the hell was her problem?

## Chapter 17

With Jess by her side (so to speak), Emma's confidence was growing. Even though Jess frequently told her how stupid her comments were, or how wrong she was, it was still wonderful to have someone in her life again. It felt right. Emma was starting to feel like a normal person again. She was even looking forward, cautiously, to she and Jess going out on their second date with Ben. Well, why not? It was what Jess wanted and it would not be so bad for Emma. At least she would have Jess to talk to.

Ben was also thrilled that a second date was to go ahead. He found Emma attractive and something of a mystery, but these were not his main reasons for asking her to go out with him. He had lived in London for four years now and had not had a girlfriend in that time. He had moved away from home when his then girlfriend, the love of his young life, ended their relationship. She had met far too many new people and was having too much fun at university to remember the boy she had left behind. Ben had been heartbroken and against the wishes of his parents had decided to move away, make a fresh start and move to London. Here he would embark on a successful career, meet loads of beautiful women and be able to show his ex exactly what she was missing.

His parents knew life was very rarely this fair, especially not for shy young men who had never really achieved any form of greatness. Undeterred, Ben left anyway.

The last four years had shown him just how right his parents were. His job paid well enough but he was hundreds of thousands of pounds short of being a city banker. He did see lots of beautiful women in the city but never spoke to them or made them aware of his existence. He met his flatmate Rob through work and they would sometimes go out for a drink or a meal, or he would go out with other people from the office. Apart from this small group he had no other friends; he never met anyone new and never met anyone he could conceivably ask out on a date (at least no one that had said yes to a date anyway). He was lonely, he wanted a girlfriend. Rob had a girlfriend and it seriously impeded Ben's chances of going out on a Saturday night as it became 'date night' for Rob and Lucy.

Ben had always been close to his parents and he could have (easily on many occasions) let them know how he felt. He could have let out all his disappointment and loneliness to the two people who loved him dearly and would have listened. But he never let on, never admitted he was wrong, never admitted the last few years had been a waste. London was impossibly expensive and lonely but to his parents he always pretended it wasn't. For them he made up a life which, whilst not quite a lie, was only distantly related to the truth.

Ben asked Emma to go on a date with him because he was lonely and wanted a girlfriend and she looked like she might say yes. Who she was, what she was like, was not as important as the fact that she had said yes. He was delighted that Emma had agreed to go out with him again, not because he desperately wanted to see Emma again, but because he wanted to go out with someone and pretty much anyone would have done.

So the foundations of Ben and Emma's relationship were not built on mutual respect, or even mutual attraction, but rather because Ben was lonely and Emma's dead best friend was bored.

Getting ready for the date, Ben had a little swagger in his step. He was feeling good, feeling proud that it was Friday night and he had a date. Rob showed unbelievable restraint in not taking the piss out of Ben a) for his ridiculous strutting about (it was hardly Claudia Schiffer he was taking out) and b) because he was going out with Emma who was widely considered to be boring, arrogant and rude. No, instead Rob showed great strength of character and stayed quietly supportive of his friend.

Jess, on the other hand, would not shut up.

"Put some music on, we need music to get ready to."

"Okay, okay... any requests?"

"Oh just put on anything!" came the snapped reply. Emma dutifully put on a tape, then went about selecting some clothes to wear.

"Christ! When I said just put on anything I meant music, not clothes!"

"Don't you think this top looks nice?" Emma pleaded.

"It makes you look ridiculous. Haven't you got anything nice to wear?" This was surely a rhetorical question. Jess had 'lived' with Emma for long enough now to know the limitations of her wardrobe.

"I thought this top would look nice with a pair of jeans," Emma reasoned.

"If you don't want to look attractive, fine! It's your life." This was a mean shot. Yes, indeed it was Emma's life but this served only to remind her that Jess had no life of her own. Emma had taken it. She still needed to pay for that.

"What would you like me to wear?" she asked meekly.

"Do I have to make all the decisions?" There was a pause whilst Jess let out a long, tired sigh. She knew Emma didn't have anything nice to wear, she never had.

"Just put on that ridiculous top and some jeans then. I guess there's no point trying to find anything nice for you, you don't have anything. In fact, I don't think any shop in the world would have something that would make you look nice."

Emma did not reply. Instead she put on her top and jeans and stood in front of the mirror. The outfit didn't look nearly as nice as it had in Emma's head. She looked scruffy and unattractive. It would have to do. There wasn't an option B. She picked up her make-up bag, dabbed some brown eye-shadow on her eye lids, a splodge of blusher on her cheeks and a smear of lipstick on her mouth.

"Didn't anyone ever show you how to put make up on properly? You look like a clown." Of course no one had ever shown Emma how to put make up on. Her mother had taken almost no interest in Emma's appearance and never considered make-up tutorials to be part of her role as mother. The only guidance she had ever had regarding appearance came from Just 17 magazine and Jess herself. She had muddled through as best she could but had never learnt to tone and blend properly.

Her heart stung at the harshness of Jess's words. She was an ugly woman painted to look silly. Ben would probably run a mile when he saw her. She got a tissue and removed a good 90% of her make up so now it looked smudged and old, as if it might have once looked nice but now desperately needed re-applying. She brushed her hair as hard as she could, trying to make it look shiny and silky. Instead she managed to produce a static effect so it looked like someone had spent the last 10 minutes rubbing her hair with a balloon. She looked at herself sadly in the mirror, then turned away. There was nothing she could do now about the way she looked so the best thing was not to dwell on it.

She grabbed her coat, bag and keys and they left for her date.

# Chapter 18

Emma had left the village far behind her now. For this part of her walk she needed to cut through a beautiful stretch of land planted with trees and ferns. When her walk neared its end she would cut back through this area but a few miles further up the coast. First she needed to get down into the estuary and walk on the soft golden sand bordered on each side by tree covered mountains. She loved this part of the walk, the seclusion of the trees, weaving her way through the undergrowth until it finally gave way to the sandy expanse below. This place always made her feel calm. It was here that she stopped for a moment and leaned against a silver birch. She had reached the part of her story where Jess's meanness had really exerted itself, a meanness that was never to go away.

Emma had always believed she was punishing herself as hard as she could for Jess's death. After the euphoria of her return it seemed Jess had decided Emma had not been punished nearly enough. A thought occurred to Emma – maybe it wasn't about her? This was a new phenomenon, for Emma to think of Jess in any way other than as connected to herself. But Jess had begun to show a mean spirit to anyone and anything they encountered together. Maybe it wasn't about Emma herself; maybe it was that death had changed Jess, made her harder and far less forgiving.

Emma pondered this as she neared the bottom of the tree-covered slope she was navigating. Then she took a sharp intake of breath. She had reached the estuary. Even though she had been here many times and had seen this sight over and again, still its beauty amazed her. She could never quite prepare herself for how spectacular it looked. The mountains on the other side of the estuary were a rainbow of greens, reds and even purples as the trees and the rhododendrons that quietly strangled the forest displayed their finest. Through the spruce could be spotted the occasional oak tree, defiantly reminding anyone who cared to look that they had once ruled this part of the world. The top of the mountain faded away into a shroud of mist.

Turning left she was greeted with the sight of yet more multi-coloured mountains weaving away into the distance. In front of her was a golden pathway made of the finest, softest sand. It cried out to be explored. The sky overhead had cleared to a soft and gentle blue and the wind had dropped to a slight ruffling breeze. When she had first visited here it almost felt like an invisible string was pulling her along, urging her deeper into this magical place. On this walk she felt as if she were pushing herself along, desperate to be part of this place again, to let it engulf her senses one last time. As she stepped on to the silky soft sand she let out a long, slow sigh of relief. Part of her had been afraid she would not make it this far.

She took off her shoes and let her toes wiggle in the warm, wet sand. She spent a moment trying to absorb as much as the view as she could, not just through her eyes, but her ears and her very breath itself.

It was time. She had to move on. She had to continue with her story.

The meal in the Chinese restaurant was uneventful enough. Somehow a conversation started about nature and walking and Emma really felt in her element. In fact after her quiet performance at the Italian, tonight Emma positively rambled on. She talked at length of walks she had been on, trees she had seen, the African Sycamore Fig, which though she had never seen one in real life, she had seen a documentary on and was enthralled by the miniature eco-system alive in each tree. Jess found this all really rather mundane and Emma had to speak louder and faster to drown out the complaints of "Boring!" echoing through her mind. Her eyes flashed as her mouth battled her mind.

Ben was impressed, and ever so slightly intimidated, by her passion. For their next date he decided it had better be an outdoor picnic. A third date was indeed arranged for the following Saturday.

Jess couldn't wait to get out of the restaurant and begin her tirade against Emma. As they walked home, she began.

"That was boring!"

"Ben's not boring." Emma almost felt a little protective of him. He seemed nice.

"Not Ben! You! You rambled on like a mad woman. 'Oooh, I love trees, oooh trees are so great'. My God, woman, what were you trying to do? Bore him to death?"

"We were having a nice conversation." Emma's bottom lip even stuck out a little as she replied to Jess's onslaught.

"No. That was not a conversation. That was just you talking and talking like a mad woman. He barely had a chance to speak! You just wouldn't stop!"

"Leave me alone."

"What?!"

"No! I'm sorry. I didn't mean leave me alone. Please don't go. Please don't go anywhere. Don't leave me." Emma was crying now. She was confused. She felt that Jess was harassing her but more than anything else she did not want her to leave. Even though she wasn't sure why anymore.

"Tut," was the only sound Jess made.

"Please, Jess," Emma implored.

"Let's just get home." This was as close to a comforting reply as Emma was going to get. As they reached her flat Emma was choking back tears, her makeup had given up entirely and was now smeared all down her cheeks. She fumbled with her keys and let them in.

Jess was silent the entire time.

# Chapter 19

If Emma had been given the chance to think clearly she might have drawn up all her strength and asked Jess why she was treating her the way she was. Why was she being so mean? But Emma couldn't think clearly, she had no space to because Jess was always there in her mind. Jess could go off and be quiet for hours, lost in her own world, lord knew where. But Emma had no such luxury. She couldn't think about Jess objectively whilst Jess was in her mind. So she never tried. She just assumed Jess was punishing her for causing her death; that Jess was angry to have died. That was justified. That made sense. So Emma left the whole issue well alone. She had been unhappy for so long now that it didn't seem out of the ordinary to be unhappy now. It was what she deserved.

The following Saturday there was a bit of a breakthrough. Jess seemed to actually enjoy the picnic. She had always loved being outside, in the fresh air and she revelled in the time they spent sitting under a large oak tree on a blanket laden with sandwiches, cake and wine.

Ben had really gone all out in preparing the picnic. He'd bought sandwiches and cakes from M&S and then discarded the packaging and re-wrapped the food in cling film so he could lay claim to it all being his own work. Emma was gullible enough to buy it and be impressed. They were sitting in Osterley Park, technically the garden to a large manor house, but far too big to be sensibly conceived of as a garden. The birds sung sweet little songs as they bobbed about and butterflies flitted amongst the flowers surrounding their spot. Jess hummed gently to herself as she did when she was happy. Emma felt the most relaxed and happy she had done for many, many years. She was in a beautiful place with her best friend. And Ben, of course, Ben was there as well.

Emma was getting used to Ben. This was only their third

date and it still felt strange to have someone, other than Jess, to talk to. They talked about books and films as they ate and whilst the conversation certainly didn't flow freely, they avoided the awkward silences of their first date. Also, Ben kept giving Emma shy little glances and sweet little smiles. Emma liked that a lot. It made her feel good and slightly warm in her stomach. After the picnic the three of them dozed in the warm spring sunshine. It was nice to be quiet and comfortable.

A sharp, cold breeze roused them from their comfortable slumber. They stirred, aching from their sleep against hard oak roots. As they stretched and reacquainted themselves with their surroundings a thought occurred to Emma. This was the first time she had ever slept with a man. The thought made her giggle.

"Do I have bad bed hair?" Ben questioned anxiously, assuming the giggle was somehow directed at him.

It didn't seem right to Emma to bring up the subject of them sleeping together so instead she countered with, "Tree-root hair, rather than bed hair, but it looks fine." She smiled up at him. Yes, he did look fine. She wanted him to kiss her. They had never shared a proper kiss on the lips and she wanted one now. But she did not want to instigate it. Oh sod it, yes she did! Why not? She wanted to instigate a long, lingering kiss on the lips so she did. Ben was a little taken aback but soon came up to speed and kissed her back. It was nice.

"Eruugh, fish breath," came the commentary from her permanent observer. Emma did not want to break the mood with Ben but she had to reply to Jess, to shut her up and just let this moment be.

"We've both been eating prawn sandwiches; I imagine my breath's a little fishy too." Emma silently tried to silence the critic.

"It was you I was talking about."

Emma pulled back from Ben, suddenly aware that she probably didn't taste so good.

"That was nice," he said, smiling at her.

"Are you sure?" Emma was filled with self-doubt.

"Of course, shall we do it again?"

"If you're sure you want to?" She was really filled with self-doubt.

Ben answered her in the only way possible; by kissing her again. His reassurances having calmed Emma she started to really enjoy the kiss. It felt soft and warm and wonderful.

Had the kiss happened anywhere other than a public park it may have led further, but there is nothing like a tube journey home to cool passion. So at the end of their date as they said goodbye at the tube station they kissed again – not quite the gentle, slow kiss as in the park but more a good bye kiss and they each went their separate ways.

The date did highlight a conversation that quite clearly needed to happen between Emma and Jess. Twice in one day Emma had to be the instigator.

"Jess?"

"Yep."

"What happens if, you know?"

"What?"

"Well, you know, if Ben, I mean, if Ben and I, you know, want to do more?"

"What, more than picnicking? Wow, you slow down there girl. What next? Ten pin bowling?" Jess's voice was rich with sarcasm. She was not making this easy.

"Look, if Ben and I want to, you know," she sort of tailed off here.

"What?" demanded Jess.

"Sex! Okay? Sex. What if Ben and I want to have sex?" Well she seemed to have cut through to the heart of the matter there.

"What about it?" Or maybe she hadn't quite cut to the heart of it.

"What about you?" Emma suddenly felt so sad asking this of her best friend. Her best friend whom she loved and wanted to be with always. Her closest friend, the one she had killed.

"What about me?" Even Jess's harsh tone did not dispel Emma's sadness.

"I just mean that if I'm going to do something like that, well, you know."

"What! Just spit it out woman!"

"Okay." Emma let out a long, slow sigh. What on earth was the best way to say this? It's not like when the time came she could give Jess a tenner and tell her to take herself off to the pictures.

"I love the fact that you and I are always together, I don't want that to change. It's just there may come a time when Ben and I need to be alone together. A time when it wouldn't be right for you to be there... you know, commenting."

Silence.

"Jess?"

Still silence.

"Jess please say something."

"So," Jess finally spoke, "you beg me to come back to you. You beg me to be with you and as soon as I do you're trying to get rid of me? Have you any idea how selfish that is?" Jess's voice was filled with incredulity.

"I'm not being selfish; I'm just trying to plan ahead."

"Oh, plan ahead! Oh, how very sensible. Yes, you must have plans. Oh yes, everything must be planned out." Jess's incredulity had been replaced with sarcasm. "Where exactly would you like me to go?" Bitterness now overshadowed sarcasm.

"Jess, I don't know. I don't know. I just thought maybe we should have, you know, guidelines."

"Oh guidelines is it now? Well of course, these would go both ways. I mean if I ever wanted to have sex you would of course make yourself scarce. As soon as I meet someone new and want to start shagging them, without a care for your feelings, I'll just give you the nod and a wink of off you'll go and leave us to it? Well?"

Jess was more furious than Emma had ever heard her be. She wasn't finished yet. "Oh no wait, that's right. I can't meet anyone new, can I? You took that away from me. You did! You made me what I am and now you find it... what? Inconvenient? Is that what I am to you now?!" She practically screamed this last part.

Emma was shell-shocked into silence. She felt terrible.

How could she ask this of her best friend, someone from whom she had taken so much already? But Jess was not yet finished and worse was yet to come.

"Why the sudden need to have sex, eh? Why is it suddenly so important to get laid, eh? You've gone without it so far, why now?" Jess was part of Emma now, could see and feel her thought process. As she asked the questions, Emma's thoughts gave her away. Any encounter with Ben would not be her first. In fact her first happened many years ago, on a night Jess remembered well.

"You dirty bitch!" she screamed at Emma, "you dirty, filthy bitch! You worthless slut! While I was having my head smashed in by a car – something that would not have happened where it not for you – you, you were getting fucked in an alley! You fucking cow!"

Emma could feel Jess's rage inside her. It burned white hot and it hurt. It intermingled with Emma's own feelings of guilt and terrible sadness. She felt like the lowest scum on earth, so full of hate and regret. As Jess's rage howled through her mind Emma started to howl herself. At first a chocked back rasp in her throat that grew to a dull noise and eventually a long, drawn out sound that was not quite a scream. There were no tears. Just Emma sitting alone on her settee, howling a sickening noise full of years of pain.

Jess should never have found out about that night. Her knowing brought home to Emma just how wrong she had been. How her every action had not only led to death but further had dishonoured that death with a random, meaningless encounter whilst it occurred. Emma had killed her best friend and then practically danced on her grave with a man whose name she could no longer remember. Emma was a worthless, stupid, disgusting person. Everything Jess said about her was true, of course she was right. Emma was pathetic to ever think otherwise. She was filled with self-hatred that manifested itself in a long, painful, primeval howl.

Emma sat for hours with her arms wrapped around her, her howls gradually turning to tears that poured as though they would never stop. Eventually paranoia and panic replaced her self-loathing. There was silence where there shouldn't be. A quiet, pathetic, tired little voice whispered, "Jess?"

Nothing.

"Jess."

Nothing. Emma's panic grew.

"Jess! Jess! Where are you?! Jess!"

Nothing.

"Jess come back! Jess!"

Nothing.

Emma was gripped with fear. What had she done? Dear God, what had she done? Her stupid, stupid selfishness, her thoughtlessness had driven away the one person she wanted to be with her. Through all of that night Emma paced her flat begging Jess to speak. Her mantra of old returned. "Jess I'm so sorry. Please forgive me."

A thousand times she thought this through that long, dark night as she paced back and forth. She pleaded and begged for forgiveness, just as she had done on so many nights before.

# Chapter 20

Denise looked at the white trouser suit being offered to her by the shop assistant. They were going to be married outside, in her fiancé's large garden and a trouser suit seemed the most suitable option. She'd never been a 'long white dress with veil and train' kind of a woman. She felt uneasy and for the life of her couldn't think why. The suit appeared to be just what she'd been after. So she took it and went to try it on.

The dressing room was as one might expect in such an expensive boutique. It was a large room with mirrored walls and a silk covered chaise longue, presumably so you could see what you would look like sitting down in the chosen garment, as well as standing up. Denise supposed that if you had a companion with you they could sit comfortably whilst you tried on different clothes. Indeed there were two glasses of champagne ready poured in the changing room, one for the bride to be and one for their shopping buddy.

She changed quickly and when she saw herself in one of the many mirrors an icy chill ran through her. Not because the outfit looked so right and not because it looked so wrong. Rather because she saw herself, alone, a 40-something woman about to be re-married with no daughter to help or guide her. *What a stupid thought*! Emma had never helped or guided her when choosing clothes, and she had never needed her to. In fact she couldn't think of single occasion when she and Emma had been clothes shopping together. She now lived in a land where mother-daughter shopping trips were the assumed method of bonding. It irked her that something so facile as deciding what to wear would bring a closer bond between mother and daughter. That was not how she and Emma had done things. She tried to take comfort from the fact that she had not had to spend money on Emma to bond with her, but the idea of them having a bond seemed false. It didn't ring true. She downed both glasses of champagne, changed back into her own clothes and bought the damned trouser suit. The quicker she chose something – anything – to wear, the quicker she could put this stupid shopping trip behind her.

# Chapter 21

The first soft, silvery light of dawn found Emma slumped asleep in a chair. After hours of wandering around her flat, she had finally sunk down into its soft cushions and succumbed to exhaustion. She slept fitfully and after only an hour or so awoke with a familiar feeling of guilt. Only now her guilt was accompanied by fear. She feared for Jess. She knew she had hurt her friend badly and she so wanted to take away any emotional pain she had caused. Oddly, she also worried for Jess's physical wellbeing, as well as her emotional. She didn't know where Jess was, and when a loved one is missing it is only natural to fear for their safety. She worried that Jess might be trapped in some lonely, far-off place, unable to return to her. Her fear and guilt were so all consuming it didn't occur to her that it was strange to be concerned for the physical wellbeing of someone who was already dead.

Because she didn't know what to do, and because she was a creature of habit, Emma started to get ready for work. It was only as she splashed cold water on her face that she remembered it was Sunday. Even the comforting familiarity of routine was to be denied her today.

She had no idea what to do with herself. She threw herself back into the chair and stared numbly at the wall. Perhaps if she just sat very still and was very quiet she might hear Jess. She strained her ears. She held her breath, lest the noise blocked the sound of Jess's voice. She wondered if she could hold her breath for long enough that she might actually join Jess, but soon found this to be physically impossible.

Vans, taxis, buses and cars all made their way past her window that day. All full of people getting on with their lives, going to places, meeting friends and doing so as loudly as possible. Emma wanted to scream out of her window, "SHUT UP!" but lethargy prevented her. So she spent her day and all of that night sitting quietly, desperately straining to hear any sound that might be Jess. All the while in a soft, near silent voice, she pleaded with her. She felt worse now than she ever had. To kill her friend was a terrible thing to have done, but to then cruelly and coldly push her away after her so longed-for return seemed to be twice the crime. Emma was scum, she didn't deserve to have a good friend like Jess, and now it seemed she no longer would. A brief fluttering of arousal from Ben's kiss had been all it took for her to again betray her best friend.

She curled herself up into a tight a ball as she could and for the next 24 hours she slept badly and cried silently.

The next morning she pulled herself up. She needed to go to work. She needed to get out of the flat. She didn't want to go out, she wanted to stay curled up here, but a kind of auto-pilot kicked in, a survival instinct of sorts that made her get dressed without really questioning what it was she was doing.

For two days she had had only the most fitful, disturbed sleep and hardly any food at all. As she arrived at work Linda in accounts noticed, without the slightest air of concern, that Emma looked like shit. Served her right for being such a cow.

# Chapter 22

Ben did not call Emma that Monday. He'd made a conscious decision to wait until the Tuesday. He didn't want to appear over-eager. He did think about her though often on that Monday and he even reached for the phone twice. But no, he would wait, play it a little bit cool and make a casual call on the Tuesday. He wondered if she was thinking about him.

Emma was not thinking about Ben. Emma was not thinking about work. The only thing Emma thought of was Jess. She sat at her desk, hiding behind her computer and dwelt on the awful things she had done and how she would ever make it up to Jess. Would she ever even be given the chance to make it up to Jess? This thought made her feel sick.

Roz, Emma's boss, was aware that her strange young data entry clerk was sitting at her desk, looking awful and doing nothing. If it were anyone else she would have gone over to them and kindly suggested that maybe they take the day off. As this was Emma though she didn't bother. She didn't want to engage her in conversation; she was a bit weird and made Roz feel uncomfortable. As long as Emma wasn't actually crying Roz decided it was not her concern, if Emma wanted to sit and stare at a black computer screen whilst holding her breath (*she was, wasn't she? She was actually sitting there holding her breath – well that was just weird*) then Roz would just let her get on with it.

It wasn't until she was walking home that Emma thought of Ben. Obviously she could never see him again. That was the least sacrifice she could make. This actually cheered up her a bit. She was making a sacrifice for Jess. Surely that had to count for something? She would return to her lonely life and then maybe Jess would feel sorry for her and come back to her. Maybe. It had to be worth a shot.

She was so pleased with her new plan, with the optimism it brought, that she even made herself some food when she got home. She dined on beans and stale toast. She'd felt too nauseated by her own actions to be able to eat before. Now she had a plan and there was nothing like having a plan to make her feel better.

She was so tired she went to bed at 8 o'clock that night and fell asleep almost immediately. Sadly her sleep brought her no respite though. In her dreams an unseen figure that Emma took to be Jess laughed at her, chased her, bullied her and made her suffer. Then in one bizarre nightmare scene Jess and Ben wrapped themselves into a passionate embrace. Her mind forced her to stay and witness as Jess turned and beckoned to her.

She awoke, suddenly, dripping with sweat. What did the dreams mean? Was Jess trying to tell her something, communicate through her dreams? If so, what the hell was she trying to say? Obviously she wanted Emma to be punished, but what did the dream with Ben mean? This disturbed Emma the most as she could not understand it's meaning. Did Jess want Emma to keep seeing Ben? Was she telling her that her sacrifice was unwarranted? Was it too small a thing to give up or was it that it was unnecessary to give up? Had the sacrifice been rejected? Jess liked Emma going out; did she want her to continue to do so?

Emma had no idea. She felt exhausted. Despite her mind-numbing tiredness she stayed awake for the rest of the night trying to decipher that which was too ethereal to understand – the meaning of a message in a dream. Without Jess's guidance she had no way of confirming what it all meant. She stayed awake anyway, desperately trying.

# Chapter 23

The next morning Emma did try to do a little work, if only to distract her from the maelstrom of thoughts battling in her mind. She felt lost. She didn't know what she was meant to do and there was no one to counsel her. At 10.30am her phone rang.

"Yes," she answered curtly.

"Hi Emma, it's Ben here."

Emma did not respond. The call had come too soon, she hadn't decided what to do yet, this was all happening too soon.

"Emma?" Ben wondered if they had a bad line.

"I'm here," she finally confessed. *Why did I do that?* she wondered. *Damn it, I should have just hung up and dealt with this when I was ready. Too late now.*

"Great, erm, I was wondering if you'd like to catch up at all this week?" He felt he'd kept that nicely casual.

"I don't know."

"Oh, er, got a busy week on have you?" He tried to sound upbeat; after all, he was being casual.

"I don't know. I mean I don't know if I can see you again."

"Oh." Ben was crestfallen, "why?"

"I just don't know okay. I need some time to think."

"Think about what? Have I done something?"

"No it's not you."

"Oh great, here comes the 'it's not you, it's me' speech."

"No that's not it." Oh dear, there was no way Emma could explain that she wasn't sure if she could keep seeing Ben as she needed to check if she had the approval of her dead best friend first and she wasn't sure how long that would take.

"So what is it then?"

"I don't know; I just need a bit of time, that's all."

"How long?"

"I don't know."

"Look Emma, if you want us to break up, just say so,

okay?"

"I don't know yet what I want."

"I see." There was an edge of coldness to his voice.

"I'm sorry."

"So we are breaking up then?"

"I don't know."

"Oh for goodness sake, Emma. Look why don't we meet up and have a chat about this? I mean if we are breaking up, then I should be involved in the decision. You owe me that much, right?" He was keeping his voice as light and cheerful as possible. There was still hope and he didn't want to ruin it by being an arse. Oddly, he had said the one thing that really struck a chord with Emma – 'you owe me' – *My God, was Jess communicating with her through Ben?* Emma's heart leapt. *Oh my God, everything was falling into place. This was amazing!* Jess was using Ben as a conduit. No wonder she was so keen for her to keep seeing him! Oh wow, life can be wonderful when everything falls into place!

"Shall we meet up tonight?" she asked excitedly.

"Sure, okay. Yes, no problem." Emma's change in attitude threw Ben a little.

"Say, 7 o'clock, at my flat?"

"No problem, erm, just give me the address?"

Emma smiled at this little game. How funny to ask for the address, of course Jess knew where the flat was! No problem, she would play along. Directions were given and the conversation ended on a high note. Emma sat at her desk, working and humming away happily to herself for the rest of the day.

On a serious note, it did occur to Emma she may have to tread carefully. Maybe Ben didn't know he was being used as a messenger, maybe Jess could only get little snippets of thoughts and conversations through to her via Ben. If this was the case, she would have to listen very carefully to everything Ben said so she could pick up on these valuable communications from Jess. No problem, she would be attentive to his every word.

Throughout the course of the day Emma had gone from

looking worried and pre-occupied, to giggly and happy and then on to thoughtful.

*Oh heck,* thought Roz, *please don't let it be drugs. I really can't be arsed to deal with it if it's drugs.*

# Chapter 24

On her way home from work Emma went to the supermarket and picked up a vacuum packed bag of mussels in garlic and white wine sauce. All she had to do was chuck it in pan and heat through for 5 minutes, yet to Emma it was like she was preparing the greatest feast on earth. She had no idea whether Ben liked mussels or not, and she certainly didn't, but she wasn't cooking for either of them. This was purely for Jess.

As she shopped she entertained quite romantic thoughts about being with Ben and growing old together. Jess would be almost like their child, they would both share her silent thoughts and commentary. She would be with them both always, binding them together. Yes, Jess was with Ben at the moment, but more normally in the future she would be with Emma. Emma would look after her and share with Ben all that she said. And Ben would understand because he too would have spent time with Jess so he would know how important her thoughts were. Their little family of three would be so happy together. It all made sense.

As she entered her flat though, worry took over. What if Ben didn't realise Jess was with him? What if Jess never spoke directly to Ben but was only with him so as to communicate with Emma? Then they wouldn't have their bond. Okay, no need to panic. They would still have a bond – it would be that Jess bought them together and if Emma couldn't share Jess with him then so much the better – she would have her to herself. It perhaps wasn't as perfect as the little family of three, but it would still work.

Emma was starting to confuse herself with so many different scenarios. She was also so excited she could burst. She couldn't wait to see how aware Ben was of Jess's presence. She convinced herself that even if he wasn't aware at all it didn't matter. Jess was still there and that was the important thing.

There was a shadow of grey cloud in the back of Emma's mind. A hint of a doubt but no more. Emma kept ignoring it, willing it away, but it would not go. Eventually she had to face it squarely. Why was Jess with Ben and not Emma, as she should be? This thought was a bit of a show stopper.

Emma carefully placed down the knife she was using to cut bread with and pondered this. Well, of course, if you thought about it, it made perfect sense. Jess must have known a time would come when she would need to communicate through a third party. Jess was so clever and wise. She must have known a time would come when, for whatever reason (she tried not to think about the argument itself) she would need to use someone else so she could be with Emma. Jess, obviously being the expert on death and the afterlife, had made sure there was always a third party available for when the time came. That was why she had pushed her to go out with Ben. Oh silly Jess, if she had just told Emma this was why she was pushing her towards Ben, then Emma would have run to him with open arms. Lovely, wonderful Jess, trying to spare Emma any worry or fear for their future together, but all the while making sure the necessary ingredients were in place for 'just in case'.

Emma went back to slicing the bread feeling much calmer and happier. Whatever the reason, whatever the logistics, Jess would soon be with her again. Not only that, but as an added bonus, Jess had given Emma a man for extra company. Jess had found Emma at her lowest ebb and given her hope and a partner and a life back. What a wonderful world.

As Emma contemplated life, death and the afterlife, Ben stood in the off-license at the corner of the street. He too was facing a dilemma that needed to be resolved as soon as possible – white or red?

# Chapter 25

At 7pm precisely Ben knocked on Emma's door. She ran to open it and stared into Ben's face. She scrutinised him for a few seconds but could see no sign of Jess. Never mind, she was there, Emma knew that much. Ben was a little surprised to be stared at in such a way, but hey, Emma had mentioned she was having a really busy week (or something like that, wasn't it?) so he just smiled and handed her the wine.

"Hi."

"Hi," she replied quite breathlessly.

"You had me worried there on the phone, I thought we were breaking up." He said it with a smile, he wanted to tread carefully as he wasn't really sure what the situation was.

"Oh no, no-no. No. Sorry I was just, you know, having a day of it and wasn't sure if I'd get to see you tonight or not."

"That's alright then." Magic, he still had a girlfriend. He gave her a big smile and a kiss on the cheek.

"I made mussels." Emma looked deep into his eyes as she said this.

"Lovely, I'm starving." Was that a sign? Was that Jess? He did look directly into her eyes as he said 'lovely' was that because the words were coming from Jess and he just didn't realise it? Brilliant! Jess was pleased by the mussels. She always knew she could win Jess round with seafood.

Ben had indeed found himself staring into her eyes as he said 'lovely'. It was an involuntary reaction he gave whenever he lied. He didn't think mussels were lovely at all, in fact he'd never eaten them because they looked so god awful. But hey, he wasn't going to be rude about it. He'd give them a go as Emma had clearly gone to some trouble.

"I'll serve up." Emma skipped off to the kitchen happily whilst Ben looked for somewhere to sit. Blimey, he didn't expect Emma's flat to be such a dump. Emma hummed to herself as put the finishing touches to dinner. When she emerged from the kitchen, beaming a big smile and carrying two plates of food, Ben was reminded of a story he'd heard about housewives using Valium to help them get through the day. Emma certainly looked happier and more pleased to see him than ever before. For the second time in one day someone wondered if maybe Emma was on drugs. Ben dismissed the thought as ridiculous.

"Looks great," Ben remarked, purely because this was what people generally said when served food.

For Emma it was no general comment, this was Jess directly thanking her for the food. She looked lovingly at Ben and smiled an even bigger smile.

Ben, ordinarily, was not particularly good at picking up signals from other people. Understanding body language was not a talent he possessed. Had he been any good at it he might have been led to believe that Emma's behaviour signalled a change in their relationship. A 'legs are shaved and clean sheets are on the bed' sort of change. Luckily he wasn't very good at picking up on signals at all. Also he was far too preoccupied with his plate. For all the world it looked like the woman sitting opposite him, smiling, had decided to treat him by serving a plate of bogies floating in a white wine sauce. Carefully he scooped one up with his fork. Emma seemed to be waiting for him to start before she did. Which made it far worse as it meant he had an attentive audience watching his first dabble with bogie-shaped seafood.

*Nothing else for it, just be brave and stick it in your mouth*, Ben told himself. A strange thing happened as his fork entered his mouth. Suddenly his taste buds came alive with the most beautiful flavours. Garlic and white wine always tasted good together, but mixed in here was a gentle hint of saltiness and a truly gorgeous flavour that he couldn't quite put his finger on but was obviously the mussels. He couldn't believe he'd never tried them before. They were wonderful! Ben's thoughts were writ large on his face, as he too now sported a beaming smile.

"These are fantastic," he said.

Emma replied with a cute, knowing smile and a gentle shrug of her shoulders. She was so happy. She tucked into her own plate. *God they were awful, but hey, at least Jess was happy.*

After the meal they sat on the sofa, talking for hours. Emma was an attentive listener, which worked well as Ben loved to talk. Rob had heard all of his stories before and, unless the conversation concerned football, tended to not get that involved. It was wonderful to talk to someone he could share all his feelings with. So, it would be fairer to say that after their meal they sat on the sofa and Ben talked for hours whilst Emma listened. She listened to his every word and watched his facial expressions and eye movements. Whenever he did ask her a question she had to resist the urge to laugh and say, 'you already know the answer to that!' because she had to remember Ben was unaware of Jess's presence.

It was 3am before Ben left her flat. They shared a nice kiss, not a passionate one, but a nice one just before he left. They both felt elated and slept well that night.

# Chapter 26

The beginning of a new relationship is traditionally a fun time. The flirting, the newly shared jokes, the anecdotes previously unheard can make the whole world seem fresh and new and exciting. Whilst this was so for Emma and Ben, it was also a very difficult time of adjustment for Emma. She had spent so many years shut away in one bedroom or another, alone, that she found this new lease of life difficult to cope with. She had lived by a strict routine for years, a routine that would not allow her time to dwell too much on past crimes (though, ironically, dwell was pretty much all she had done during these years). Her schedule consisted of waking, showering until she felt she had washed away whatever last night's nightmare was, having breakfast, going to work where she would try to avoid talking to anyone (avoiding people could take as much concentration and effort as actually starting a conversation would do) and then returning home to eat dinner and lose herself in the TV schedule.

TV was her god, her saviour. She watched her shows with almost religious devotion, though she had to be careful, she avoided any program that might rekindle painful memories. Anything that might include any sort of car accident or that might show friends, especially female friends, bonding and having fun was to be avoided at all costs. This meant *EastEnders* and *The Bill* were definitely out (far too many car accidents). Gardening shows and nature programs were fine and indeed watched with such intensity so as to block out the niggling, dark thoughts always on the edge of her consciousness, that she developed a bit of a crush on David Attenborough at one point. Comedies were okay but when, a few years ago, she saw a listing for a new show called *Friends* she felt betrayed by her TV and her ever-present feelings of self-loathing deepened markedly. TV was for escape and should not include programs showing happy people her age bonding and supporting each other, no matter how funny. That was out of the question. But she forgave her TV and simply avoided the show; how could she stay angry at the one thing that kept her sane?

A relationship with Ben meant disruption to this routine. Being with Jess of course made the effort worthwhile, but Emma still struggled with this major disruption to her life. Also, she was far from ready to take on other friends or confidants. She was only just taking the first tentative steps towards re-joining the rest of humanity in living a life; she wasn't about to change overnight. She found so many excuses to avoid going out on a Saturday night with Rob and Lucy that in the end Ben gave up asking. (Rob was now convinced that Emma was a cow and his friend insane for wanting to be with her, but as he didn't really give much of a rat's arse he never bothered to voice this opinion).

All Emma wanted was to just be with Ben (and Jess). Ben accepted that Emma didn't like going out much, or didn't like Rob, or something, either way he wasn't bothered, he was just as happy to sit in with her at her flat watching videos and eating take-away.

Another problem Emma had was that Jess was becoming increasingly cryptic. Sometimes it was hard to know what she really wanted. Sometimes Emma even wondered if Jess were still there at all, but she had to dispatch with this thought as soon as it arrived. She had to believe Jess was still there or it would have meant she had lost her forever and there was no way that could be. Her mood went from elation to despair in the blink of an eye. She had to fight hard to not let Ben see that she was struggling, the time was not right yet to introduce him to Jess. He had to be completely in love with her before she could share Jess with him. Sure, Jess had chosen Ben, but Emma still had to be absolutely certain he was right for both of them. It did occur to her that the path to 'completely in love' may involve physical love. The whole sex matter still needed to be addressed.

Ben was also contemplating an issue he wanted to discuss with Emma. Sex was something that had occupied his thoughts and he did wonder when they might eventually get around to it. They had shared some lovely cuddles and the odd kiss but nothing further as yet. He didn't want to push the matter and was happy to wait; however, he did wonder if there might be something he could do to gently lead things in this direction. He wanted to take Emma home to meet his parents.

Now, okay, this may not be the traditional path to seduction but there was some logic to it. Ben felt that if Emma met his parents she would see the relationship was progressing and that he was serious about her. Then maybe she might feel that the time was right for the relationship to move along in other ways. It was a subtle plan. A more direct route would be to book a table for two at an expensive restaurant followed by an evening in an expensive hotel room. However this was a stupid plan as why on earth would a woman want to have sex with him simply because he had paid over the odds for an evening out? It made no sense and also would be extremely presumptuous, to the point of downright ego-mania, to assume the plan would work.

No, he much preferred his plan. It would make Emma feel more comfortable with him and help things to naturally develop. Also, he liked her so he thought it would be nice for his parents to get to know her and like her also. Which was ironic really as Ben himself did not know her that well at all. She never spoke of her past, never told anecdotes about her childhood, in fact in their time together she rarely spoke of anything that had happened more than a month ago. Ben was aware of this but it didn't really bother him. He didn't feel like he needed to know everything and anything that had ever happened to her. He liked the woman she was today and, hey, if it was in her nature not to share too much of her past then that was okay by him. It wasn't as if she knew everything about his past either. He admitted to himself that he did have a natural curiosity to know a bit more about her, but that would come in time. For now he was just happy to spend time with her. Now all he had to do was broach the subject of a weekend away in sunny suburbia with his parents.

After the success of their trip to Osterley Park, and with

the nicer weather coming in, Ben and Emma spent almost every weekend on long walks through London's various parks. They both always had a bit of a soft spot for Osterley and visited often but they also went to Hyde and Regents Park, St James' and Green Park as well as Hampstead Heath. Anywhere that offered a green and pleasant place to walk, preferably with trees to sit under and a lake or river to wander by became their destination. One Sunday in June as they walked along the edge of the Serpentine in Hyde Park Ben made a suggestion.

"I was thinking of going home for a weekend soon."

"Home? We just came from your house." Though she avoided going to Ben's as much as she was able, circumstances meant she did have to go there sometimes.

"No, not that home. Home-home, you know, the place from whence I came."

"Ah, methinks you have a hankering for some home cooking!" Quite why they both would occasionally slip into theatrical, mock-Shakespearean speech neither of them knew, they just did from time to time. All couples have their 'thing' and this was theirs. Besides it helped to keep the conversation flowing, having something to hide behind, when otherwise there might be silence. Luckily they grew out of it after a few months.

"Is this a frozen lasagne I see before me!" said Ben giving possibly the worst Macbeth rendition ever.

"Yes okay, that's enough now. So when were you thinking of going home?"

"Well, that's the thing; I wasn't so much thinking of me going home, more 'we' going home."

"'We'?"

"Yeah. Are you up for it? Would like to come and meet the olds? Laugh at my Thomas the Tank Engine wallpaper?"

"You do not still have that in your room!" exclaimed Emma.

"No, not really, would be funny though wouldn't it?"

"Only to your bizarre sense of humour."

"Thank you. But would you like to come back with me for

the weekend? It'll just be Mum and Dad there and they would really like to meet you." This threw Emma a little. Ben had obviously discussed her with his parents. She hadn't discussed him with anyone, who would she discuss him with? *What had he been saying about her? What did they think? Blimey, this suddenly all seemed a bit serious. Would I like to meet his parents?* She was silent as these thoughts whirled through her mind.

"Christ! I'm not asking you to marry me. Just would you like to come and meet my parents?" Emma's silence had, in turn, thrown Ben a little off balance.

Strangely, his comment about marriage stung Emma a little. Not that she had been thinking about it, but still, no one likes to hear that they are not being asked. However, she decided to err on the side of magnanimous.

"Yes, I would," she said with a determined nod of her head.

"Alright then, we will."

"Okay then."

"Good."

"When?"

"What? Oh, yes, erm, how about not next weekend but the weekend after? Go up Saturday, come back on Sunday, just overnight."

"Sounds good to me."

"Great." Ben gave Emma's hand a little squeeze and they stopped to kiss before continuing on their walk.

They spent the next few hours wandering until they found a nice spot for a picnic. Ben noticed that during the rest of the day Emma did not, as might have been expected, ask him anything about his mum and dad. She did not seem curious as to what they are like, what sort of people they are. It was as if the conversation had been cast from her mind. In fact the very opposite was true. Emma thought of little else. Emma had a tendency towards excessive worrying and the prospect of meeting Ben's parents worried her a lot. It did not, as first, occur to her that they might not like her. Instead she worried about the fact that Ben had parents at all. She wanted him to herself. She wanted him to be like herself, alone in the world, with only each other and Jess for company.

The idea that he belonged somewhere to some people about which she knew nothing bothered her. She felt jealous, not so much that he had someone, but rather that they had him. They had an entire life with Ben from which she had been excluded. They had shared experiences with him, knew all his likes and dislikes, had seen his formative years go by and that was something she could never have with him. His parents felt like a wedge between them. They highlighted the differences between them, because he had a happy loving couple of parents at home, looking forward to seeing him and his new girlfriend and she had nothing.

Emma, of course, knew Ben had a life before he met her; she just did not want to recognise it or accept it. The more he shared of himself with her, the more he took her into his life and let her see who he was and where he came from, well, that would surely lead to an expectation of reciprocation. He would naturally want to know more about what made her the person she is, what experiences she had had. Emma was still not ready to open herself up like that. Though she had not consciously formed the thought, what she really wanted was for her, Jess and Ben to exist in a vacuum, with no past and no future, just today.

## Chapter 27

A few days after their picnic Emma and Ben were sitting on her old settee.

"Oops," said Emma as she poured the last of the wine into her glass, "I'll get another bottle." Ben followed her into the kitchen and gave a little sigh as she put the empty bottle in the bin.

"What?"

"What, what?"

"Why did you just give that little sigh?"

"No reason," said Ben, trying to sound casual.

"No, go on, what?" Emma couldn't let anything be, she couldn't let a sigh go unrecognised in case it had come from Jess. She had to know what it meant.

"Well, it's just… I wish you wouldn't put glass in the bin. That's all."

"Why on earth not?"

"Because you can recycle it. There's a bottle bank just near your office."

"You want me to walk to work with a big old bag of all our empty bottles?" That just seemed stupid to Emma when she could far more easily just put the bottles in her own bin. It would be many years before recycling bins became something every household had.

"Yes, but it's far better to recycle them."

"Why?"

"It's just a better thing to do." Ben reasoned. A little light went on in Emma's head.

"Okay," she beamed at him.

"Really?"

"Yes, of course, from now on we'll recycle all our bottles. It can be our thing. We can recycle together." Then she gave him a huge bear hug. "You are wonderful you know," she breathed into his jumper.

"Great." Said Ben though he found Emma's sudden change of heart when it came to saving the planet a touch confusing.

Of course he was confused. Emma wasn't telling him he was wonderful, she was telling Jess. Jess was always looking for ways to save the planet and here she was using Ben to ensure Emma kept up the good work. Dear Jess. Emma was as sweet and attentive that evening as she ever could be.

Despite his negative points and because of his positive ones, Emma was growing increasingly fond of Ben, as was Ben of Emma. Of course it was hard for Emma to see Ben as much more than a conduit for Jess, but it seemed Jess had indeed chosen a worthwhile conduit. Someone she should spend the rest of her life with, besides Ben had been Jess's idea and so of course she was falling for him, it was what she had to do.

This suggestion to meet his parents though, where did that come from? Was that Jess or Ben? Emma spent a lot of her time alone analysing all the things Ben had said to her and trying to work out which came from him and which from her friend. Was it Jess that wanted her to meet his family? Was she gently leading Emma towards a world where she would have family and friends and be happy again? If Jess had forgiven her their previous argument then why wasn't she back with Emma now? Why was she still with Ben?

Emma's mind whirled with questions yet simultaneously she chided herself for questioning any of this. Jess was back, it was a miracle and it should not be questioned. Emma would just go with the flow. It was the only thing she could do. Go with it and see where it led her. So with a mind full of doubts, fears and queries, she went to meet his parents.

# Chapter 28

A strong breeze whipped down the mountains and along the estuary, catching Emma's hair and ruffling it. It felt good to feel the air speed past her; it brought with it a sense of freedom. Apart from the lines left by the now retreated waves, Emma's footprints were the only impressions in the sand. She could hear nothing but red kites and crows angrily chasing each other away, protecting their nests and the sound of the wind in the trees on either side of her. She could honestly believe she were the only person in the world.

She looked longingly at the trees. As a child, whenever they had driven past woods or large clumps of trees, Emma had always felt an overwhelming urge to run into them. She yearned to lose herself amongst the trees and live with the fairies and pixies she knew dwelt in forests. It was an odd compulsion that stayed with her even now when she knew the forest dwellers were squirrels and not fairies. She still had a strong desire to run up into the trees, build a small fort and live out her days surrounded by nature instead of people.

It was too late now. Her problems too huge to just run away from. They would catch her and be with her always. So, she turned instead to stare at the mountain in front of her and forced herself to stop imagining a life where flowers could act as clothes and nectar as food. She had to think about Ben's parents, because maybe that was where it all had gone so wrong. She so badly needed to discover where that slippery slope had begun, the catalyst that was the beginning of the journey that had led to today.

Slowly, very, very slowly, Emma was starting to suspect that maybe it wasn't an event that turned her fortunes, but just her reaction to all that had happened that had brought her to this estuary today. But Emma did not like that train of thought and so instead let her mind wander back to the day she met Mr and Mrs Brookes, Ben's mum and dad. If somehow this could be their fault, then that would suit Emma very well.

Mr and Mrs Brookes lived in a perfectly nice three-bedroom semi, on a nice estate, in a nice suburb – so far it seemed Emma had nothing to fear.

When meeting a new partner's parents there might be a number of different, hidden motives. It may be that Emma really liked Ben and want to meet his family in the hope that they might like her and so make for an easier relationship all round. It may be slightly more cynical, perhaps she liked Ben but ultimately want to see what sort of background he came from before making any major commitment. Or, in reality, like Emma, it might be out of a fascination for what, or who, your partner was before you met them. Whilst the latter was certainly true with Emma, in the two weeks leading up to the meeting, her desire to learn more about Ben's past became almost an obsession.

She could not quite pinpoint why she felt so nervous about the meeting or why it became so important to her. Perhaps if she knew herself better she might realise that she wanted to know his past so that she might defeat it. Yes, that did sound ridiculous, but Emma wanted the present to be all that mattered to Ben. She wanted to see his past so that she could lead him away from it, away from his parents, away from his past experiences so that he could exist only in the present with her and Jess.

To say Emma had been a little tetchy on the journey to Ben's home would be an understatement. Ben silently prayed that Emma was not in one of her moods. For all the fun they had together, Emma could occasionally be a bit of a spoiled brat, taking everything and anything said to her as an implied insult. Ben really did want his parents to like her but her mood did not bode well. He tried flattery and jokes to bring her round but she seemed stuck in a dark place he could not reach her in.

Until they turned into the drive of his parent's house; then a smile appeared on Emma's face. Not a real smile, but rather the kind you see on waiters' or waitress's faces. The sort of smile that says 'I do not want to be here, I've been on my feet for the last 6 hours but I have to be nice to you as you may leave a tip'. Ben found it a little discomforting but hey, at least she was smiling, that was a start.

Emma's smile was borne out of an understanding that she had to at least pretend to like these people, she had to be the one to start off on the right foot so that any subsequent falling out would not be her fault. Please understand, Emma was not completely callous, she did not have a master plan to drive Ben's family away, rather she had a vague feeling there was a certain way she should behave right now and that things would perhaps work out to her advantage. Frankly, she wasn't sure what that would be, or even what she wanted it to be.

Emma was a little disarmed when she met Tom and Ellen Brookes. If you took the best of both their features and mixed them together, the result would be Ben. Their physical connection to him was unmistakable. They had made him and that fact was impossible to escape. If Emma had been keeping score it would be 1-0 to Tom and Ellen. Also, if Emma's smile was fake, then theirs was genuine, full of warmth and welcome. 2-0.

"Come in! Come in!" Ellen greeted them. Then in true mum-style she asked far too many questions to ever be answered in any one visit. "How was your journey? Was the drive okay? Are you hungry? Have you eaten? Are you tired? Did you stop anywhere on the way?"

"Mum." Ben stopped her roll with a great big bear hug. "We're fine and this is Emma."

"Emma," said Ellen, holding out both her arms to embrace her in an unexpected hug, "hello Emma."

"Hi." Emma's breath was cut short by the hug. Tom now joined them in the hallway.

"Dad!" Tom and Ben embraced with hearty back slaps. *(Why do men do that? Is a hug between men okay, and made less feminine, if they try to paralyse each other with a sound beating to the spine?)*

"Ah, this must be the lovely young Emma we've been

hearing such nice things about." Tom warmly shook Emma's hand. Actually, this was kind of nice. They were so welcoming and kind. Maybe this would not be so bad after all.

"No she's in the car; I'll go and get her." Laughs all round. "Kidding," Ben breathed with a very pointed look at Emma, whose withering glance indicated she did not find that at all funny. May be this was not going to be good after all. Ellen distracted them from Emma's dive from one extreme emotion to the next.

"Come into the lounge, I've baked biscuits. Would you like some tea?"

Over tea and biscuits Tom and Ellen quizzed their son on his job and life in London. They also asked Emma polite and only very gently probing questions about herself and her family. They immediately sensed that family questions were answered only very vaguely and so had the sensitivity to leave the subject alone. They kept Ben up to date with the latest news in his brother's life and generally it was a pleasant afternoon tea.

After tea Ben showed Emma around the house (both boys' rooms were both blue, no sign of Thomas the Tank Engine or any other fictional characters on the walls). They then took a leisurely stroll around the small back garden so Ben could point out where the swing had been and what changes his mum had made over time.

So far this was going okay. Emma felt welcome and at ease. She couldn't wait to have some time alone in Ben's room so she could look through his books and find out more about his life before her. But on the whole, this was fine. Ben had a past and at least she was getting to see it before casting it out. Maybe it wouldn't even need to be cast out? Maybe Emma could be part of a family again? Time would tell.

When someone is as sensitive as Emma – and lord knew that her isolation and self-absorption over the last few years had certainly made her sensitive – it could take only a word or a sentence, misconstrued, to turn their evening up-side-down.

The evening meal was going well (from a social point of view, from a culinary standpoint the beef, vegetables and even roast potatoes were well over-cooked, only the Yorkshire puddings were under-done), the four of them shared a couple of bottles of full bodied red wine and the conversation was flowing. Ellen, ever the romantic, something which a few glasses of wine accentuated nicely, wanted to know more about Ben and Emma's relationship. She tried a subtle start.

"So, you two met at a work outing, is that right?"

"Yes Mum, we bonded over pudding."

"Pudding?" Ellen was a touch confused.

"Yep, we shared a… oh, what was it again?" Ben looked at Emma.

"Men!" interrupted Ellen, "you never remember the important little romantic elements do you?"

"Chocolate mousse," Emma interjected quickly before Ellen could continue her verbal rampage on men's inabilities to remember desserts. Emma was grateful that Ben had doctored the story a little; it was true they had shared a dessert, it was probably for the best that he had missed out the part where she stole it from his plate.

"That's right," said Ben, picking up his story again, "we shared a chocolate mousse and, having caught Emma's eye, I asked her out on a date." Ben expected his mum to not be satisfied with this version of events and demand a more detailed account of their meeting and subsequent relationship. Ellen, however, decided on a far different tangent.

"Sharing a dessert!" she exclaimed, as if the idea astonished her. "A nice, healthy looking girl like Emma, you should have had one each! Not like that flimsy Claire you used to go out with, she could barely look at chocolate without whining on about calories."

"Claire?" asked Emma, trying to keep her voice as neutral as possible. Ben's attempt to answer was drowned out by his mum.

"Oh yes, you must remember him telling you about Claire?" Ellen had clearly not been a fan of Claire's and to be honest was relishing the idea of a bit of light-hearted bitching. "Happiest day of my life when she broke off the engagement, honestly! What you were you thinking getting engaged so young?" She gave her son a smile and shake of the head as if to say 'kids eh? What's a parent to do?' She paused to take a sip of wine, to clear her throat and prepare for a good old badmouthing session. Emma used this pause to excuse herself from the table. Ellen was surprised to notice the deep scarlet colour she had gone.

"Leave it Mum." Ben said, but not unkindly, as he went to follow Emma.

He found her sitting in his old bedroom. She had planned to go and lock herself in the bathroom for a while, but this seemed childish even to her. She couldn't quite rationalise why she was so angry, all she knew was that she was bloody furious. She didn't look up as Ben walked into the room.

"Listen, Emma," Ben began.

"What?" Emma still did not look up at him. She didn't plan to make this easy for him.

"I suppose…" Ben started again, with a different tactic.

"You suppose you should have told me you were engaged to be married?" Emma interrupted, her voice heavy on the sarcasm.

"Oh Emma, this is not a big deal," (possibly a dangerous tactic here from Ben, it was clearly a big deal to Emma) "it was years ago for God's sake. Claire was a girl I knew at school, we got engaged on her 16$^{th}$ birthday. Christ, I didn't know what I was doing, I was just a kid. I was too young to know what love is," (actually, not true, Ben had loved Claire deeply and was heartbroken when she left him, however half-truths seemed like a safer option at this time), "it was just a playground thing. We got older, grew up and realised what a stupid idea it was."

"You mean she realised, she broke it off didn't she?"

"We *both* realised," Ben said emphatically, "she was going off to university and we knew it wouldn't work out," he tailed off.

Emma, if anything, looked even more furious now than before he'd started to explain. Of course she was bloody furious, from what she had learned of Claire so far she was thinner and more intelligent than Emma. No ex-girlfriend should ever be thinner or more intelligent than the current one.

"So, how do you feel about her now?" Oh, this was a pointed question, Ben had to tread carefully.

"For God's sake Emma! I haven't thought about her in years!" Again, not true, but certainly the safer option. Ben was frustrated by this ridiculous argument but he felt he was getting onto more secure ground now.

"Why the hell would I be thinking about her when I've got you?"

Emma may have been oblivious other people's feelings and opinions for many years, but even she could see how patronising this was.

"Oh, I don't know why you may have thought of her. Maybe because you planned to bloody marry the woman? I do not have an ex-fiancée but I believe they tend to stick in the mind." Emma was looking straight into his eyes now, arguing with him through gritted teeth. She was practically foaming at the mouth she was so angry. She had come here to find out about his past, an ex-girlfriend was not what she had wanted to find.

"Emma this is bloody stupid, we're arguing over something that happened years ago before I even met you," he was getting angry himself now. "Okay, maybe I should have told you, maybe it seems important to you, but to me it means nothing. That's why I didn't mention it, because it just isn't important."

Actually, Ben wasn't sure why he had never mentioned Claire before. She had been a huge part of his life for years. He liked Emma, a lot, and he did want to be with her. In fact he was falling for her; why else would he bring her home to meet his parents? (In his anger he conveniently forgot about the whole 'possibly leading to sex at some point' plan). He had loved Claire very deeply and she had hurt him a lot. Perhaps he had just not been ready to share this part of his life with Emma; perhaps he was still working through his feelings on the subject. The sheer irony of Emma's anger at Ben's lack of disclosure was, of course, lost on both of them. Ben, however, was self-aware enough to recognise that part of his anger was borne out of guilt. Yes, perhaps he should have told Emma about Claire. He felt like he had been caught out. In a sense, he was technically in the right, Emma had known he was not a virgin when they met, of course there had been women before her, Christ, he assumed she wasn't exactly a virgin either. But points for being technically correct rarely count in any relationship. If one person has an ex they actually exchanged rings with, then the other person, whether they are male or female, generally wants to know about it. They feel it is their moral right and moral points always seem to count much higher than technical points in relationships. Ben realised his anger was only going to exacerbate this situation. Tact and diplomacy now seemed like the most sensible options.

"Look," he said gently, "would you like me tell you about her now?"

Whoops! Emma's look told him in no uncertain terms that this tactic was a definite no-no.

"Emma, I'm sorry, okay? I didn't mention it before;" (good choice of words, referring to the situation as 'it' rather than 'her' might help to remove some of the fraught emotionally tension) "it was something I haven't thought about in years, it just didn't seem important anymore. I would have sung like a bird if I'd known that not telling you was going to upset you. I would never want to upset you." He tried to hold her hand, she had gone back to staring at the floor and he wanted her to look at him. "Em? Love? Are we okay about this?" He felt like he had done enough now. This was tiring and he just wanted to go back downstairs and finish off a nice evening with Emma and his parents. As with any confrontation, Emma reverted to type.

"I'm going to bed now." It was said with such finality. The conversation was indeed over, for now. She turned her back on him and started to undo her shoes ready for bed.

It was 8.30pm.

Emma lay awake for a long time staring at the stupid blue walls in Ben's stupid bedroom. For the first hour or so she wound herself up by thinking of every negative aspect there was to Ben. He had kept important information from her. He was secretive. Okay, she only had one example to base this on, the goddess-like Claire. But that was enough to keep her going for a while. Then she remembered the time he had kept her waiting in a restaurant. He'd been almost an hour late. That was unforgivable. That was just plain rude. How dare he treat her like that? Bastard. She'd only waited because she wanted to see Jess, not that idiot Ben. Though actually, thinking about it, he had been late because an old lady had slipped getting off the bus and had twisted her ankle. Ben had called her son and then waited with the woman until he arrived to take her home. Emma knew this wasn't just an excuse because when he finally showed up at the restaurant he was carrying a home-made cake the old lady had made for her grandchildren but had *insisted* Ben take in exchange for his kindness.

Okay, so that was a bad example of what a bastard he was. So Emma contented herself instead with obsessing about Claire. Just how beautiful was she? How intelligent was she? What was she studying? What was she like? Emma managed to build up a picture of a stunning girl with brown-honey coloured hair and blue-grey eyes, picking up her Nobel Prize for services (to medicine probably – how could she? What a bitch!) whilst laughing about the young boy she had left behind, destined to go out only with plain, stupid girls. It was a pitiful train of thought.

Oh! And another thing! (Emma couldn't believe she hadn't picked up on this earlier) What the hell was Ellen doing talking about Claire anyway? It was obvious she had only mentioned Claire to wind Emma up and show her what a disappointment she was in comparison. That was so bloody rude. Ellen had seemed so nice but really she was just a scheming cow. Just waiting for the chance to humiliate Emma. Pretending to like her and being friendly when all the time she was setting her up for this horrible fall. Ellen had deliberately brought Claire up so that Emma and Ben would argue. What a manipulative, nasty cow it turned out she was.

Yes indeed, Emma had a talent for misinterpreting and misconstruing pretty much everything so that it might support her belief that the whole world hated her and was punishing her for her past crimes. If there was a Nobel Prize for having your head stuck up your own arse Emma would have surely won. No question.

The force of Emma's anger was completely out of proportion to the events at hand. She felt Ben had betrayed not only her trust, but far worse, he had betrayed Jess. What sort of conduit was he if he couldn't be upfront and honest about who he was? He had been in love before, he was spoiled goods. He should have spent his life waiting for her and Jess. Okay, this thought would have seemed irrational even to Emma so she didn't think it in her conscious mind, but essentially that was what was driving her rage.

Part of her anger was reserved for Jess. She had supposedly given her a perfect man but when it came down to it he wasn't as perfect as he could have been. But as ever, Emma couldn't consciously be angry at Jess so instead this feeling was also turned against Ben.

What Emma was really feeling was a little bit insecure that Ben had once had a pretty, intelligent girlfriend. Of course Emma didn't realise this, she'd never had a relationship with a man, so instead she turned her insecurity into anger. And boy, what anger it was.

Ben, thankfully, had the good sense to leave it as long as possible before going to bed, so that Emma was already asleep when he got there. No point inviting a midnight row. Besides, his mum had been beside herself that she had caused an argument and needed lots of hugs and a fair few rueful smiles from her son and a good long chat about it before she felt better. She was a kind-hearted soul and there was no way Ben was going to let her spend the night feeling bad.

The next morning Emma was up, dressed and ready to leave by 7am. She had had an awful night's sleep and felt bleary eyed and incredibly bad tempered. Ben was of course awake. How could he sleep with the racket Emma made as she was getting up? She banged and crashed around, partly to take some her frustration out on inanimate objects, but also to make sure that Ben was awake. There was no bloody way he was getting a lie-in after the night's sleep she'd had. Ben lay very still and very quiet in bed, delaying the inevitable argument, musing on how it was possible for a person to make so much noise just brushing their hair. He had hoped this would have all blown over by this morning.

Some hope. He could feel Emma standing over the bed, looking at him. He knew the longer he took to respond the angrier she would get. *Oh well, here goes nothing.* He opened his eyes.

"Morning," he opened, trying for a neutral start. Emma said nothing, but she had stepped back from the bed so Ben knew at least for now he wasn't in any physical danger.

"Sleep okay?" He was going to keep it neutral until he got some sort of sign from her as to how things were going to be played.

"No, I did not sleep okay." There was a dangerous edge to her voice; she pronounced each word, somehow managing to make them sound ominous.

*Screw this*, thought Ben, *I might as well just get straight to the point.*

"Are you still angry about last night?" If he wanted to open the floodgates to disaster he certainly chose the right question.

"Oh, I'm just fine about last night, I mean, of course I am. I come here to meet your bloody parents and what happens? Your mother," she practically spat the word mother, "invites me in and then ends up going on and on about how beautiful and wonderful and smart your gorgeous ex-girlfriend, oh no wait, I'm sorry, *ex-fiancée* is. But no, I don't care about it. I'm fine actually."

Lord, that was quite a bit for Ben to take in. He wasn't sure which part to tackle first. The ex-girlfriend bit, well, they'd had that argument last night so it seemed a bit pointless to go back over that territory. The bit about his mum and Emma's blatantly fictitious version of what had happened, now that really pissed him off. How dare Emma talk about his mum like that? She had done nothing wrong. Rather than get into that now, with his parents just across the hall in their room, he decided to play Emma at her own game.

"Great, well, if you're alright, I'm alright. I'm going back to sleep. See you in a few hours. Kettle's downstairs if you want to make yourself a cup of tea." And with that he rolled over and did a damn fine impression of someone falling asleep.

Ten minutes later, Emma was indeed sitting in the back garden drinking a cup of tea. Ben's reaction to her this morning had practically floored her. She had stood over him with clenched fists, her expression contorted into an angry look of rage. But he steadfastly refused to open his eyes. He had gone back to sleep for God's sake! Emma had remained staring at him for a few minutes, utterly speechless. She was stuck in a house full of enemies with nowhere to go. She would have jumped in Ben's car and headed back to London but she had never learnt to drive. So here she was, stuck. She didn't even know where she was. Didn't know the address so she couldn't order a taxi to take her anywhere.

As the stupidity and enormity of her situation struck her she could have laughed, but she was still too angry. So instead she had walked out of the bedroom door, down the stairs and into the kitchen. It occurred to her that perhaps if she had a cup of tea and sat and thought about things she could figure a way to leave the house and still maintain the moral high ground (something she had a sneaky feeling she had lost this morning). It was a beautifully sunny morning, so here she was, sitting in the garden drinking tea and listening to the birds sing as if it where the most normal morning in the world.

Normal apart from the boiling rage bubbling inside her. How dare Ben treat her like this? How dare he keep things from her? How dare his mum be such a cow? How the hell did she end up in this stupid situation? This was everyone's fault except hers. She had to fight the urge to storm out of the house. She had nowhere to go and would only end up having to storm back later in the day, tail between her legs, to get a lift home with Ben. No, it was far better to stay where she was. This way she could take up a defensive position as soon as anyone else stirred. She could hold her ground, say nothing to anyone and as soon as that bloody idiot Ben got his stupid, selfish, uncaring arse out of bed they could leave.

She was angry with Ben now because of all his faults. She was angry with him for daring to have such a mean mother. She was angry with him because he obviously did not care for her the way she had thought he did. In fact she had lots of reasons to be angry with Ben, but actually none of them were particularly good reasons. Emma certainly did not recognise this and sat seething. If she'd bothered to think it through she would realise that she was no longer angry with him for having an ex-fiancée, as much as she let herself believe this was the problem. The truth is, the ex-fiancée had no bearing on their relationship now. So what? He had gone out with a girl when he was younger and believed himself to be in love. He thought he might marry the girl. So? This had happened years ago, it had no impact or real relevance on his relationship with Emma. Yes it would have been nice if he had told her, he should have told her really, but to be fair it wasn't really any of her business and it is ridiculous to get so wound up about something that really has no effect on your life.

That was what Emma would have thought had she been able to disengage from her anger. The truth of the matter was she had been embarrassed by his mum knowing more about Ben's life than she did. That was all last night had been about. To make such a huge drama out of it, well that was ultimately Emma's choice. She had chosen to completely over-react, of course it wasn't a conscious decision, quite the opposite, it was made with almost no thought whatsoever. Her sitting alone in the garden, without a friend in the world, was a situation she had brought upon herself. If she had not over-reacted, if she had just quietly let Ben know she was a bit hurt by his not telling her himself (which would have been a very fair reaction) right now he would be all over her like a puppy, trying to make up for making her feel a bit hurt. He would be out in the garden trying to make her laugh, or at least smile, to show her that she does mean the world to him and making sure this whole matter was put behind them. Instead he was up in bed wondering how he had got himself involved with such a drama queen and she was in the garden wondering how she had got herself involved with such a bastard.

Walking along the estuary, Emma realised now what a ridiculous situation she had created that day. Why hadn't she had the sense at the time to just accept that Ben had an ex-girlfriend (fiancée – whatever)? She wished she could shout at the young woman sitting in the garden 'grow up and get over it!' Emma had matured a little since that day, it was just such a shame it had not happened in time, such a massive shame. Emma didn't want to think too much about that day now.

Ben had got out of bed as soon as he heard his parents stir. He made their excuses and they left. Ellen had tried to apologise to Emma but to her it just sounded false, as though Ellen where further compounding last night by making fun of her now. So they had left and driven back to London in silence.
    It was a long while before they were to see each other again.

# Chapter 29

Emma stopped walking and leaned against the jagged rocks which lined the estuary. She didn't feel particularly tired, but her head hurt. The beauty around her, the calmness and the fresh air should have prevented the dull ache in her head. There was a sense of urgency, a sense of tension inside her that contributed to the pain. She still had so much to work through but she was plagued by a dim, distant sense that time was running out. It made her feel a bit sick. She had apologised for the way she had blown Claire-gate (as she referred to it to herself) out of all proportion and most particularly the way she had been so rude to Ellen. But the apology had not been heartfelt. Emma always believed that she had been wronged and only apologised to be magnanimous.

Today, however, she saw the incident for what it really was. It was one tiny slipped comment from Ellen, innocuous in itself with no malice behind it at all. Why the hell hadn't she seen it as such at the time? Perhaps if the row had not have happened all the subsequent events might not have happened. Today might not be happening. One thing was for certain however, looking back over events she could not find any reason at all why Tom and Ellen might be responsible for her current situation. She would have to keep looking for an answer. She had to keep looking for someone else to blame.

Ben had dropped her off back at her flat, without a word, she had stormed out of the car, slamming the door behind her. Anger got her through the first few days without him. In fact she was very happy not to have him around. But once the anger subsided it was replaced by the old recognisable loneliness she had felt for so long. Only now it was far worse. Because in pushing Ben away she also, yet again, pushed Jess away.

How was it that she could keep being so mean to the one friend she loved above any other person? Jess had been such a true friend. She'd forgiven Emma for killing her, she'd presented Ben to her to show their most recent argument was also forgiven (the thought of that day, the day when Jess had discovered what Emma was doing at the moment she died, still made Emma feel sick to her stomach), yet still Emma had thrown Jess out of her life again. This couldn't be. She had to do something about it.

So, she mounted a sustained campaign to win him back. She begged, she pleaded, she cried. She asked Ben for his parents' address so she could send flowers to Ellen. She apologised and apologised. It would be easy to say this was not Emma's finest hour – desperately fighting to win back a man, not for his virtues, not for any shared happiness, but so that she might instead be closer to Jess – but actually looking back over her life these past few years, it probably was. Ben, mistaking her desperation for sincere regret, eventually forgave her and agreed to see her again on Friday night.

They met in the Italian restaurant where they had spent their first date. Emma had spent hours getting ready, though with her limited wardrobe and lack of skills in applying makeup, she actually looked just as she had on that first date. Emma felt sick. She was so nervous. She wasn't just here to win Ben back but also to win Jess back. After all she was with Ben now – the two came as a package. As long as Emma remembered not to talk about trees, she had to remember not to bore anyone.

They sat down and looked at the menus. Ben almost immediately discarded his. He knew what he wanted to order.

"I think I'll have the mussels," he said.

Emma stared at him for the longest time. Her brown eyes looked like they were filling with tears yet a happy smile played on her lips. This was it. This was the sign she'd been looking for. Jess was communicating to her via seafood. She was saying, "I'm here, it's okay, we're back together. Be with Ben, it's what I have decided for you. Take him, don't worry, I'll still be here in the morning." Their previous argument was fully forgiven.

"Would you like to come back to my flat?" Emma asked.

Ben just looked at her.

"Let's go, now, come on, we haven't ordered yet. Let's just leave."

Ben looked at her for a long time before saying, "Okay."

In her haste Emma practically dragged Ben back to her flat. As soon as the door closed behind them she kissed him passionately, whilst manoeuvring him to the bedroom. She tried to take his shirt off as they kissed but her fingers moved awkwardly and with too much to concentrate on at once she stumbled. She had no experience, of course she'd had sex, but she'd never made love before. She basically had no idea what she was doing.

Luckily Ben, whilst not a seasoned pro, had been planning this moment in his head for the last 6 months, he regained their balance, kissed her and moved back gently so he could lift his shirt over his head. Holding her hand, he led her to the bed and removed from the pocket of his jeans a condom he had optimistically bought along with him.

Emma wasn't sure what to do next. Should she remove her own clothes or let him do it? She tried not to over think the situation and sat down on the bed. Ben lay down next to her and kissed her again, with more passion and urgency than before. It didn't matter now who took off whose clothes; they were both naked, pressed against each other. Emma had kind of assumed they would just go straight for it, as with her previous encounter, but instead Ben gently cupped her breasts. He moved his head down and started to kiss and suck her nipples. *Oh boy, that felt good!*

His hand moved further down her body. Emma was now a mass of tingles. She had never felt such a sensation before and it felt wonderful. Like really, really good pins and needles. Ben, sensing the time was ready from her gentle moaning, slowly and carefully entered her. Emma's previous sexual encounter had been something akin to the Duracell bunny on Viagra. This was so different. It started slowly and then gradually built up until they were frantically writhing together, gripped to each other. And then it happened. For the briefest moment Emma reached orgasm. It lasted less than a few seconds, but she'd felt it. Ben ejaculated moments later and they lay clinging to each other. Emma started to cry.

"What is it? Are you okay?" Ben looked distraught. What had he done to make her cry? But in response Emma smiled him the biggest, most beaming smile he had ever seen from her.

"That was amazing," she said, as she smiled at him through her tears. It was the nicest thing anyone had ever said to Ben after sex. They lay wrapped up in each other, until they fell asleep. He didn't even take off the condom until the next morning.

# Chapter 30

In her endless quest to be with Jess, Emma became over-eager to please Ben. But it was a double-edged sword. As soon as he gave any sort of indication, any tiny gesture that to her meant she was not the centre of his world, she would fall into a disconsolate, depressed state. Then she would hide herself away.

For the most part Ben did not see the full extent of her mood swings but he was aware that she could go from over-excited puppy to silent statue in a heartbeat. Somehow Emma, without actually knowing it, would bounce back just in time. Just as Ben started to wonder if perhaps she was too high maintenance she would shower him with love and affection. He would then remember that she was a great girlfriend really, I mean, look how she had admitted she was wrong over the whole Claire thing. Then they would once again be happy with each other. Somehow Emma managed to keep Ben in her life. They both believed themselves to be in love with the other.

To say Emma was happy during this time would not be quite correct. She thought she was happy. She thought Ben made her happy, but in reality she was too tightly wound to be anywhere near happy. She searched constantly for any sign that Jess was with them. She took comfort in even the smallest gesture (Ben liking The Cure, for instance), and was distraught each time she was unable to find such a sign.

As it did every year, Christmas approached. No matter what Emma did to block out its impending arrival, each year she would be subjected to a loathsome period where she would be inundated with images of 'festive family fun'. She hated Christmas more than any other time of the year.

This year was worse than any other as Ben was prone to mentioning it, reminding her of that she sought so hard to avoid. What she would like for Christmas? It hadn't even occurred to her that she would need to buy Ben a present. She hadn't bought anyone a present for such a long time. What on earth did people buy their boyfriends for Christmas? Luckily TV provided the answer – aftershave. A nice easy present that didn't require much thought at all. Perfect.

Then of course came the much greater hurdle. Where would she be spending Christmas? Well the answer was simple, of course, she would spend the day wrapped in a blanket crying, as she always did. Emma grew ever fearful that an invitation would be thrust upon her at any time. Every time Christmas came up she would change the subject. Throughout all of the last week in November and the first week of December she was as jumpy as a kitten on hot sand. How could she possibly avoid the horrors of a family Christmas at Ben's parents' without offending anyone? She despised the idea of being forced into a happy social holiday. She hated the whole wide world for putting her in this position. Maybe she could break up with Ben just beforehand and then make up in the new year? No, too risky, she might lose him altogether.

Such were the strength of her feelings that she hadn't noticed yet that Ben had not actually invited her to go anywhere. In fact Ben, showing remarkable sensitivity, had not brought the subject up for a few days. It was on his mind though. He knew Emma would bring with her ill feeling and animosity and frankly family Christmases were stressful enough without bringing along a known instigator. However he knew if he didn't invite her she would most likely do – well what? – spend the day wrapped in a blanket crying? In all good conscience he could not allow for that either. So they were both left with a quandary.

Oddly, it never occurred to either of them to spend Christmas on their own, together.

Neither could have possibly foreseen that help would come in the way of a botched furniture delivery. All the offices, bar Emma's, had received their new purple chairs with orthopaedic back rests, matching footrests and pine-effect desks. Emma's office still worked from their miss-matched desks and uncomfortable chairs. The only way the furniture company could possibly make good on their promise to have everything in place by the new year was to deliver on the Saturday before Christmas. Volunteers were needed to help move the old desks away. The finance director winced at the number of good-will bottles of wine this was going to cost the company.

On the Monday of the second week in December the subject was broached at an office meeting. On the Sunday, just the day before, Ben had very casually mentioned what a nightmare the roads would be the Friday before Christmas, the day he'd be going to his parents. Completely against type Emma volunteered for desk-removal duty so quickly Roz almost fell off her chair.

Later that same evening Emma and Ben came as close as they were ever going to get to a proper conversation on the matter.

"You know our desks still haven't been delivered?" Emma broached the subject.

"Really? We've had ours for ages."

"I know. They're only just going to get them in before the holidays." If at all possible Emma avoided even the word 'Christmas'. "The thing is, they need me in on the Saturday morning to help move out the old stuff." (Emma carefully chose the phrase 'they need me' as opposed to 'they need volunteers').

"That sucks, having to go in on a Saturday."

"Mmm, I know, never mind though. Hey who knows, I might even get a bottle of wine out of it." They both smiled at this. Ben then looked closely into Emma's eyes.

"Are you sure you're okay going in then?" He studied her reaction.

"Yes, it's no problem." Emma's reply was as bright and breezy as she could fake. They both knew what this conversation was really about.

"More wine?" she offered.

And that was that. The live grenade that was Christmas had been disarmed. Emma felt greatly relieved. She also felt a tiny bit cross but couldn't quite put her finger on why. Perhaps because on some level she realised Ben did not seem at all upset at not spending Christmas with her. After all he'd never actually invited her.

# Chapter 31

Christmas day started early for Emma. At 2am to be precise when her neighbours, drunk from an eve of revelry came home. After that she lay awake, worrying about the one task she had to get through that day. She knew she had to call Ben. Tradition stated that a couple parted at this time of year would have to share a mid-morning phone call. She rehearsed again and again the conversation. She would need to sound bright and breezy, as if being alone were the most natural thing in the world. Under no terms what so ever could she sound upset or depressed, both of which she felt. She wanted to get up, walk to the phone box on the high street and get the call over and done with so she could begin her own traditional celebration.

She looked at the clock to see if were yet late enough to make the call. It was 3am. Okay, so she had more time to plan. She would ask about his family, she would ask about the presents they had each given. She would ask him what they were having for lunch. In fact she would just keep asking questions to ensure he did not have time to ask her any. Then she would tell him she loved him, her money would run out and she would hang up. Then she would return to her flat, open a bottle of vodka and just wait for the day to be over.

She looked at the clock again to see if it was late enough yet to make the call. She just wanted that part to be over. She wanted to get on with hating Christmas, herself and the whole world and she couldn't do that until the fake happy phone call was made.

It was 3.15am.

Any other year she had the freedom to wake up in a bad mood, have spirits for breakfast and just wait for the whole thing to end. This year she was forced to put her own plans on hold just until she could get the call out of the way. She hated being made to do things; she hated having her plans spoiled. She was angry with Ben for daring to be her boyfriend and thereby putting her in this stupid situation. Her angry musings killed time until 5am when she finally got out of bed. She made herself a cup of tea and sat on her old settee, staring out of the window. She tried to put her mind into neutral, to not think of anything, just let the street scene below wash over her. She soon realised she didn't have that kind of mental control so instead she stood up and paced around her flat. The kitchen and bathroom needed a clean, she noted, without ever even beginning to form a thought as to when she might do that. Dust lay thick on all the surfaces and the carpet was covered in specks of dropped crumbs, which served to cover the stains of spilled wine. This was all observed casually, but again, with no thought of ever actually rectifying it. She decided to count the wine stains on the carpet and was surprised to find 15 in such a small room. *I must be clumsy*, she thought, which was about as close to self-realisation as Emma ever got. Given that all her time was spent thinking about herself and her problems, Emma actually knew very little about herself at all.

Finally the clock turned to 9am. Emma had wanted to wait until 11 before making the call, but lacked neither the patience nor discipline to wait any further. She opened her precious vodka bottle, poured a very large shot (Dutch courage) and gulped it back in one. That felt interesting on an empty stomach, a feeling Emma was used to. She put on her coat, popped the 50 pence piece she had been saving for the call into her pocket and headed outside.

She was pleasantly surprised to find it was a beautiful day. The cold nipped her nose and cheeks but the sun was shining and the day felt fresh.

"Hello, Ben?"

"Hello Emma!"

"Happy Christmas!" She managed to say it without gagging.

"Happy Christmas!" Ben replied.

Okay, now for the question marathon…

During her 50 pence's worth of time she ascertained that Ben loved the aftershave, his brother had bought him a novelty tie, everyone was fine and they were having turkey for lunch.

As the beeps sounded the end of time they both managed to fit in a quick 'I love you' before the line went dead.

She'd done it! She'd actually done it and it hadn't been that bad. She had survived a Christmas day conversation. She felt elated, even a little proud of herself. Now she could get on with her traditional celebration. Her blanket awaited her.

In a flash of sheer spontaneity, however, rather than turn directly back to her flat, she began to walk the other way, towards the canal. It was such a nice day and she was feeling about as good as she ever could at Christmas, so rather than trot back to her spirits, instead she made her way to the only nice part of the suburb. The canal never felt like part of London; there were green fields with some horses and the water itself, whilst brown, did have a calming effect.

*A novelty tie, honestly what a stupid present,* Emma thought as she stomped along. One simple object that epitomises the futility of the festive period. Family law states that presents must be bought and nothing says 'I couldn't be bothered to think of a present you might like when I saw this for less than a fiver and thought, sod it, that'll do'. Something that would be appreciated for a nanosecond, worn for half an hour and then discarded. All the effort and resources that went into making this pointless object would be for nothing. The novelty tie – the perfect symbol of the over-commercialism of Christmas. Dickens and Hallmark had a lot to answer for. Perhaps buying the tie was a defiant, ironic act against Christmas itself – or just a really naff present. Having never met Ben's brother she could not be sure.

Emma was actually enjoying herself on this day, of all days. It was nice to be out walking and she liked having a random item to get worked up about. *Novelty tie, honestly.*

As she walked along a thought hit her, quite hard. This was the first proper walk she had been on, by herself, since getting her GCSE results. Which meant it was the first proper walk she had been on since… well… you know. She had walked *to* places of course, but hadn't actually been for a walk by herself. A walk that wasn't designed to get anywhere, just a walk for thinking's sake and for the beauty of being out. She wasn't too sure how she should feel about that. Obviously she felt guilty about it, that went without saying. Here she was walking along when Jess no longer had legs of her own. Of course she felt guilty. But she didn't feel like she wanted to collapse into a screaming heap because of it. So she kept walking.

She noticed pigeons landing nearby, pecking for food. *Lucky pigeons who don't have to celebrate Christmas.* She noticed a plastic bag caught in a tree and felt a flash of anger that anything so mundane and out of place should be in a tree, but it was only a flash. Not the sort of boiling rage that would keep her happily hating the world for the rest of the day. In fact, no matter what she spotted and no matter what day it was, Emma realised she didn't feel angry at all. She felt calm. She liked the wind whipping her hair, she liked the bright winter sunlight, she even liked the cold nipping her gloveless hands. Had anyone been around to notice her, they might have assumed she was out for a quick breath of air before enjoying a full day surrounded by family and friends. She wasn't even scowling, her usual default facial expression.

She was now about as far from her own suburb as she could be without actually starting to walk through the next. Here was a brief interlude of water and greenery and, not wishing to break the mood by retuning to a built-up area just yet, she sat down.

She felt empowered by her ability to be out, almost happily, on her own on today of all days. Of course, any emotion in Emma would trigger thoughts of Jess. *How was she feeling? What was she doing? How come she was enjoying Christmas with my boyfriend when I'm here on my own?* Oh, she didn't expect to have that last thought. It had a tinge of jealousy about it. Emma slowed her breathing down and tried to control her thoughts. She had been speaking to Jess, Jess had been with her. Now she wasn't. She was with Ben. But what if she had never really been with either of them? Emma's eyes opened wide with fear. What if Jess's return had only ever been just a construct of her over-wrought mind? Because if Jess had really been with her for those few weeks, why wasn't she with her now?

There was a shadow of a thought whispering in Emma's mind. It was too confusing and frightening to address directly, but it was there. It was the realisation that maybe, just maybe, Emma had pulled Jess back to her when she needed her most. At a time when she was slowly losing her mind, she had created Jess from her memories, dragged her across the chasm of death and used her help to create a more stable mind-frame, a more stable life.

She had to believe it was really Jess and not just her own mind. Admitting she had created Jess would be to admit that she no longer lived in the world of the rational and Emma didn't want that to be so.

Her mind battled itself, split into two opposing camps. Part of her needed to believe she had spoken to Jess and part of her began to see that could not be so. The battle was too hard; it was not a war Emma wanted to engage in. So she skirted the issue. Who or what she had been speaking to could not, would not, be resolved, but either way, which ever path she had been on at that time there was one inescapable truth – the path had led to Ben. She was meant to be with Ben. She understood that now perhaps better than she ever had before. Ben was hers and he was hers for a reason.

Jess was quiet again now. She had helped Emma find her saviour and now she must rest again. She'd given Emma the opportunity to be saved. Oh, how she loved the good and kind Jess. *Rest now, my beautiful friend.*

Guilt again stabbed her heart. *My god I killed the most wonderful person.* But soon, soon that guilt would be gone.

Ben's job was not to bring her closer to Jess; it was to save her from her. It was to save her from the guilt, from the depression and the pain she had carried with her since 1989. Ben was to be her saviour. It was an epiphany. On that most hated of days, Emma had taken the first tiny baby step towards moving on, to see her life as something other than revolving around Jess.

It was getting dark now. Emma had sat by the canal all day as her mind worked through complex calculations bringing her to a new understanding. It started to rain. Emma felt cramped from sitting for so long so she stretched out her arms and tilted back her head, allowing the rain to pour down her cheeks. It stung slightly as it hit her forehead, but it felt good. As she sat there, stretched out and staring upwards, as though supplicating herself to the heavens, she realised that this was perhaps the start of a new era.

She was going to be saved from years of heartache and loss and, most importantly, guilt. And Ben would be her saviour.

# Chapter 32

They had been together (bar a short time apart) for just over a year now and summer time was fast approaching again. Ben was shocked to hear that Emma had never been overseas and so decided they should take a holiday together. Friends of his parents had a villa in Spain they would rent him for a week cheaply enough. So (with mounting excitement on Emma's part) they booked their tickets and went to Spain for a week.

At the estuary, Emma still leaned against the jagged rocks. Her head was feeling worse now. The sense of urgency had increased. She knew she had to face thinking about Spain but she really didn't want to. However, if this walk was going to have any benefit at all she had to think about it. About what it had meant to her and about what had ultimately happened.

The villa, high in the Spanish mountains, was beautiful; one of the most romantic places imaginable. The sort of place that looks really nice in the brochure but when you get there actually takes your breath away. A rare find – somewhere that is actually better than advertised. Inside the lounge was all white but it didn't look clinical, the furnishings were too soft for that. Instead it looked luxurious and fresh. The bedroom however, was the real jewel of the interior. It had a large queen-sized bed draped with a cream linen mosquito net; the sheets were gold coloured satin with matching pillows, so soft it felt like they were filled with marshmallow. To complete the effect the furniture was antique pine that gave the room a regal effect. It was the sort of room Emma, when she was much younger, imagined she would make love in for the first time. Next door was a huge en-suit bathroom covered in mosaic tiles of a subtle blue-grey hue, so it looked like a 5-star hotel bathroom. A door off the en-suit led to a dressing room, this in itself almost as big as Emma's bedroom back in London. The whole place was finished to the highest standard and made Emma feel special just to know it would be theirs for an entire week.

If the inside of the villa was nice, this was nothing compared to the surroundings outside. There was, of course, a private pool for just the two of them to use. They were so remote up here, who else would be around to use it anyway? From the pool they could see down the mountain below them and across to the mountain range to the north of them. On the drive up to the villa all Emma had been conscious of was how bumpy the road was and how uncomfortable the journey had been. But now looking down they could see splashes of bright yellow broom, swathes of deep purple sweat pea, fragrant wild honeysuckle and vibrant patches of bright red poppies all nestled between gnarled, ancient olive trees with dark green leaves and the faintest hint of pale, pale yellow blossom. It was as if Mother Nature had conspired with all the elements to make this the most romantic place on earth.

"Did I do good?" asked Ben.

"Oh yeah." Emma breathed her reply so softly, hardly daring to make a sound in a place that should be revered for its beauty. She turned to look at him, gently moved a step closer and embraced him. She reached up and joined him in a long, lingering kiss. Not a passionate kiss, but one filled with love and utter contentment.

Oh yes, this was definitely set to be a great holiday.

They spent their week in Spain lounging around the pool sunbathing, with, of course, the occasional water fight. They took long walks along tracks cut across the densely flowered hillside and they drove to little tavernas for lunch. All in all, it was a wonderful, relaxing holiday. They both felt closer to each other than they ever had. They were a young couple in love in a beautiful place. It felt like nothing could possibly spoil their happiness.

On their last full day there (they were due to fly home at 2pm the following day) Emma was quiet. She had a big decision to make. In the end she decided, *Yes*. Yes, she would take the final step and tell Ben all. Over the past six months she had grown to adore Ben, adore him for what he was going to do for her. Now it was time to make sure he fully understood his mission. She had to tell him about Jess and about her part in her death. Only once he knew everything could he really begin his quest to save her. So, in the early evening she poured them both a large gin and tonic and led Ben to the pool where they both dangled their feet in the refreshing water, under the shade of a large umbrella.

"Ben."

"Yes love, what is it?"

"I've never told you about Jess, have I?" The question was clearly rhetorical so Ben stayed silent, looking at her and wondering what was about to come.

"Jess was my best friend. She was wonderful; you two would have really got on well. We met when we were about 13 and became really close, like sisters but without the fighting." Ben smiled at this, but now he was really starting to wonder where this was going.

"She was one of the kindest people I have ever met, funny, sweet, good natured, a really, really good friend." Emma paused. Ben wasn't sure whether to say anything or not. He also wasn't sure if he should be feeling at all jealous. In the end he waited for Emma to continue.

"When we were 16 she died."

Ben looked alarmed and so full of sympathy, he reached out to take Emma in his arms.

"No," she very gently pushed him back. "I need to tell you why she died."

Emma then recounted the tale of Jess's last night alive. Did she start the story when they were already in the pub, or did she tell it properly, from the beginning? Looking back on it now she couldn't remember. Either way when she reached the end there were tears slowly rolling down her cheeks.

Ben pulled her into his arms and held her against his chest, gently rocking her back and forth. Eventually he softly spoke, "Oh my angel, I am so sorry. That must have been awful, losing your best friend like that. It's not fair when people die so young."

Emma pulled back a little so she could look up at him. "No, it's not just that it's…" she trailed off.

"Fear of losing people you love?" He enveloped her in another big bear hug. "I won't leave you my angel," he whispered into her hair. Emma pulled back more forcibly this time.

"No, you don't understand!" she snapped at him.

"What, don't understand what?" he asked, a little hurt.

This was all going so wrong. He was meant to understand. He wasn't meant to give her sympathy. He wasn't meant to be gentle and full of 'understanding your loss'. He was meant to realise it had all been her fault. He was meant to realise her guilt. He was meant to understand it all because he was meant to be the one to forgive her. Emma loved Ben but for that love to work he had to be the one who would finally absolve her of all the guilt she had carried around for so long. How could he forgive her if he couldn't even grasp that it was all her fault? He couldn't see the crime.

"You don't get it, do you?" she accused him.

"Get what?" Ben could not understand how this conversation had turned all of a sudden.

"You don't get the fact that it was my fault. My fault she died. She is dead because of me." Emma had pulled her feet out of the pool and was standing up.

Ben grabbed her arm. "What are you talking about?"

"You just don't get it, do you? You just don't understand. If I hadn't acted the way I did that night Jess wouldn't have been where she was. She wouldn't have died alone next to the road because I would have been with her."

"That's ludicrous!"

"It's not bloody ludicrous because it's true!"

Emma ran into the villa and locked herself in the bathroom. She sat on the cold tiled floor and sobbed huge, heart-rending sobs. She felt like her world was closing in on her. Ben was the first person she had ever told about Jess. It had been a difficult decision to tell him. She had only done it so that he would understand her guilty part in the whole sorry tale and forgive her. That was what should have happened but it hadn't. She still had her guilt. It did not feel better. All she felt was betrayed. Ben was supposed to understand. He was supposed to help her and he couldn't. She was winded by disappointment and bitterness.

So Emma cried. Emma howled in pain as the sobs ripped out of her throat. She lay on the cold floor and cried and cried until hours later she fell asleep in the foetal position.

All the while Ben talked to her through the door, pleading with her to open it. He pleaded with her to let him in so they could talk. He still couldn't quite understand what had happened but Emma was obviously in pain and he wanted to help her. But all that existed in that bathroom was Emma and her guilt. She couldn't hear Ben trying to talk to her. That night, all that existed in the whole world was Emma and her guilt, raw and new.

# Chapter 33

Denise never told her new husband about Emma. He knew about her first marriage but he'd never directly asked her whether she had children or not and so the subject never came up. Denise never needed to justify her decision not to tell him because it wasn't a conscious decision. So much time had passed that her thoughts were almost never on her daughter so the need to discuss her just wasn't there. If she had wanted to analyse why she never mentioned Emma it might be because well, first of all, it was very difficult to raise the matter of a grown up, estranged child. Also, Emma was not part of her life anymore so mentioning her would be academic. Finally she might also have realised that in not being able to carry on her relationship with her daughter into adulthood she had somehow failed as a mother. That would give her an unwelcome and little experienced feeling of insecurity. The box in her mind containing Emma was too heavy with too a big a lock to be opened easily and so it stayed shut.

Only when she was feeling run down, or couldn't sleep, then sometimes the shadow would break out of the box and catch in the back of Denise's throat, so that her heart would thud painfully until the lid could be closed again.

# Chapter 34

Back at the estuary, Emma started to cry. She remembered how alone and wretched she had felt that night, lying on the floor of the bathroom in a Spanish villa. Ben could have been her salvation that night, he could have saved her from her own demons, but he didn't. She had continued to carry them. There was no absolution, no relief from the torment of her guilt. To Emma, that night had ripped open all the wounds of the night Jess had died. She had not believed the wounds had started to heal but lying on that floor she felt their full force again and realised that perhaps she had healed a little only to now find them raw and bitter once more.

She allowed herself a little time to cry at the memory of her loneliness that night and then continued slowly to walk along the golden sand of the estuary. It was time now to think about this place, the place where she now walked and how she had ended up here.

After their return from Spain, Emma had become insular once more. She barely spoke. Ben tried all he could to bring her out of herself but she seemed locked in a place emotionally where he could not reach her. He had managed to glean from her that he was the first person she had ever told about Jess. So, he believed the story she had told that night had opened up unresolved grief. He believed that her silences and long periods of just sitting and staring, forgetting even that he was in the room with her, were down to grief. She was finally grieving for her lost friend. Something she should, perhaps, have done a long time ago he felt. So he was patient with her.

Of course, he was wrong. Yes, she should have grieved for Jess a long time ago, but that was not what she was doing now. Instead her silence came from a realisation that she had nothing to say to him. He was not to be her salvation, so what else was there to say? On her part she allowed him to visit her, to sit in her flat with her quietly, because she didn't have the strength or gumption to tell him to go. If he wanted to be there, then fine, it meant nothing to her whether he was there or not anymore. Besides, no one had ever shown her such patience before. Whilst his presence made no real difference, or so Emma believed, it was in some ways better than being alone. She had started to drink a lot more though.

After about six weeks of Ben's patient attention even he began to feel that he was having no effect on her. He didn't want to give up just yet so he decided a weekend away might help. It might seem a bit naïve to think a weekend away could wipe out years of grief (well guilt, actually) but he couldn't think of anything else to do. So, one Friday evening he packed an overnight bag for himself and one for Emma, put the bags and Emma in the car and headed west.

Emma was pretty much operating on auto-pilot. For the last few weeks she spent her days at work and her evenings drinking in her flat with Ben sitting beside her. She had become numb. Nothing seemed to mean anything to her anymore. One morning she had walked to work without her coat, not realising it was raining. So to be sitting in a car on a Friday night, heading off to lord knew where, really did not mean much to her at all. She didn't ask where they were going. She didn't really care.

As they drove along the landscape changed, subtly at first, but soon what had been hills turned to mountains. What had been scattered copses of trees turned to densely wooded forests. Emma noticed the trees first, as her old desire to run into them and lose herself re-emerged.

The woods were the first things she had really looked at for the last six weeks. There was no sudden miraculous moment where Emma turned to Ben, with eyes aglow, and proclaimed her new-found love for live. That would have just been silly. But at least she was, for now, taking note of her environment. That was something.

It was near the end of their journey when they turned left at a small roundabout. Here the road followed the course of the estuary, the same one Emma now walked along. The trees became much thicker here. The road had been cut out of the hillside, through the trees, making it look like a secret pathway to a mythical place. It made Emma think of Sleeping Beauty and the path the valiant prince had cut through the forest. At a sharp bend in the road was a clearing in the trees.

For the first time Emma was able to see the sea and she gasped. She actually gasped. The scene was stunning. The setting sun had turned the sea into a huge golden expanse. Between the trees she could see the estuary, itself turned gold, snaking its way to the vast stretch of sea beyond. Around another bend in the road and the scene shifted with the angle of the car. Now Emma could see the sun setting into the sea. A massive ball of gold tinged with pink slipping into the water. Another bend and the scene altered again. It seemed the cooling water had turned the sun from gold to pink and the sea was now a soft, luxurious, subtle shade of pink. Emma did not actually know where she was. But she knew she liked it.

As Ben checked them into their B&B Emma was already getting ready to go for a walk. It had been so long since Emma had talked he had become used to her silent signals. Without a word, Ben also changed his shoes and followed her outside. Though the sun had now set the scene was, if anything, even more beautiful. The thin whispers of cloud, covering the sky, had kept the sun's colour even though the sun itself had gone. The sky was streaked in a magical rainbow. With the softest pink, through orange, to the darkest purple, all set above a now silver sea the world looked beautiful. A late summer breeze played about them as they walked.

Silently Ben offered Emma his jacket. She looked right at him for the first time in weeks. Just looked at him for what seemed like ages and then, most unexpectedly, she smiled at him, just a small smile. Then she gently shook her head, to refuse his jacket, and they continued on their walk.

They bought cod and chips (just one portion of mushy peas) and took them down to the sand, where they sat and ate them. The colours above them were becoming darker now, no more pinks, rather shades from purples through to grey. The rhythmic sound of the sea gave a tempo to their silence. Occasionally a seagull would land near them, but was too unaccustomed to tourists to beg or steal their chips. So they were left alone, each in their own separate world, together on the sand.

They both slept well that night, better than they had done for many weeks. Over breakfast Ben mentioned he thought they might drive to the next beach, further down the coast, and spend the day there.

"Fine," said Emma, but her voice did not have that dead quality to it, the only one she had seemed able to speak in of late. Instead she sounded, well as she said, fine really. Ben took solace in this.

After breakfast they took the car and headed back along the estuary, turning right at the small roundabout. They soon doubled back on themselves so they were driving down the other side of the estuary, towards the beach to the south. They stopped in a small car park and headed toward the sea.

The beach here was part sand and part pebbles. It was obvious the sand would be covered as the tide came in so instead they chose a spot to sit on the pebbles, moving some of the larger ones out of the way to make for a more comfortable base.

Ben tried a conversation starter, "Beautiful here, isn't it?" but all he got for his effort was a vague "Mmm". So for the next hour they sat quietly and watched the movement of the sea. Eventually, as the tide drew closer, Emma picked up a rock and threw it as hard as she could in to the water.

"Nice shot," remarked Ben.

"Thanks." Emma had now doubled the amount of words she had used this weekend. Ben felt encouraged.

"Okay, let's see who can hit that piece of wood first." He threw a pebble at a branch floating in the water. He missed. Emma tried. She missed. Ben picked up a larger pebble and threw harder. His shot was closer, but also a miss. Emma threw again and clipped the side of the wood.

"Wahey!" shouted Ben, "good shot!" They both picked up

large a handful of pebbles and started throwing them as hard as they could at the unfortunate piece of wood. Emma's original throw had been one borne of frustration. Even she was getting bored with the prolonged silences, but had nothing to say to break them. Her throw had been an act of defiance against the world. But this was actually getting to be kind of fun. As they pelted rocks Ben started to laugh at each failure and triumph. Then finally Emma let out a laugh.

Ben almost stopped throwing at a sound so alien, unheard for so long but he knew better than to break the mood so he kept on pelting. The act of throwing was releasing some of the pent-up tension and frustration. They had thrown so many they were having to reach further out to find good rocks to throw, having practically cleared the area immediately around them. They threw harder and faster and laughed more and more. Caught up in the moment Ben impetuously leant over and kissed Emma on the cheek.

"I do love you, you know."

In reply she looked at him and smiled. She still didn't have much to say but she was slowly breaking out of her self-imposed isolation.

Slowly and gently an idea was forming in Emma's mind. It seemed a little too impossible to begin with. However, as she let the idea form and fed it with other thoughts it began to grow. It began to seem possible, more than possible in fact. It began to seem necessary. She didn't say anything, she simply continued to throw rocks and cast sidelong glances at Ben.

That evening Ben and Emma drove to a little Italian restaurant, which had been recommended to them by the owners of the guesthouse they were staying in. It was a beautiful place, the outside was decorated with a multitude of hanging baskets and pots filled with a bright array of flowers all still in bloom. Inside were wooden tables and chairs, soft lights and soft music. A picture of Pavarotti suggested he'd eaten there but it somehow seemed unlikely. They ordered two sea bass, garlic bread and a bottle of Frascati.

This time it was Emma who tried a conversation starter.

"Beautiful here, isn't it?"

Ben wasn't altogether shocked to hear a complete sentence from her; it was what he had been waiting for.

"Yes, it is a nice place," he agreed.

"No, not just this restaurant, I mean the whole place, the village, the beach, even the drive up here." They had followed the coast road north to reach this little restaurant and it had been a wonderful drive. The road had twisted and turned past empty beaches with long stretches of golden sand and past emerald green fields full of fluffy white sheep.

"It is so nice to get out of London," Ben agreed. He wasn't sure how far to push the conversation. He didn't want to start gabbling like an idiot but he also didn't want them to fall back into silence. He tried to continue with neutral comments.

"There are some beautiful cottages around here."

"I thought so too." Ben was surprised to see Emma's eyes gleam as she said this. Perhaps this was the perfect place to choose for their weekend away. It really seemed to have invigorated Emma. He felt so relieved. Perhaps he was going to get his happy girlfriend back. The one he could talk to and have a laugh with. That was all he wanted.

Throughout the meal they continued their neutral conversation, not touching on anything too emotive, instead just sharing observations about the place, the food and the surrounding area. Ben felt the evening had been a great success. So did Emma. She was coming back out of herself, emerging from her isolation. But that was because, unbeknown to Ben, she had a plan. A plan that would have a profound impact on him.

At the estuary, Emma sat down on the sand. She was trying to remember when she and Ben had first come here. Was it last year or the year before? She couldn't think. She wasn't sure. One thing that did seem blindingly obvious was just how naïve her plan had been. At the time it had seemed like the most brilliant plan ever formed. Now it appeared stupid and childish. So very stupid. She felt so tired sitting on the sand. Why did everything seem so much clearer now in retrospect?

Why hadn't she been able to see things more clearly back then when it would have made a difference? How was it that she was only able to realise her errors now that it was far too late?

The Sunday morning, after the Italian meal, Emma had crept out of bed early, so as not to wake Ben. Armed with the guest house's complimentary stationery and pen she wandered through the village noting down the relevant telephone numbers from where they were displayed outside of businesses she thought might prove useful. She took the numbers of two estate agents, a solicitors and the tiny tourist information centre. She then quietly crept back into the guesthouse and snuggled back into bed with Ben.

She lay still, trying to be as quiet as possible. She didn't want Ben to wake up yet. She wanted time to think. She was so excited with her plan but she needed time to mull it over and figure out exactly how it would work.

To Emma it all seemed simple enough but she had always been plagued by a tendency to worry. There were still details to be worked out. She couldn't wait to tell Ben about it, but she had to work out some of the logistics first. She had to suppress a giggle, so excited was she with the brilliance of it all. Ben had initially failed her, he had not been able to understand (and therefore forgive) the enormity of her guilt. It was a barrier in their relationship, one that Ben was unaware of. But that would change.

Once they moved here together, away from Ben's family and friends, once she had him all to herself in this romantic and remote village she could slowly and gradually make him understand. It would be just the two of them against the world. There would be no other distractions. Obviously they would need to work, but that would be a simple enough matter. The rest of their time could be spent walking through the dramatic scenery and stunning beaches that surrounded them. Over time Emma would articulate all that had happened with Jess until Ben could understand what really happened, not just what he thought had happened when Jess died. She had dumped too much information on him in Spain; he hadn't been able to take it in properly. She wouldn't make that mistake again. Instead they would live out their days in isolation, together, until that happy day when finally Ben would understand and forgive her. That would be such a fantastic day. After that they could plan for their future, maybe even children. This would be a wonderful place to bring up children.

Emma's mind certainly raced as she lay quietly in bed next to Ben. She felt like she had found the answer to all their problems. She felt that she had it all figured out.

Emma honestly believed that if she uprooted them both and moved them half way across the country everything would be all right. She was too wrapped up in the idea to even consider that the location had never been the problem. It was her guilt that was the problem and she would be bringing that with her. It wasn't Ben's forgiveness that she needed, it was her own. But she was far too wrapped up in her brilliant plan to ever consider this. To her there were no obstacles to happiness now, just a few practical issues, easily dealt with. Poor Emma's delusion marched on unabated.

# Chapter 34

By the time they returned to London on the Sunday evening Emma looked more refreshed and relaxed than she had done for a long time. She still did not say much, though rather than depression causing her silences it was now excitement. She had too much to think about to be able to hold a regular conversation. Ben was happy that Emma seemed happy and so contended himself with the belief that the weekend had been a great success and now they could go back to normal. No more tears, no more silences, this was what Ben looked forward to.

Over the next couple of months life returned pretty much to what it had been pre-Spain. They went walking together at weekends, they went out for meals, and they went to the cinema. Ben was pleased that the status quo had returned. Any periods of silence between them now were comfortable and no longer fraught with tension. Emma did seem a bit excitable but he had learnt to live with her often-erratic mood changes.

When he received a call from Emma one day at work inviting him to come to dinner on Friday night he was a little surprised. They had been together long enough now to not really invite each other anywhere anymore, it was usually assumed they would be together. When he put the phone down he checked his diary. No, it wasn't their anniversary, it wasn't Emma's birthday and it certainly wasn't his.

*Well that's nice,* he thought to himself, *she's planned a romantic meal at home for no reason whatsoever.* Ben believed that sort of thing kept the spark in a relationship so he was touched by the gesture.

Emma took the Friday afternoon off work. She scrubbed the flat to make it as clean and inviting as possible, which was certainly no mean feat. Then she got to work in the kitchen. The starter was easy enough, open vacuum pack of mussels in garlic and white wine sauce and chuck in a pan, no problems there. The main course wasn't anything too taxing either. Chicken breasts were stuffed with cream cheese and chives, wrapped in bacon and ready to be served with asparagus and roasted red peppers. For old times' sake she had bought a chocolate mousse for them to share for dessert. She enjoyed preparing the meal. It gave her something to take her mind off the mounting excitement, bordering on tension, she was feeling.

Having got everything ready for the meal she got to work on herself. She spent a good hour plucking, shaving, clipping, trimming and painting until she looked the best that she possibly could. With everything in perfect order, she paced the flat, waiting for him to arrive.

Ben was pretty punctual and arrived with a big bunch of flowers, which earned him a long, passionate kiss. His compliments to Emma for the way she looked and the smell of the food meant there was quite a bit of kissing before the wine was finally opened and they sat down to eat. Emma had spent a long time planning how she was going to open this conversation and had decided on waiting until after the starter and then beginning with, "I have a surprise for you." It was said just a little seductively.

"Oh?" said Ben, looking pleased and wondering if she had finally thrown away her regulation knickers and gone for something a little lacier and a little racier.

"You remember when we went to the coast a little while ago and we both said how nice it would be to stay there forever?"

"Yes." Okay, maybe this wasn't going to be about underwear.

"Well," Emma paused for effect, "now we can!"

"Sorry, what?" Ben was smiling at her. He hadn't the faintest idea what was going on.

"I've sorted it all out!" Her eyes were shining, she could have looked beautiful but was coming off as maybe a little manic. "I've rented us a house!"

"What do you mean?" Ben wasn't sure he could take more

time off work for another holiday.

"I've rented us a house, given my notice on this place and I've resigned at work! We can move there full time! We can live there, it can be our home!" Emma very nearly said 'ta-dah!' at the end but decided against it. Ben was staring at her, clearly not planning on saying anything.

"The lease on the new place starts next month, so if you give your notice at work on Monday we can move 4 weeks from today. Isn't that amazing? Isn't it great?!"

"What are you talking about?" This had to be a joke, surely.

"Us, you and me, moving away from London to start a new life together." Wow, Ben was being really slow on the uptake.

"Are you serious?"

"Yes, of course, it will be amazing! Just imagine, our own little place, living together, no distractions. Just you, me and that beautiful place. It was so hard keeping it from you, I wanted to tell you so many times, but I thought I would wait until it was all finalised and surprise you."

"Well, you've certainly done that." Ben was trying to stay calm, this was obviously a wind-up and he didn't want to fall for it too hard.

"So, what do you think then? Are you amazed at what your clever, wonderful girlfriend has done?"

"If you mean this chicken, then yes, it is very good. If you mean moving, well I'll have to get back to you on that." He was smiling at her again now, playing along with the joke. But this was no joke to Emma.

"What do you mean, 'I'll have to get back to you on that'?" There was a hard edge to her voice.

"Eh?" Emma was taking this joke a bit too far.

"What do you mean, 'I'll have to get back to you on that'?" she repeated, the hard edge a little harder this time. "It's all arranged, we're moving. Me and you, we're moving, we're going together to start our new life."

"You can't just tell someone they're moving half way across the country!" The whole notion was absurd.

"What? You want me to ask you then?" This was said with a whole new level of sarcasm.

"That would have been a nice start!" There was no hard edge to Ben's voice; he was far too flummoxed for that.

"Well I don't see what your problem is."

"My problem?" His voice had gone up an octave. "My problem is that you think I'm going to give up a perfectly good job and a perfectly good life to move to… to,,, some bloody back water." Okay, now there was hard edge to his voice.

"It's not like I'm asking for a kidney! I thought you'd be pleased. I thought this would be just what we both wanted!"

"Jesus! You can have a bloody kidney if you want one. That's not a problem. Telling someone you're about to turn their whole life upside down, now that, that is a problem!"

"Well excuse me for trying to make a better life for us!" Emma stood up as she said this. This was not going at all how it had in her head. They should be making love at this point, joyous, happy sex to celebrate their new life together.

"Make a better life for us! Who the hell are you to decide what I should do?" Ben downed his glass of wine in one gulp and stared at her.

"You bloody ungrateful bastard. I've gone to all this trouble to sort everything out and all you can do is sit there and complain!"

"If my sitting here and trying to talk, oh I'm sorry, complain, about you trying to take over my life and tell me where I'm going to live and what I'm going to do is not to your liking then sod this!" Ben got up to leave.

"Yeah, go on fine, piss off then! If that's what you want then bloody well go. You bloody stupid bastard!" Emma screamed the last part of this sentence.

Ben stared at her. He had no idea what to say. He was so angry with her. How could she not see how insane this all was? He grabbed his coat and stormed out of the flat. It seemed like his only option, Emma had clearly flipped and there was no way he could talk to her like this. He left just in time. As he closed the door a half-full bottle of wine smashed against it.

# Chapter 35

It pained Emma now to think of that argument. Though she still couldn't completely see it yet, his ingratitude at her careful planning still stung, but Ben had been right. She couldn't just decide she was going to change someone's life forever without considering what they wanted. But he had said he'd wanted to stay in that little village forever. He'd *said* that. But then, people always say that when they go to somewhere nice for a visit. The very rarely actually mean it. Why hadn't Emma realised then and there that she had gone too far?

After Ben had stormed out Emma was too angry to realise anything. He had once again let her down. She had planned the perfect evening to celebrate the perfect plans she had made and he had been too bloody stupid to realise it. Emma was in a rage, a full on rage. Smashing the bottle of wine had not been nearly enough to sate her anger. She threw the dinner plates across the room; she threw the knives and the forks before she dragged the table to the ground. That was still not enough so she destroyed her flat. Rampaging through the tiny space she called home she embarked on a project of utter destruction. She felt nothing but rage, even her ever-present guilt bowed silently backwards, out of the frame, to allow anger its fair share in the spotlight. Everything was an affront to her, every object, every reminder of who she was, had to be destroyed. She wanted to rub out her existence, she wanted to nullify this life. Her entire being was consumed with aggression and violence. Everything had to be destroyed and the tiny pieces that remained smashed out of existence. That night she was vengeance and destruction personified. When she smashed the TV she ground the remains with her hands and feet into the carpet. The clothes Ben had left at her house from many nights stayed over were dragged from the wardrobe and ripped. Emma tore at buttons and thick material until her hands poured with blood. Then she smashed the wardrobe itself to the floor.

Still she was not satisfied. She smashed every cup, glass, plate and saucer in the flat. She broke doors by hurling herself at them. For hours she rampaged through her home and destroyed it. The only thing she didn't break was a bottle of vodka from which she drank long, heart-burning slugs and clung to, like a child with a teddy. Eventually when there was nothing left to break she sunk to her knees, sobbing, the sound guttural and barely human. Once again Emma sobbed herself to sleep that night.

She woke up next to a pile of her own sick. She could have died, vomiting in her sleep like that, but life was too cruel to give Emma such an easy exit. No, she had to wake up and face what she had done. The devastation in both the flat and her head were phenomenal. She crawled to the bathroom and drank cold, clean water from the tap. There were, of course, no glasses to drink from. She sat on the toilet and tried to piece together what had happened last night.

The fight with Ben came back to her easily enough but the rest of the evening was a blur. Her throat hurt from crying so much. She felt too ill to be surprised or appalled by her rampage. She crawled from the bathroom into her bedroom, dragged the ruined clothes from the bed and sunk under her duvet, painfully slashing her thigh on a piece of broken glass. She lay very still and through nightmares and fitful dreams she slept until Sunday.

When she opened her eyes on the Sunday morning it was clear her sleep had brought her no rest or refreshment. She had never felt so ill in her entire life. Her feet were cut from the broken glass strewn around the flat, her hands were red and swollen from cuts and bruises, her chest and throat felt ripped apart by a night of wailing but these were mere trifles compared to the pain in her head.

She honestly felt that Sunday morning like she might die. She lay in bed hoping perhaps she would. When, after a couple of hours had passed, it became clear she wasn't going to die she got up. First, she had to re-hydrate herself. Without any glasses the only way to drink was to tip her head under the tap.

The dizziness that ensued from tipping her head to the side made her throw up. With nothing left in her stomach it felt like her stomach lining was coming out through her mouth. In utter hopelessness and despair she went back to bed. What else was there for her to do?

Emma lay in bed for hours. It got dark again but she couldn't sleep, it got light again and still she couldn't sleep. She just lay there somewhere between life and death. Her entire world, both physically and emotionally had collapsed. Ben had let her down again and at this point Emma had neither the strength nor the will to do anything about it. So she lay there, crying when the tears would come and silent when they would not. She didn't have a plan anymore and felt too despondent to hold a thought in her head. So she just lay there.

Eventually, even when you want to die, your body gets fed up with the lack of signals coming from the brain and so decides to take charge. Or perhaps it is part of the brain that is concerned only with survival, that is disconnected from the emotional side, that gets fed up. Either way Emma was way past feeling hungry, or feeling anything but a dark emptiness. But her body and/or brain had had enough of this so finally, gingerly it propelled her towards the kitchen where she ate a slice of dry, stale bread. She kept it down for a full five minutes before throwing up again. This was okay though because her survival instinct had now taken over and it made her stay in the kitchen alternatively nibbling bread and drinking water until it was convinced she would survive the night. Then it allowed the emotional side back in to take over.

Emma needed to decide what to do and as she had a plan already in motion, one for her and Ben, the simplest course of action seemed to be to follow that plan on her own. It appeared to be the path of least resistance. She would get out of London, get far, far away from anyone that knew her and start again, alone. She would crawl back into herself, leave life behind and disappear to a remote corner of the country without ever interacting with anybody ever again. There she could wilt away without ever having to go through the pain of disappointment again. It wasn't much of a plan but it was the only one she had.

# Chapter 36

In the weeks leading up to her departure she did not try to contact Ben. The very thought of him disgusted her. Though it should be noted, he didn't try to contact her either. The very thought of her freaked him out.

She also didn't bother to return to work. She only had a few weeks left until her notice ran out and as she felt no loyalty to the company whatsoever she didn't bother to turn up for work. Also, going to work meant seeing Rob and there was no way Emma was going to put herself through that.

Instead she spent her time trying to figure out the unbelievably convoluted train route she would have to follow to reach her new home. She also cleaned up the broken glass in her flat. She didn't do a particularly thorough job, the holes she had bashed into the walls and doors meant it was clear she was never going to get her deposit back; she cleaned up just enough to prevent her cutting herself any further. She also went through her wardrobe (not that this piece of furniture itself still existed) to see if anything was salvageable. She still had the clothes she'd been wearing when Ben came for dinner but they were splattered with her blood.

Everything else was ruined. Underwear was even trickier. She hadn't ripped anything but she had thrown it across the floor and then smashed the drawer against the wall. This meant her knickers had been lying amongst broken glass. As you might imagine it only took one near fatal incident with a clean pair of knickers and tiny fragments of glass before she decided to throw the lot out and start again. Thankfully she hadn't cut herself but it was close enough to set her heart racing. She had to buy more clothes.

She dragged herself to the high street, picked up the first top and pair of trousers she found in her size along with a pack of knickers and that was her retail therapy complete.

Emma did find one item of Ben's clothing that had

escaped unharmed. It was a jumper that had been thrown into the back of the wardrobe at the end of last winter and not touched since. It was a green woollen jumper, very snuggly and cuddly. It had been Emma's favourite of all of Ben's clothes. Emma sat and stared at it for a long time (after all, she had nothing else to do). She stared at it as if it might at any moment jump up and do something interesting – a little song and dance perhaps? She didn't know what to do with it. She couldn't quite figure out how it made her feel. Finally, in a moment of sheer practicality she packed it with her own clothes thinking that perhaps her new home would be cold and she may need a good jumper come winter.

Emma had no possessions of any value; in fact after her recent rampage she had no possessions at all really. Her clothes and toiletries fitted into the small backpack she had moved to London with.

Once packed she cancelled all of her utility bills and left the flat. She wanted to avoid seeing her landlord; her deposit would cover the damage she had caused, so she felt herself to be all square on that front. Rather than going to the lettings agent she popped the key into an envelope with a note to say she was leaving the flat as per the notice she had given earlier in the month. She did not give a forwarding address.

On her way to the tube station she put the envelope in a post box and left London. There was no one to say goodbye to so she began her arduous train journey without any fond farewells or best wishes for the future. She never looked back, she was finally moving forward.

# Chapter 37

*Moving forward! What a joke,* Emma now thought with bitterness. She may have left London carrying only a small backpack, but her emotional baggage could have filled Pickford's largest van and trailer. She dragged it all across two different tube lines, four separate connecting trains and a taxi before she finally arrived many hours later at her new home. The agent had been very good about letting her move in early. Truth be told the agent was just amazed that anyone would rent out such a small, run-down house and was happy to bend over backwards to ensure it all went smoothly. When she arrived it was already dark and the lack of street lamps didn't make finding the house any easier. Eventually however she stood outside her new front door, found the key under the doormat as arranged and let herself in.

Never having seen the house before Emma was initially confused to find the bedroom and bathroom downstairs and the kitchen and lounge upstairs. Thankfully the house had been rented fully furnished so all Emma had to do was throw her bag on the floor, settle down on the bed and open the bottle of vodka she had picked up earlier. Sadly the fully furnished house did not include bedding so Emma sat on the bare mattress wishing she had a pillow and drinking herself to sleep. It had been a stressful day with so much travelling. It would have been an exciting adventure had Ben been with her, but alone Emma suddenly feared she had made a massive mistake.

What the hell was she doing here? How was she going to build a new life for herself? Did she even want a new life or just somewhere to hide away? These thoughts crowded her mind but her best friend, vodka, helped her to accept that this was her life now and it was the best thing for her. She didn't cry herself to sleep that night. She did however lie on the bare mattress wishing she had bedding and wishing above all she had had the foresight to pick up loo roll before she got here. Staring a new life might have been wonderfully exciting or fantastically frightening, but ultimately it was the little things, like loo roll, that determined how easy or comfortable it was.

The next morning Emma woke up feeling stiff from travelling and from being hunched up for warmth in her new duvet-free bed. She also had a nice tingling feeling: she was out of London, she was away from all the mistakes that had been made there. She was in a new place where nobody knew her and she knew nobody. She was truly alone. She found comfort in this. No one could judge her past crimes because no one knew of them, nor would they ever. She would live here away from the world. Alone felt good.

There was no food in the house so she wandered into the village for supplies. The small local shop met most of her food needs. A camping shop provided her with a sleeping bag; without a car Emma had no way of travelling to the nearest town for a duvet, especially since the twice weekly bus service was not running today. A picnic set with plastic plates and cutlery served as her new tableware. She also managed, somewhat incongruously, to pick up a pillow from the hardware shop. She now had all she needed.

After a breakfast of Coco Pops (which she had never grown out of) she went for her first proper individual walk along the beach. Her shopping trip had emphasised to her the need to get a job. Emma had some money saved up but not enough to live on for more than a month or so. She needed an income. So her first walk was spent trying to decide where it might be best to apply for a job. Living in a small village without a car seriously limits income-related opportunities.

She thought of all the possible places where she might find work. On her first trip here with Ben she had taken the number of the solicitor's office, thinking she may be able to pick up some office work but that avenue had been closed many weeks before during a call made from her then-place of work to her prospective place. Mrs Jones had covered all of the administration needs at the solicitors for the last 15 years and nothing was about to change there. She thought about asking the estate agent if they had any vacancies. But working there would mean talking to people, guiding them through the highs and lows of house buying and frankly Emma couldn't really give a rat's arse about other people's highs and lows. She didn't want to be that involved with anybody, so she put that idea on the back burner.

Then an idea struck her – the library! People weren't supposed to talk in libraries. Okay, she would have to get used to being around books again but the silence would suit her well. Besides she had missed reading and felt it was time to forgive books, she wanted them in her life again. Getting a job in the library was the perfect plan. Emma felt a small lump in her throat as she thought of the 'perfect plan'; this whole mess was part of her 'perfect plan' that had gone so horribly awry. She was here alone and alone was good, that was what she had to keep telling herself. The fact that she was not meant to be here alone, had never planned to be here alone, well that just had to be ignored. This was the way things were. There was no point in being disappointed by the way things had turned out. It had been her fault for trusting and relying on someone else. Other people were not for trusting or relying on. Alone was good.

Emma contacted the library the next day. It was a miraculous and unbelievably rare moment of good fortune. The library had just had their funding increased meaning they could take on someone to help sort and categorise the books. They had advertised the position but had had no takers. Emma had the wherewithal to lie about having experience in a library (a white lie, surely, I mean she had been to a library before and she had read books so it wasn't the worst lie ever told). After a brief interview Emma was hired on a short-term trial basis. She was to start the following Monday. The pay was bad, very bad, but it would cover her rent and food (and vodka if she only bought generic brands) and since she rarely ever spent money on anything else the situation was fine with her. She left the library feeling pleased; actually, properly pleased. She hadn't felt this way in a very long time. Getting on for ten years, to be precise. True, she may have at times felt happy during her time with Ben, but that was not her recollection of it now.

Before Emma started her new job she spent her time making her new house feel more homely. On the whole this just meant hanging up her few clothes, but she did also buy a TV set from a small electronics shop in the village. The rest of her days were spent walking. In fact it was in those first few days that she discovered the walk she was now on. It took a whole day to do and had to be timed carefully to miss the incoming tide, but it was a beautiful walk and well worth the effort. Emma felt a sort of contentment during these first few days. She had found a place in the world, tucked away, where her isolation, far from feeling punitive actually felt positive. It felt good to be out in the fresh air, away from other people. Here she couldn't hurt anyone and they couldn't hurt her. She felt that this was how her life was supposed to be.

Her first day at the library taught her that just because a place is supposed to be quiet doesn't necessarily mean it will be. It seemed the local library was the place for the old, the lonely and the unemployed to come and have a good old gossip about village affairs. Emma was initially disheartened by this discovery. However she found something of an unlikely ally in Mrs Timbers, the old librarian. She was possibly the village's most prolific gossip and had loved her many years working in the library building it up as the centre for tittle-tattle. The only thing she didn't like was that occasionally she would have to do some work and this interfered with chatting to the customers. The arrival of Emma meant that all the work could be passed over. This suited them both perfectly, Mrs Timbers took care of gossip (a valuable community service) and Emma took care of the books.

Categorising the books was actually much harder than Emma had thought it would be, but Mrs Timbers kindly and carefully explained the system to her, whilst Emma frantically scribbled notes. Mrs Timbers was happy to train her sad, quiet assistant as it meant she would never have to categorise again. The library had actually qualified for the extra funding because of the many people who came to visit it regularly. The fact that these people only took out books to justify the long gossip they had had was of no consequence to the funding committee. Emma and the octogenarian Mrs Timbers almost never spoke to each other. This was not out of any rudeness or mutual dislike but rather that Mrs Timbers was too busy with her regulars and Emma too busy with the shelves. Their lack of communication suited them both well and they got along together brilliantly.

Emma believed it to be the most natural thing in the world to never talk to anyone. She slipped back easily into her silent ways. She did her best not to think about Ben. Jess had clearly not given him to her so as to forgive her, but rather to punish her further, to ensure she suffered in her guilt. It was strange because whilst she was still angry with Ben her feelings were not solely directed at him. Ben was no longer the central figure at whom her disappointment and hurt were aimed at. Instead she felt as if the entire world had let her down. Ben was no more or less to blame than any stranger she might see in the street. Even these intense feelings were dissipating slightly. Now that she lived in a place where she felt comfortable and had other thoughts to occupy her mind it was like she could no longer be bothered to be angry. She still had her guilt. That would never leave her. She had killed her best friend and it was only to be expected that the world, personified in Ben, would let her down and spoil her plans. She had no right to be happy. Oddly, in accepting this she felt calmer. Her acceptance of the isolation and the silence felt like a comfortable old cardigan she had slipped into. The status quo had returned to her life.

She began to take pleasure in simple things. On the rooftop across the road from her lounge window a pair of seagulls had built their nest. Emma would watch it for hours on end, worried she might miss the moment when the young gulls finally hatched. She liked her seagull neighbours far better than her human ones. Her human neighbours had tried to engage her in conversation but she had politely yet firmly stopped them in their tracks. She would nod or smile at them but resolutely keep walking to show that whilst she wasn't being rude, she was certainly not about to engage in a long chat about the weather. It was a joyous day when three fluffy grey bundles finally emerged from underneath their mother in the seagull nest. They seemed to get bigger every day and Emma couldn't wait to rush home from work to check on their progress. It was her own private avian version of the soap opera *Neighbours*. Her utter joy at the new arrivals was massively tempered as they got to about a week old and their appetite outgrew their food supply. This meant the birds would wake up with a voracious hunger they could only express through very loud cheeping. This was fine during the day but the damn birds had a habit of waking up at 4am so until they fledged they became Emma's alarm call. An alarm that went off very loudly, could not be switched off and started three hours before she needed to get up was no one's idea of fun. Despite this, on the day they fledged Emma felt like a proud parent sending her child off for its first day at school.

Emma's life settled into a familiar routine. Though with her evenings predominantly spent walking the time she spent drinking and watching TV were cut dramatically. She felt far healthier than she ever had in London. It would be easy to believe that Emma's life was all peaches and cream now that she had moved to her countryside retreat. That would be wrong, of course.

Even when she was happy she felt bad about it. Whatever she did with her life had been at the expense of Jess's life. If Emma felt happy it was always tinged with the feeling that she was being disloyal to Jess's memory. Her peace and contentment made a mockery of the fact that her actions had led to the death of a beautiful, vibrant girl who never had the chance to fulfil her potential as a woman. Emma struggled with her contentment, it felt wrong. She should not be allowed to feel happy. She had reneged that right on the night Jess died. In turns she would feel guilty for feeling happy and at other times she was terrified that something or someone would take it all away from her. It wasn't hers by right. She hadn't earned it. Quite the opposite in fact, she had earned the right to suffer and be punished. As long as she lived she could never be truly happy because every good thing that happened to her was a reminder that nothing good would ever happen for Jess again.

It had been so many years now that Emma had trouble remembering exactly what Jess looked like; but the guilt, *that* she remembered with laser-like precision. Sometimes she would feel angry at Jess for dying. How dare she die when Emma needed her so much? How dare she die and make Emma feel so bad about it? In her mind she would lash out at Jess for being so stupid and selfish that she had gone and got herself killed. Then she would calm down a little, the anger would subside and Emma would be left sobbing, wracked with guilt that she had ever been angry with someone she had loved so much and had wronged so badly. Emma's memory of Jess herself had become distorted; she thought of her almost as a saint, only better. She'd had no negatives points at all, everything about her character had been perfect and had she been allowed to live she would surely have saved the world. Emma had denied the world of someone who would have achieved greatness, someone that would have put right all the wrongs. Jess was the yardstick by which Emma measured herself and obviously no one could measure up to such perfection. So even in her happiest times she carried with her a ball of self-loathing in the pit of her stomach.

# Chapter 38

Emma was getting tired now. Whilst the walk was not especially physically exerting, the emotional journey she had been on today was starting to take its toll. She dragged her feet along the golden sand of the estuary. She had to keep looking to her left so as not to miss the small gate she would need to climb over. From there she would be able to find the path that led through the trees, up to the road that would take her back to the village. If she missed the gate there was no way back up to the road. So she had to keep looking out for it. When she had done this walk previously, finding the gate had been no problem. Today she was distracted by her thoughts. Did it usually take this long to find the gate? Emma couldn't remember. Her anxiety about finding the gate was overshadowed by the fearful, dark memories of this morning and what had led to it.

Whilst living here, hidden away in this remote village, a new plan had occurred to her. During her many months of long walks vague notions had come and gone, sometimes her train of thought distracted by a bird flying low past her or the spectacular cloud formations above the mountains. Despite the distractions, or perhaps because of them, because of the life that surrounded her, she had started to develop thoughts that were less negative. Ben had very nearly saved Emma. With him she had begun to see a time when she would no longer be bound by her guilt, a time when she could start to look to the future, to make plans and to think about actually having a life. This had, of course, been cruelly snatched from her when it transpired that Ben was not of the same mind set; he did not want to be her saviour. But the possibility of redemption remained. If Emma could somehow make amends for causing Jess's death then perhaps she might be forgiven. Perhaps she might be able to leave behind the half-life she had imprisoned herself in.

She struggled with these thoughts. To be forgiven would mean leaving Jess behind, no longer making her the centre of all her thoughts and actions. That seemed wrong. However, if she could leave her guilt behind maybe she could just let Jess rest in peace. Something Ben had said about her never having properly mourned Jess hit a chord with her. Had she denigrated her friend's memory by never properly mourning her passing? If she could get past the guilt perhaps she would be able to say goodbye to Jess, let her rest, and then get on with her own life. It seemed too radical. It was wrong. She wasn't ready to let Jess go. So, she would put these thoughts to the back of her mind and continue on her way.

But the thoughts gnawed at her. They would not leave her. She wanted to ignore this train of thought. What good would it do her? To consider usurping Jess as the centre of her life made her feel even guiltier and for what purpose? Why take on this extra guilt when there was nothing she could do about it? How could she possibly expunge not just her guilt borne from the actual act of sending Jess to her death, but also the guilt that had built upon it? Jess's death had laid the foundations and she had slowly and carefully been adding to it for many, many years, building it up like a well-constructed skyscraper. What act, what deed could possibly knock that down? So, all in all it was best not to continue along that train of thought. She should forget it. It scared her; she didn't know how to live without her guilt so why try to find a way to do so? She should crawl back under her warm familiar blanket of despair and forget such stupid notions as forgiveness and redemption. They were not for her. They were alien and wrong. She felt some contentment in convincing herself of this.

Then, one night (why, why did it have to happen?) Emma had a dream, or rather a nightmare. To begin with it was familiar enough. She felt herself drawn into a grey and dusty place, she could barely see through the half-shadows surrounding her and she knew she should be afraid, but this dream had stopped scaring her a long time ago. She knew that when she approached an area so filled with dust it choked her, she would find Jess's body there. She knew she would hold Jess's body and try to put it back together but as she did so her bones would crumble and add to the dust around them. Sometimes she didn't even try to put Jess back together anymore, sometimes she would just hold her dead body and wait until she could wake from the dream.

As she approached the designated spot Emma was amazed to see that Jess was no longer there. Suddenly she did feel afraid. What new nightmare was this? What terror had come to punish her now? Then she heard a sound, very soft and gentle at first. She had never been aware of any noise in the dream before. But she could hear a gurgling. She looked around her; it was too hard to see into the shadows, they were too dark. She started to grope around on the floor, feeling her way through the dust, trying to dispel her growing nausea at running her hands through a dust which had once been her best friend's body. She had to find out what was making that noise, where it was coming from. Then she felt something soft. Her hand recoiled. She gingerly reached out again, and there it was still, something soft. She crawled towards it on her hands and knees. As she saw what it was the noise stopped and Emma woke up suddenly, drenched in sweat. She was shaking; the nervous exertion of the dream had terrified her. She couldn't understand what she had seen.

It was a baby.

It was a befuddled few minutes before Emma could pull herself fully into waking, out of the dream. Crazy thoughts ran through her mind. *Had Jess been pregnant? Had she killed an infant as well? No, of course not! Jess had never had sex, never mind been pregnant.* She eventually managed to slow her breathing down and to feel a little calmer. It was just a dream. That was all. Finally she managed to drop off to sleep again.

The next day the feeling of the dream would not leave her. Even after the details themselves had faded, as is so often the case with a strange dream, the feeling remained. She felt disturbed; she had only ever seen death in that dream, why would see now see life? A new life at that. The baby disturbed her far more than seeing Jess's body ever had. She understood why she would dream about Jess, that made sense, but a baby? That was just insane. It didn't make any sense. She was able to force herself to stop thinking about the dream itself, but the feeling of unease remained.

After work she headed for the beach before she went home. A good long stomp would shake away that bad feeling. There was a cold north wind blowing and it felt good, despite the chill it was refreshing. She made herself take notice of all the things around her. She watched the seagulls gliding on the wind. She watched the waves rising and falling as they made their way to shore. She looked at the mountain behind the village, trying to commit its shape to memory. She concentrated on everything around her so she could dispel what she felt inside her.

After an hour of walking along the beach she did start to feel a bit better. As she headed home a little voice in her mind was laughing at her for being so upset by a nightmare. She listened to that voice and began to accept the wisdom of forgetting the dream, not letting it get to her. She let herself in the front door convinced that she had banished the bad feeling. Now she could settle down to her usual evening activity. She made her way up to the lounge and flicked on the TV. Fantastic, Animal Park, just what she fancied. She settled back on the settee and let the TV do the thinking for her.

# Chapter 39

A month later the dream was nothing more than a vague memory, easily pushed aside. Walking, TV and vodka had done their job well and Emma was now numb to the strange feeling the dream had inspired. She even managed to think less and less about redemption now. It was a stupid notion. What if she did somehow manage to make amends for what she had done? What would be the point? She had no way to kick-start her life. What was she supposed to do, run through the village shouting 'I'm back!' as if everyone in the village would then drop what they were doing and run out to congratulate her, welcome her back into the world of the living?

Stupid, stupid thoughts. There was no way back for her now. She hadn't made a new friend since she was 13 years old. She had no idea how to make friends. Obviously there had been Ben but that was different. He had come to her. She had no idea how to reach out to new people, make friends with them, share thoughts and activities with them. No, redemption was out of the question. She successfully pushed such thoughts away. Well, almost successfully, for some reason she couldn't fathom, when her mind was at rest, when she wasn't keeping vigil on what was running through it, then it would turn, without her permission, back to the idea of being forgiven, back to the idea of having a life again. It was as if she were battling with her own mind, forcing it to stay within the parameters she set for it.

She missed conversation. Occasionally, not often, but occasionally she would think of something funny and she wished she had someone to share it with. There she would be, happily (well, not happily, this is Emma after all) getting on with her day and suddenly a thought like that would pop into her head. Why on earth would she want to have a conversation with anybody? Where did that little desire come from? For goodness sake, she had spent years avoiding conversation. She had done everything she could to ensure that other people were kept at a distance and now all of her sudden her mind was telling her she was lonely. Utter nonsense. She really had to keep better control of her thoughts, stop letting such idiocy into her mind.

The thing was, she couldn't quite rationalise Ben. Okay, he was supposed to have been her saviour, but she hadn't thought of that when they had first met. Of course Jess had been with her then to insist she go out with Ben, that was the reason she had been with him. But if Jess had only ever been a construct of her imagination (and she did still struggle with this notion) – well, how did Ben fit into that? Why had her imagination pushed her to be with him? Sure, his interest in her had been flattering, but that was such a shallow reason to get involved with someone. Especially when her life was dedicated to remorse. When they were together she had, for a time, pushed away the suffering she was duty bound to feel and instead allowed herself a little happiness. In the end she was able to justify his presence in her life – he had a purpose to serve, but to begin with that purpose did not really exist. She had spent time with him because she wanted to. She enjoyed his company, enjoyed being with him. These were not the thoughts and actions of someone serving penance. So she found it hard to understand why he had become part of her life.

The passage of time allowed her to see Jess's return more clearly now. Her mind had not been as rational then as it was now and perhaps – maybe, just maybe – she had imagined her friend was with her. This served as yet further proof to Emma that she was pathetic. She had dragged her dead best friend across the chasm of death just to be her companion. She couldn't even let Jess rest in peace; she had to continually keep disappointing her.

Poor Emma, still too blinded by her own pain and ego to see that she was not a martyr. She hadn't caused Jess to die. Her influence over life and death was just not that strong. She was still too convinced that her actions had caused a death, so convinced she should be punished, even convinced that she was successfully punishing herself, that there was purpose and meaning to her unhappiness. Because of this she did not understand she had spent time with Ben because she was lonely and wanted love – much like any other person on the planet. She was with him, because that was what people generally did; they pair up. With any luck they would pair up with someone they actually love and respect. But because happiness, love and companionship were not part of Emma's all-consuming crusade against herself she really could not rationalise why it was that she and Ben had first got together.

It bothered her. Now she was out of the relationship she could look back on it and examine it. At the time she had been too swept up in it to be able to really cross-examine what was happening. Now that she did look back she couldn't understand how she had let the relationship begin. If Jess hadn't chosen Ben as her saviour then why the hell had she been with him? She wanted to understand because she was worried, very worried.

It seemed to Emma that her recent thoughts about redemption were wrong – not just wrong but evil. Evil because to be redeemed she would have to make amends for Jess's death. How could she possibly make amends? It was something she could never do because she was not a good enough person. She could not offer the world all that Jess could have, so to think of redemption was to tarnish the memory of Jess. To make her seem less than she really was. (The irony, of course lost to Emma, was that she had distorted the memory of Jess beyond recognition. Jess had been a lovely girl, but not necessarily the saviour of all man-kind). So her recent thoughts of redemption just showed what a weak character Emma really was – she had always suspected it, but this helped to confirm it. Her thoughts rolled around and around, endlessly covering old ground, forever repeating, forever leading her back to the inescapable truth that she was scum.

Furthermore (she was really getting on a roll of self-loathing now), her relationship with Ben had been a sign of real weakness. At a time when she should be punished, what had she been doing? She was out having fun. She'd been enjoying herself. Emma was disgusted with herself. She had imposed a sentence on herself that she was too pathetic to serve. She had fallen off the path of penance straight into a good-looking man's arms. Oh, she had been so disloyal to Jess; she had failed her.

Emma wasn't out walking when she put all these thoughts together. Instead she was sitting at home. She had turned the TV off because there was nothing safe for her to watch, nothing that fitted her strict criteria of what was acceptable. She had eventually turned the lights off also because she was sick of seeing her own reflection in the dark TV screen. So she put all of these thoughts together whilst sitting alone in the dark drinking. She sucked her bottle of vodka like a dummy. To Emma it seemed she had now gained full control of her thoughts. She was recognising where she was going wrong and she would ensure she did not fall off the path of penance again. Redemption be damned. Oh yes, she would keep a much tighter vigil over her thoughts and actions.

Any interested observer watching this scene would not have seen a woman finally gaining full control of herself. They would have seen a very sad, lonely person cradling a bottle of drink whilst descending into the darker depths of self-hatred.

That very night she had the same dream again, the baby dream. What cruel trick was this? What was her mind doing to her? Was it a message? Did it have meaning or was it just random pieces of information put together by her dreaming mind to send her mad?

She threw back her sleeping bag and lay naked in the dark. The cold felt good, it dragged her away from her dream and back into reality (or at least a version of it). The room was silent, she couldn't hear the sea and there was no bird song at this dead hour. Emma jumped out of bed and went to the loo, more out of something to do than necessity. She shivered as her feet touched the cold vinyl flooring of the tiny bathroom. She had to concentrate on feeling cold; it helped distract her from her fear.

*Okay,* she thought, *okay, my mistake; I had cheese on toast for dinner. Cheese gives people bad dreams.* So the baby, far from being a message was just a symptom of difficult-to-digest food. She comforted herself with this thought as she snuggled back into her sleeping bag. It was 1am and she needed to go back to sleep. She curled herself into a tight ball and recited her times tables until she was able to doze off again.

She found herself in a bright white room. She didn't recognise it at all, yet she knew where she was. She was in Jess's room. Jess stood smiling at her, saying nothing. Emma tried to speak but was unable. All she could do was to smile back at Jess. She became aware of a heavy weight in her arms. As she noticed the weight Jess came towards her and gently stroked the side of her cheek, she then looked down into Emma's arms. Emma knew she must look down, she must see what it was that Jess saw. In the middle of this beautiful, tender scene Emma felt fear. She didn't want to look down, she had a feeling it would break the moment and she wanted to stay here forever. But she had to look, she had to know. There was, of course, in her arms, warm and weighty, a baby.

Emma awoke, drenched in cold sweat. There would be no more sleep tonight.

For the second time that night Emma threw back her sleeping bag, the cold sweat that clung to her made her shiver and did not feel either good or refreshing. She quickly dressed; she was so cold she pulled on the old green jumper she had brought with her. Soon she left her house and headed for the beach. There was only the light of the full moon to guide her. She broke out into a fast trot, keen to leave her house far behind, wanting to reach the water's edge as quickly as possible. Within minutes the out-going tide lapped gently against her feet. She wasn't sure what comfort she expected to find at the shoreline yet was still disappointed to feel only the full strength of her torment. She turned around the face the full moon.

"Leave me alone, you bitch!" she called out to the placidly-staring orb.

Emma knew now what all this meant. She understood it and yet hated it. It had all been forced upon her so quickly. It didn't seem fair. She knelt down in the wet sand and sobbed. She had been given a mission, one that she did not want to carry out, one she wasn't even sure she could fulfil.

Emma had been searching for signs of one sort or another for so long now that she was unable to recognise coincidence. As she ran to the water's edge her thoughts had been of Ben. This was unexpected for Emma, given the current circumstances, but not unexpected to anyone that could see she was wearing an item still enveloped in his smell. The old green jumper served as a locus for memories of Ben. It wasn't a sign, it was science. Emma managed to expertly misinterpret the flashes of Ben she saw in her mind. However, she wasn't daft enough to rely solely on her mind's wanderings. Having never been on the pill her cycle had fallen into that of the moon and she was at her most fertile now, ovulating even as she sobbed on the sand.

This was enough for Emma. Her dreams, her memories and even the moon itself had all combined to show her what she had to do. She needed to have a baby and it needed to be with Ben. She didn't fully understand why she had to do it, but she knew it had to be done. She sat hunched on the cold, wet sand, crying and confused until the water had retreated far out to sea and the soft first light of dawn broke behind her. Then she pulled herself up and walked home slowly carrying the knowledge of what she must do. It was a heavy burden. Emma was now far removed from anything Freud or Jung had intended. She was not interpreting her dreams; she was using them to justify her choices.

Over a bowl of Coco Pops she decided she had to stop feeling sorry for herself. She was lucky. She had been given a mission. In fact she should be delighted. All this meant that Jess was still with her, guiding her thoughts and actions. Emma no longer had to worry about her own weakness in getting together with Ben; it had all been part of Jess's plan. She now had a goal to work towards. Instead of self-pity she now had to turn her thoughts the logistics. What was the easiest way to get pregnant by a man who lives hundreds of miles away, who never wanted to see her again and whom she would like to avoid seeing again if at all possible? The logistics would certainly require some thought. On the plus side, she did have 28 days to find and implement a solution.

# Chapter 40

Feminine wiles were something Emma had heard of but never employed. She had never knowingly manipulated anyone. Okay, not true, she had engineered it so that other people would ignore her – but that wasn't really manipulation, was it?

She pondered this for a while before deciding that dwelling on what she had or had not done in the past was not going to get her pregnant. She needed to convince Ben to visit her and the visit had to take place three weeks from Saturday. She could call him and tell him she loved him and wanted him back but she had a strong (and correct) feeling that this would not work. They had ended the relationship so badly, why would he contemplate their getting back together? Also, it had taken a long, sustained campaign to win him back before and Emma had the strangest feeling that she was on a deadline. Conception needed to happen and it needed to happen soon. Understanding that Ben might be reticent to help her fulfil her plan was quite rational for someone whose sole aim is to get up the duff so they might save themselves from their own self-created damnation.

Maybe she could call him and start with apologising for upsetting him the last time they spoke? No, that would mean admitting her plan to move them both here had been wrong and she wasn't prepared to take that step.

Many a good long stomp across the beach was spent in trying to figure out a way to convince Ben to drive up and see her. The meeting now had to take place two weeks from Saturday. Time was running out. She needed to make the call. Eventually she decided that whilst she had no plan, no script to work to, she would just have to make the call.

"Hello?"
"Hello, Ben?"
"This is Ben."
"Hi Ben, it's Emma." She was incredibly nervous but

actually sounded quite matter of fact.

"Emma." Ben sounded cold and distant.

"How are you?" She had to get him talking.

"Fine. You?"

"I'm okay. I'm okay." She repeated herself, desperate that they not fall into silence. Ben said nothing. Idle chit-chat was clearly not the way to go.

"Ben, I wondered if you would come up and see me?" Oh crap, that sounded so contrived.

"Why?" Ben was not going to make this easy for her, why should he?

"Because I would really like to see you."

"Why?" Not in the least bit easy.

"Look, we ended badly. The way we left it, I don't think either of us wanted to leave it like that…"

Ben interrupted, "I'm okay with the way we left things."

"Look, Ben I just need to see you."

"Why?" Good grief he sounded like a three year old, always wanting to know why. Emma was getting angry. She had to stay calm; she could not screw this up.

"Because I just want to see you!" she snapped at him. Her voice had gone up an octave. She had to keep it together.

"Why?" *Oh for fuck's sake,* thought Emma. *Why couldn't he understand how important this is? Why couldn't he just stop asking stupid questions and get his arse up here? This isn't going to work, this isn't going to work.* Oh dear god Emma had to make it work. Her resolve to stay calm was breaking down. She was desperate. She had to get him up here. It was the single most important thing in her life.

"Ben!" she shouted into the telephone, "I'm dying." She took a sharp intake of breath and just stopped speaking. She had meant to say I'm dying to see you, but she didn't, she just stopped. Her heart raced in her chest, she could feel all her major veins throbbing. She couldn't believe what she was doing, but carried on any way. She compounded her sick lie by letting in hang in the air in the silence between them.

"What?" asked Ben softly.

"Please come up and see me." Emma spoke softly as well.

She felt dizzy. She felt disgusted by what she was doing.

"Emma, are you really...?" All the anger had gone out of Ben now.

"Yes." She almost choked on the word.

"But how? Why?" He sounded so sad. She could almost hear him shaking his head, willing it not to be true.

"I have a disease. In my kidneys. They can't cure it." Ben had once shouted at Emma that he would give her a kidney if she wanted one. How he wished he could take those words back now.

"Please come up and see me," Emma again repeated. She had to end this conversation. She had to get his agreement to come up and then get off the phone. She was shaking and needed to throw up. Maybe she really was sick?

"Sure. Of course I'll come up. Of course I will. Shall I drive up now?"

"No, no, I don't want to put you out." This was beyond sick. "Why not come up in a week or two? Weekend after next perhaps, let's say the 12$^{th}$. Come up then."

"Of course. Oh Emma I am so sorry, so, so sorry."

"It's okay, honestly it's okay. Here let me give you my address."

Ben couldn't believe how brave she was being. He took down her address and promised to be there by 2pm on Saturday the 12$^{th}$.

Emma put down the receiver and rested her head against the cold steel of the phone box. What had she done? It had worked, but at what cost? Oh lord, what had she done? Her hands trembled and her stomach heaved. She turned around and threw up in the bin just outside the phone box. She walked slowly back to her house. Well, at least phase one was successfully completed.

# Chapter 41

*She had succeeded. She had done what needed to be done. The ends justified the means.*

Emma clung to these clichés as if they were a guiding philosophy. She needed them, they were a barrier between herself and the lie she had told. It didn't matter what is was that got Ben here – the important thing was that he would come, they would have sex and she would fall pregnant. She had to keep her mind on the main goal. After her euphoria and revulsion at achieving the first step, her mind turned naturally to phase two; the great seduction. Perhaps the great swindle would be a more appropriate description? For the sake of authenticity she would need to look ill. Luckily her recent return to a poor diet and excessive drinking meant this was not a difficult bridge to cross. She considered that she would also need to look attractive enough to be sexually alluring. This careful balancing act could have been difficult to achieve, but thankfully it was unnecessary. Emma remembered that Ben had never baulked at having sex with her before and she had certainly never been alluring then. Available, it seemed was a more important element than alluring.

She spent hours trying to imagine what would be the best thing to say, where would be the best place to sit so the light might catch her and give her the appearance of illuminated beauty. She tried to see herself as some poor 19$^{th}$ century heroine, felled by consumption, yet still beautiful and brave. She was certainly no such thing however and whilst she was prone to the irrational she still had a tiny modicum of self-awareness. So, after much time was spent deliberating the best way to get him into bed she decided that clean sheets and shaved legs were her most powerful tools. If all else failed she could make it her dying wish. Sympathy sex was as likely to get her pregnant as any other kind.

The sex would have to be the unprotected kind of course,

something they had never engaged in before. Emma did spare a moment or two to consider if that might be a problem for Ben. She didn't have any condoms in the house and Ben was unlikely to bring any. What sort of man would pack condoms to go and see his dying ex-girlfriend? So all she had to do was ensure any overtures where made after 5pm when the local chemist closed. As long as she could get him feeling very sympathetic and very turned on by about 5.30-ish the plan should work.

It never occurred to her that once might not be enough. They could have sex and she still might not get pregnant. Some couples tried unsuccessfully for years. But of course, they were not on a mission handed to them from the dead. Emma had to get pregnant and therefore she would. It was not a matter that even warranted consideration.

So many hours over so many days were spent planning the act itself. In this time Emma allowed herself brief day dreams of buying the pregnancy tester kit, coming home, peeing on the relevant little stick and receiving the joyous news that she was indeed with child. However over all this time she never once considered what would happen when the child was born. She never once thought of being a mother, of having the responsibility of raising a child. It just didn't occur to her. Her mission was to get pregnant, that had been made clear to her.

But why? For what purpose? What would happen when the child arrived? What was her mission then? These questions never entered her head. How she would cope as a single mother was never formed as a conscious thought. She was too consumed with the details of her immediate plan to ever see anything resembling the bigger picture.

# Chapter 42

On Friday the 11<sup>th</sup> Emma took the day off work. As her seagull neighbours had long since fledged (in fact it would soon be time for a new nest to be built) she awoke at her usual time of 6.30am. She immediately regretted taking the whole day off. The hours stretched before her, needing to be filled. She had to keep busy for the next 31 and a half hours before Ben's arrival.

She got up and had breakfast. Well, that was 15 minutes killed. The plan had been to spend the day cleaning the house but only now did it occur to Emma that she had a very small house. There just wasn't enough of it to fill a whole day of cleaning. She decided to have a walk first, that would help a bit of time pass. Emma left her small house behind, crossed the car park and headed down to the beach. The high tide had just turned and the waves were starting their retreat. Today would be the perfect day to do her long walk, the one that took her along the beach, through the village and down to the estuary, then back up through the woods and all the way home again. Just at the turn of high tide was the perfect time to start the walk.

Emma indulged in a brief moment of annoyance. She would have loved to have today to herself, to be able to walk where she wanted oblivious of any deadlines. But her time was not her own. She had plenty to do and the long walk would take far too much of her precious time. Instead she contented herself with a quick stomp in the other direction, up to the lifeboat tower. She chastised herself for wanting today to be any other way. She had been chosen and she must follow her mission. To think otherwise was selfish. Oh how she hoped she would be up to her task, that she would succeed. Of course she would, she had Jess guiding her and supporting her. How could she possibly fail?

Emma's obsessive thoughts kept her from noticing where it was she walked and what it was she passed. She didn't see the red kites circling the mountain behind the village. She didn't see the playful majesty of a pod of 8 dolphins leaping and swimming through the sea to her left. She didn't hear the locals calling out to each other, excited by the rare sight of dolphins in an area they did not naturally frequent. She didn't see the mist clear out to sea allowing the sun to glint off the headland there. She did see the lifeboat tower and when she got to it she turned round and stomped back home again.

Once home she set to her task. She scrubbed, bleached, rinsed, dusted and hoovered her little house like never before. She had to open all the windows as the unaccustomed smell of cleaning products made her feel a little dizzy. She chose to ignore the long strips on the wall where the wallpaper was missing. They zigzagged across each room like gaping wounds. Evidence of every time she had failed to stop herself ripping large sections of wallpaper away, just as she used to as a child. It was her house; she could do what she bloody well liked with the wallpaper. Besides it was too late to do anything about it now.

When she had finished she made herself a sandwich. The butter knife left in the sink and the crumbs on the surfaces did not match her idea of how the house should look so she scrubbed the kitchen from top to bottom again. Then she realised she'd forgotten the skirting boards so she filled a bucket with hot soapy water and washed down all the doors and wood work in the house. Then she polished it again. Emma was unaware whether scientists had ever found a correlation between clean houses and pregnancy but as she had nothing else to do she cleaned as if her life depended on it. Finally she finished. She decided against having a shower as it would only mess up the bathroom again. Rather she would have one in the morning, then clean the bathroom again and then set about making herself look as if she were dying beautifully.

As evening fell Emma sat on her sofa. She sat very still; her only movement was that of raising her bottle of generic brand vodka to her lips to take long drinks. She had decided against having dinner, or using a glass for her drink, or any other activity that might in any way spoil the cleanliness of the house. She had no idea why it was so important, it just was. So she sat very quietly and very still until it seemed like a reasonable time to go to bed.

## Chapter 43

Emma did not sleep well that night. She was a bundle of nerves and excitement. She needed to get a good night's sleep and worrying about sleep itself kept her awake for most of the night. Eventually the clock passed midnight. Well, that was it. Today was the day she was going to get pregnant. It was today already.

Sleep then escaped her entirely and for the next 6 hours she tossed and turned until eventually she threw back her sleeping bag and decided to get up. Her sleeping bag, oh crap it was still on the bed. She had intended to buy some nice new sheets and maybe even a duvet to make the bed look all the more inviting. She could not believe she had forgotten. There was no way now she could get the bus into town and back again in time. She felt utterly miserable. She had planned today so carefully and yet had forgotten one vital element. How could the plan work now? How could she possibly create the child she was destined to have with a stupid polyester-lined sleeping bag on the bed? The day had only just begun and the task was failed already. She shook her head sadly and then slapped her face to pull herself together. All was not lost. She would just have to make do, make the best of it. She would bloody well convince Ben to lie down on this crappy bed and make love to her. It was her mission and she had to do it. She sat on the toilet and had a quick little cry at her own wretched stupidity, then she splashed cold water on her face and got on with the plan. Waking up and having a quick cry was nothing new to Emma.

She ate breakfast very carefully over the sink to avoid spilling milk or getting Coco Pop crumbs anywhere. Then she showered and removed as much body hair as seemed applicable before wiping down the entire bathroom to return the gleam she had achieved yesterday. Only it didn't seem quite as shiny as yesterday and that bothered Emma. So she grabbed the furniture polish and sprayed and rubbed down all the tiles on the walls and floor. That looked better. It smelled good too.

So, now what? She still had 7 hours before Ben was due to arrive. It was not the first time she had spent hours pacing her abode waiting for Ben. She had to keep that previous encounter out of her head. She could not allow herself to be angry with Ben. She needed to seduce him, not shout at him.

At 1.30pm Emma walked over to the car park where she had arranged to meet Ben. The street in front of her house was too narrow to get a car down so he would need to park in the car park and then she would walk him to her house. It was only a 30 second walk and Ben wasn't due for another half hour so Emma arrived at the meeting point far earlier than she needed to. She leaned against the car park railings and felt incredibly uncomfortable.

People walked past, families on a day out to the seaside, and they all seemed to be looking at her, accusing her. There was the woman who was pretending to be dying so she could manipulate her ex-boyfriend. Whilst she knew they couldn't possibly know of her plan she still saw judgement in their eyes. She stared down at her black shoes and studied them intently until the church clock chimed quarter to the hour. Her stomach leapt at the sound. She felt nervous and also angry, she knew she could not be angry with Ben so she turned her feelings inward and chastised herself again for forgetting about the duvet. She had no idea of how today would turn out and what she really wanted to do was hide away and have a good cry, but that option was denied her. Looking up she saw Ben's blue car pull into the far end of the car park. Show time.

Ben spotted Emma and pulled the car into an empty space near where she stood. He got out of the car carrying a small overnight bag. As planned in her mind Emma walked to him and gave him a big hug which he returned. She breathed in the smell of his clothes and his aftershave (he was wearing the brand she had bought him). She was surprised at how nice it felt to be in his arms. She had not expected to feel such relief at his presence. It went beyond the feeling of relief at a plan well executed. She realised now she had actually missed him. They walked back to her house hand in hand.

Once inside she made them both a cup of tea and they sat on her two-seater settee together.

"So, how is everything?" Well, they had to start a conversation at some point.

"Everything's fine with me but what about you?" Ben looked deep into her eyes as if he might be able to see her illness and somehow root it out.

"I'm okay. But look I didn't want you to come here to talk about me. I felt really bad about the way we left things and I just wanted to see you again, to make things right between us." She was playing the part of magnanimous dying heroine really rather well, she thought.

"Sure." said Ben, but then he felt at quite a loss. He could think of nothing to talk about except her illness. It had occupied his thoughts ever since she had called.

"So, do you like the house?"

"Yes, yes, it's lovely." He paused. "It's upside-down." At this Emma laughed and Ben finally felt a little more at ease.

"Yes, it really threw me when I first moved in. The kitchen and lounge are here and the bedroom and bathroom are downstairs." As the first thing Ben had done when he arrived was use the toilet this was an unnecessary explanation. Also, it bordered on talking about when and why she had moved here. Emma needed to steer off this conversation quickly.

"Why don't we drink our tea and then we can go for a walk along the beach?"

"Sounds lovely." Ben felt sad looking around her little house. She had obviously started to decorate; large sections of the wallpaper were missing. He guessed that project was on hold indefinitely now, now she was dying. Oh God, how awful.

"So, how's Rob?" Emma could not give a rat's arse about how Rob was but at least he was a safe conversation. They drank their tea and Ben regaled Emma with stories of how Rob was (boring), how things were going at work (boring) and how his parents were (slightly less boring).

Emma felt agitated (and bored) by the conversation. She wanted to get on with the main event but knew she had to bide her time. Once their cups were drained they put on their shoes and headed down to the beach. It was a lovely spring day and they walked far along the water's edge, skimming stones as they went. They then walked all the way back to the village, bought some fish and chips and sat on the beach to eat them.

They chatted far more than they had the last time they had sat on this very beach with fish and chips. Emma told him all about working in the library. They laughed at Mrs Timbers' gossip-orientated community service. Ben decided he wouldn't have liked having seagull neighbours but Emma highlighted their positive points and eventually he agreed it must have been nice to see the chicks grow. All in all they talked a lot yet they talked about nothing. They sat in silence as they watched the sunset into the sea, both realising this was far too beautiful an event to spoil with idle chatter. The breeze picked up as the sun disappeared and they decided to leave the beach. The main event approached at last.

"I should probably check into a B&B," Ben said as they crossed the car park.

"What?" Emma stopped in her tracks.

"I should, you know, probably check into a B&B, it's too far to drive back tonight."

"No!" Emma had to regain her composure. "No, I mean, you've come all this way to see me, the least I can do is give you a bed for the night." She forced a light-hearted smile. Ben hadn't spotted the spare room at Emma's house, most likely because there wasn't one, but he agreed to her kind offer. Bullet dodged.

Back at the house Emma poured them both a glass of wine. A very, very large glass of wine.

"To old friends," she toasted. She gave him what she thought was a seductive smile.

"To old friends." Ben toasted, oblivious to her seductive

smile. Ben didn't like to ask whether it was okay for her to drink, he sadly guessed her condition had gone beyond the point of it mattering whether she drank or not.

Over the next few hours, like a hostess on a mission, Emma filled and re-filled their wine glass until they were both pissed. Ben had to keep one eye shut to keep Emma in focus and Emma had pretty much lost her ability to articulate properly, her words instead slurring together. They had almost reached the point of no return, where sex would become infeasible, when Ben stumbled down to the toilet. Emma followed him down and as he left the bathroom she invited him into her bedroom.

After quite a bit of fumbling and wine tasting kisses they managed to have sex. They were both too drunk for it to be particularly good sex, but then Emma wasn't in it for the orgasm.

# Chapter 44

Ben awoke with a pounding red wine hangover. It took him a minute to work out where he was. Slowly last night came back to him. Oh heck, they'd had sex. That was bound to complicate things. It probably shouldn't have happened but right now Ben's main priority was getting a glass of water and two Paracetamol. He'd deal with any post-coital fallout after that. He rolled over and reached out for Emma, surprised to find she was not there.

Emma had woken up early. She didn't even have the merest hint of a hangover. In fact she felt fantastic. She had achieved her goal, mission completed, sex had been had. She felt so proud of herself, so capable and happy that she had done what she set out to achieve. In a life bereft of achievements she relished the unfamiliar joy of a job well done. As Ben awoke, Emma was in the bathroom taking a pregnancy test. Okay, part of her knew this was utterly redundant as no test could possibly be accurate enough to know if she were pregnant or not yet, but she enjoyed the pantomime of taking one anyway. It came back negative. Okay, that was to be expected. She felt disheartened by the result but comforted herself with the fact that it could just as easily be a false-negative and she was more than likely carrying a child even now. She gave herself a little hug before returning to the bedroom. She had never planned how she would act with Ben the next day but for now she felt great and was happy to share her positive mood.

"Good morning sleepy head," she greeted him.

"Mornin'," he mumbled back.

"Would you like a cup of tea?"

"Mmmmm, yes please, definitely."

Emma tidied up last night's wine glasses whilst making the tea. She hummed a little tune to herself as she pottered in the kitchen.

"Here you go, a nice cup of tea in bed."

"Thanks Em."

"Why don't you drink your tea and then have a shower whilst I make us a nice fry up?"

"Thanks Em. You're a star." Ben still wasn't quite sure how he felt about last night or quite what direction this morning was taking, but hey, anyone who was willing to make him tea and a fry up to ease his current pain was a wonderful human being in his mind.

As Emma fried, toasted and buttered upstairs she heard Ben go into the bathroom. Perhaps after breakfast they could go for a walk, maybe have some lunch in the pub and then Ben could head back to London. She wondered idly whether he would come back for another visit. Did she want him to? Would he perhaps play a part in their child's life? She had never planned to tell him about the baby, but it had been so nice to see him. Who knew what might happen. She could have a miraculous recovery, or a cure could be found for her disease. She filled her head with happy day dreams and fantasies as she bustled about.

Down in the bathroom Ben sat on the edge of the bath. He did not feel well. He had no idea how much they'd drunk last night but he seemed to have a vague recollection that once the wine ran out they'd started doing vodka shots. Eerrgh. He pulled off his t-shirt and got into the shower. Blimey, Emma was not exactly a big person but surely this bathroom had been designed for pixies! It was tiny. He gratefully felt some relief as the water poured over his head and down his body. He was starting to feel a bit better now.

Getting out of the shower was not easy, there was far too little floor space between the sink, toilet and shower and what floor space was available was slippery from Emma's excessive use of furniture polish. His foot slipped as he tried to gingerly place it on the floor. Christ! What sort of person had a bathroom floor that was this slippery? Luckily his descent was halted as his foot hit hard against the bin, toppling it over. His heart pounded as he realised he could have quite easily had a nasty accident then. With slight revulsion he picked up a couple of used tissues and a little plastic stick that had fallen from the bin and piled them back inside. Not usually one given to going through other people's bins, he did make a slight exception for the little plastic stick. What was that? Ben sat on the side of the bath and stared down at the object in his hand. It couldn't be. Why would it be? Needing to know more he looked back into the rest of the bin contents. There was the box belonging to the little plastic stick. *Bloody hell.*

He dried himself off as quickly as possible, went to bedroom and pulled on his clothes. His mind was whirring. He had no right to question Emma. *Lest he forgot, she was very ill.* Her life was her own; Ben had no right to ask her about it. But he had to ask her. No matter how hard he tried to reason with himself that the stick had nothing to do with him, he could not escape the fact that last night they had had unprotected sex and this morning there was a pregnancy tester kit in her bin. Ben had the strangest feeling he had somehow been set up but he couldn't believe that. That couldn't be true. The stick obviously had nothing to do with him. Coincidence. That was all. Emma could have had sex last week for all he knew. Besides, everyone knew that pregnancy tester kits didn't work for the first few days. Didn't they? Or did they? He couldn't stand this. He had to know. He had to confront her.

"Emma!" he called as he made his way up the stairs, "what's this?" He held the offending object out in front of him.

"What's what love?" she asked as she met him at the top of the stairs. "Oh!" She saw the object in his hand. She felt blindsided. He was never supposed to see that. No matter what decision she made about their future together he was never to know that last night had been planned. Her mind raced as she looked wide-eyed at the stick. What explanation could she possibly give? Even as her mind flailed wildly for a plausible excuse she couldn't help but think that Ben would need to wash his hands before breakfast. There would be germs on that stick. Germs. Perfect.

"It's mine; I took a home test not so long ago. I was having strange pains and I wondered if somehow I might be pregnant." She spoke slowly and calmly, trying to make this seem like the most natural thing in the world. "Oh course, the pains were not from pregnancy – see look, it's blue which means it's negative. So I went to the doctors to see what else could be causing the pain and then I found out..." she let that hang in the air for a moment, "I found out I am sick. But you know my illness isn't really something I like to talk about. You know?"

She looked directly into his eyes. She felt her last comment had been a nice touch. He'd accused her, she had countered and even managed, hopefully, to make him feel a little guilty in the process. She resisted the urge to let out a sigh of relief. "Now come and eat your breakfast, but please wash your hands first."

Ben watched Emma as she went to fetch the plates and carry them into the lounge. He was in a difficult situation. He knew, he was sure, he was being fed a line, yet how could he push the topic any further? He couldn't force her into talking about her illness if she didn't want to. He dutifully washed his hands, having discarded the stick in the kitchen bin, and sat down to eat his breakfast.

Hang on a minute. When did she take the test, how long had she known she was ill? The bathroom bin looked like it had been emptied recently. After all the time they had spent together he knew her bathroom habits well enough to know that this just didn't sound right. His sensitivity and curiosity battled all through breakfast.

"Emma, how long have you known that you're sick?" He couldn't stand it anymore. Something was going on here and he needed to know what it was.

"A while now." She blushed just ever so slightly as she answered. She did not like this line of questioning. Ben equally hated this line of questioning but he'd started to pick at a thread and now he needed to unravel the whole story.

"Are you on a lot of medication?"

"No."

"Oh?" Ben queried. Emma didn't respond. This morning had started so well and now she felt like she was being interrogated. She felt defensive and made a snap decision that no, Ben would certainly not be part of their child's life.

"No medication at all?"

"What I have cannot be cured so there is no point in my taking any medication." Her attempt to keep her voice light and soft failed. Instead she sounded as though she were talking through gritted teeth.

"Don't you need any pain killers or anything?"

"The pain comes and goes."

"What's the name, I mean, what is it you have?" Ben felt awful for asking this. Emma felt worse, it hadn't occurred to her to look up a name for her 'disease'.

"Look, I really don't like talking about this. Okay?" She should have just left it there. At this point Ben would have still, despite his reservations, respected her wishes and left it. He already felt like he had pushed too far. But no, she continued, she felt accused and wanted to make him feel bad for it.

"Why is this so important anyway? Why all the questions? I'm the one who is ill." She went into the kitchen and slammed her empty plate into the sink. Ben followed her; he stood, almost nervously, at the top of the stairs.

"Are you?"

"What?"

"Are you sick?" He couldn't quite believe that he'd asked her that, but he needed to know and it was out in the open now. He didn't even realise how much he doubted her until the question was said allowed.

"What the hell kind of bloody question is that? How dare you ask me that?"

"Look Emma last night we had sex and this morning I find a pregnancy tester kit in your bin. You can't blame me for being curious. I need to know if this is just coincidence or what."

"I don't need to explain myself to you!" she spat at him.

"My God, why are you being so defensive?"

"Me? What about you! Why are you being so bloody inquisitive?"

"Because you still haven't answered my question. You've

got to admit this whole thing looks a bit bloody strange. You ask me into coming up here and now you won't answer any of my questions!" They were both shouting now.

"Manipulate you! How the hell have I manipulated you? My God, if visiting your sick ex-girlfriend is too much to ask of you, then I am so sorry for having troubled you!" When in doubt, she went with sarcasm. Ben had never mentioned manipulation; Emma had inserted that into his sentence herself.

"Are you really sick? What illness do you have?" His eyes bored into hers. He realised now, with utter clarity that Emma was not sick at all. She had used that as a horrible, unforgivable excuse to get him up here, but why? Emma just wanted to get him out of the house, he had served his purpose. She had no further use for him now. But before he went she wanted to hurt him.

"I never should have chosen you."

"What?"

"I never should have chosen you to get me pregnant."

"What the hell are you talking about?" Even though it was as Ben feared, he still couldn't believe it was true.

"Yes, Ben dear, that's all you are to me, sperm. I just needed to get pregnant and chose you to do it. I'm so sorry if having sex with me was such a chore. Don't pretend like you didn't get anything out of this. All you are to me now is sperm. I don't really give a shit about the way we left things before; don't flatter yourself that I do. Choosing you was stupid, but it's done now, so now you can fuck off!"

"What kind of crazy bitch are you!?"

"The kind you slept with last night." Emma really felt like she had the upper hand now. She was hurting him and it felt good. If she hadn't been so angry she would have laughed in his face.

"You crazy bitch!" He wanted to get as far away from her as possible but she was holding his arm, digging her nails into his skin. She wanted him to hear this. She had years of hurt waiting to come out.

"Oh please! You used to love me, remember? I was only

with you because Jess wanted us to be together. You never meant anything to me; you were just a tool to be used."

"Jess? Who the fuck is Jess?" Then it dawned on him. Wasn't Jess Emma's best friend? More to the point, wasn't Jess dead?

"What do you mean who the fuck is Jess!" Emma was screaming at him now. How dare he not remember the most important person in her life? "Jess is worth a million of you You're nothing! You're below nothing! Your just bodily fluids that I needed!"

"You used me because it's what your dead best friend wanted?" He shook his head. He couldn't believe this. He was too angry to fear for Emma's sanity. He just wanted to get as far away from her possible. As he tried to back away Emma yanked him back towards her, she was not nearly done with him yet, she had so much more venom she wanted to drown him in.

"Get off me!" Ben screamed at her. As he again tried to pull back, Emma again tried to pull him towards her. Rage gave her strength. His foot slipped on the top stair and his entire weight tried to project him down the stairs. All that was stopping him was Emma's nails, ripping the skin from his arms. As gravity tried to claim Ben she was his only chance of salvation.

Emma let go.

As he fell backwards he tried to twist his body round so he could use his hands to stop his fall. But the stairs were too narrow. His head smacked first against the wall on one side and then against the railings on the other side. At this final jolt he came to rest. The impact of this second hit snapped his neck. He lay sprawled on the stairs and he just didn't look right. His head was at such a strange angle. His eyes were wide open, staring up at her, unseeing.

Emma sat with a heavy thump on the top step. She stared back at him. The living and the dead stared into each other's eyes for a long moment. Still sitting, Emma backed away from the stairs and crawled into the kitchen. She scrunched herself up to be as small as she could and sat on the cold kitchen floor.

She was only aware of two things – her own heavy breathing and Ben's lack of breathing. She breathed harder, as if she might compensate for Ben. She looked out at the grey flint wall behind her kitchen window. It seemed to suck the air right out of her, so grey and menacing. With the air sucked out of her, Emma sat on the cold, hard floor and did nothing. Useless and motionless, she sat for a long time, unaware of anything until a single thought entered her mind. She needed to get out of this house. More than anything she needed to get out.

# Chapter 45

Emma's birthday was always a bit of a hard time for both Steve and Denise. Each year on the 14th March they would both become a little despondent, a little distant to their respective partners. Denise liked to spend the day in her garden if she could. They had a much larger garden now she was married and though a gardener was employed to look after most of it, Denise kept a small patch for herself. She would spend hours weeding and planting to create the effect she was after. Often on the 14th March though she could be found just sitting staring at the flowers with a trowel in her hand, neither weeding nor planting. She would just sit and stare for hours, with lord knew what going through her mind.

Steve would generally choose that day to go out for a long drive by himself. He would never have a destination in mind; he'd just drive and see where he ended up. Usually he would find himself in a remote green, beautiful spot. Then he would get out of the car, walk until he felt himself truly alone and then just stand and stare, with lord knew what going through his mind.

For the rest of the year however, they were both able to live contented lives, without a thought for their daughter. She had been lost for too long to be able to find now. Besides, she was kept safely in little boxes that resided in each of their minds, locked tight and only very rarely able to creep out.

# Chapter 46

Had she already passed the gate she needed to go through to get out of the estuary? Oh lord, by going forward was she getting further and further from where she needed to be? Emma turned to look back along the estuary, to see if she could get some clue as to her bearings. She froze. What she saw behind her terrified her. She felt rooted to the spot. She could not react. What she saw, getting closer and closer with each passing second, with each second she stood frozen, unable to move, had the power to destroy her. Should she run forward or back? Which way should she go to escape? Where was the gate? Where was the path that led to safety? She just didn't know which was the right way. She had to get out of here because coming up behind, with the force and fury of a thousand eons, was the sea.

She had misjudged her walk. She had started it too late. She hadn't been thinking about the tide and now it was coming back in. The sea was flooding the estuary on which she stood. It would not be long before it came crashing down here. She had watched it once before from the safety of the bank and been amazed at the speed and ferocity with which the sea returned. Soon it would come, smashing over her and washing her away. She would drown. She stood trembling, incapacitated by her own stupidity. She couldn't believe she had put herself in such danger. What should she do? Go forward or back? Apart from the gate there was no way to get out of the estuary, the way up was blocked by sharp, jagged rocks, covered in slimy seaweed, there was no way to climb them. She was stuck; trapped in a wide, open space.

Going back would take her closer to the incoming tide, so Emma started to run forward. Sand is a difficult medium to run on and she kept stumbling. Though compacted by a thousand tides it was still sand, soft and yielding, trying to claim her. Each new step was a miracle. Her feet felt so heavy and tired but she had to keep running. The sea was getting closer and closer. At first her feet would just get wet, making running even harder, but within a few minutes the waves would crash around her, sucking her under. She would die. She had to keep running. She had to get away.

As she ran it felt like she was in a nightmare. A horrible dream where you run, desperately trying to escape but even as the full force of your will and all your might is concentrated on getting away, other elements come to play. Perhaps the sight of an old school teacher, or your boss standing just outside your field of vision, screaming about a late report, distracts you.

For Emma it was exactly the same. Even as her whole being propelled her forward, parts of her mind skipped away from her current predicament and random thoughts popped into her consciousness. Glimpses of this morning's scene seemed suddenly to rise up in front of her before she could cast them away; images of death distracted her as she ran. Both her own death and death caused by her mingled into one in her mind. Still she ran, she had to beat the incoming tide. The sea was too close now, she had no option but to try and scale the sharp, slippery, jagged rocks. Her hands and feet slipped as she tried, until she could no longer propel herself forward.

The cold, briny waves washed over Emma as she clung to the rocks. She was so scared she started to cry. Tears poured out of fear and self-pity, she didn't want to die here. She knew that with utter certainty. So many times she had wanted to die, to sink in to a comfortable oblivion, but this was not one of them. Waves choked back her sobs, the salty water catching at the back of her throat. She could only breathe in stolen gasps, when the sea allowed. She was freezing cold and her constant dunking under water made the world seem very dark. She gasped out a scream for help whenever she was able, misjudging every time so that more water crashed in to her mouth and rushed down to her lungs. Still she clung to the jagged, sharp, slimy rocks.

Each battering from the waves made her shoulders feel like they would dislodge entirely from her body. Still she clung on. The waves seemed to carry in them an immense and ancient tiredness which they imparted to Emma each time they hit her.

She closed her eyes.

Amidst the cold and the dark and her fear, part of her mind escaped. It took Emma far from this place and far from this time. In flashes it showed her own life. It took her back to a funeral she had attended in 1989. She stood in her black dress, apart from the other mourners, her head down. When she did look up she saw Sarah, crying. *She hated Sarah.* Sarah had been in the pub with them that night, she'd left early. She had been Jess's friend that night, not Emma. Emma hated her for ever having come between them, even if only so briefly.

Her mind took her further back, to Jess. To them sitting happily in Jess's room, putting the world to rights. She felt a contentment she had not felt in a very long time. This life felt so close and real.

Emma opened her eyes to experience what her mind showed her, but all she saw were the waves washing fear all around her. She was not part of that comfortable life anymore.

The path she was on came to a stop against sharp, jagged, slippery rocks being consumed by the incoming tide. A massive jolt passed through her body as one of her hands slipped suddenly. She gripped tighter, pressing her body as far as she was able to against the rock.

She did not want to die here.

She gripped tighter still as the waves hit her again and again. They seemed to be coming in faster and there was so little respite in which to breathe.

She gripped the rocks tighter, holding on until her fingers poured with blood.

For so many years her life had been unnecessarily consumed by death and guilt, until finally life caught up. She was responsible for Ben's death and at long last had every reason to feel guilty. Similarly, her life had been eaten away by death, consumed by it, so often wishing for it. Now here was death and Emma retaliated. She fought for life with every fibre of her being.